The School of Beauty and Charm

Also by Melanie Sumner

Polite Society, *Stories*

The
School of
Beauty
and
Charm

a novel by

Melanie Sumner

Algonquin Books
of Chapel Hill
2001

R

A SHANNON RAVENEL BOOK
Published by
Algonquin Books of Chapel Hill
Post Office Box 2225
Chapel Hill, North Carolina 27515-2225

a division of
Workman Publishing
708 Broadway
New York, New York 10003

Library of Congress Cataloging-in-Publication Data
Sumner, Melanie.
The school of beauty and charm : a novel / by Melanie Sumner.
p. cm.
ISBN 1-56512-286-0 (hc)
1. Teenage girls—Fiction.   2. Runaway teenagers—Fiction.
3. Georgia—Fiction.   I. Title.
PS3569.U46 S38 2001
813'.54—dc21   2001034341

10   9   8   7   6   5   4   3   2   1
First Edition

I dedicate this novel to my husband,

David Marr

David Marr

Mary Ruth Sumner

Roger Sumner

Georges Borchardt

Shannon Ravenel

DeAnna Heindel

Faith Shearin

Adrienne Su

Darrach Dolan

Uli Gratzl

Scotti Bloom

Costas Corytsas

Patrick Marr

Zoe Page Marr

Cleveland Storrs

The Whiting Foundation

The Authors League Fund

Change Inc.

Pen American Center

Zeke's Auto Supply

Sadie Christmas Sumner-Marr

Tinman

Thank you for your support in the creation
of *The School of Beauty and Charm.*

The School of Beauty and Charm

PREFACE

My sponsor, Regina, says I've never had a problem as bad as my solution for it, and that is more or less how I ended up in the Wapanog County Jail on the night after I was supposed to marry Zane Wilder. She says God saved my ass. She should know—she's been married nine times. "Why did you marry all of them?" I asked her once. She said she didn't want to hurt their feelings. Regina has been sober for a while. She carries a cane decorated for each season and raises it to any man who hits on one of her sponsees—"My babies," she calls us. We call her Mom. She asked me to come here tonight and tell you my story.

Chapter One

I WAS BORN AGAIN, for the first time, when I was seven. That
year smiley faces covered the country and people ended con-
versations with "Have a nice day." In March of that year, a
string of tornadoes whipped through Counterpoint, Georgia,
lifting pine trees as if they were birthday candles stuck in a cake,
then scattering them willy-nilly across the roads. Houses flew
to new yards, and cars sailed through the sky like lost kites.
Dogs landed in trees; cats went bald, and hamsters left the
hemisphere. For the entire month, the wind whirred and sucked
with relentless fury. It was obvious, at least to the Baptists, that
God had taken out His vacuum cleaner. Clearly, He had found
me, Louise.

"Remember who you are," my father warned me each time
I left the house. Not one to leave anything to chance, he would
add, "You are a Peppers." Then he straightened his shoulders
and smiled hard, demonstrating the posture of a Peppers facing
the world.

Pepperses are white, not albino or Swedish or anything like that, but regular white. We are also white on the inside. Except for my mother, Florida, who is high-strung, we never raise our voices or blow the horn of an automobile. We have no rhythm, and when we watch others dance, we tend to blush. Spicy food burns our tongues. Every other November, we vote Democrat, which, down South, used to be the same as voting Republican. Florida is always careful not to cancel Henry's vote by voting for a different candidate. The whole family avoids discussing sex, politics, and religion, favoring the topic of the weather, which averages seventy-five degrees in Counterpoint year-round.

A Peppers is smarter than the average bear, as Henry likes to point out, with a stern reminder to be grateful because God could just as easily have given our brains to other people. According to Henry, most folks don't have a lick of sense. He doesn't know how they survive. There are a few people smarter than us—geniuses, probably, but they don't have much personality.

That's how God made the world; Henry doesn't know why. God is white, upper-middle class, and Southern Baptist. He has sideburns like Henry, and small, straight, white teeth like everyone else in our family, but whereas the Pepperses are on the short side, God stands about twenty-one feet tall. Inside Bellamy Baptist Church, His head grazes the faux cathedral ceiling, forcing Him to bend down to see His flock up close. He wears square glasses from Revco and one piece of jewelry: a gold Masonic ring. In His back pocket He carries a small black comb and an ironed white handkerchief. He drives a four-door Ford without electric windows.

God's son, Jesus Christ, looked like a Hell's Angel in every picture I ever saw, but Florida explained that these portraits were done long after His death and may not have been accurate. "Jesus lives inside of you," she said. "Your body is His house."

For some reason, perhaps because we received extra portions of brain, God made all Pepperses tone deaf. I swear that Henry sang "Home on the Range" to me when I was a baby, but no one believes me. Every Sunday morning at Bellamy Baptist, we'd rise from our pew bench and lip-synch, lifting our chins and stretching our mouths wide to accommodate the whole notes. Florida made herself the exception. With her shoulders back, eyes bright, and red mouth open, she emitted a brave warble, having once done so in a beauty contest before walking away with the Miss Western Kentucky title.

Had anyone in the family been albino, it would have been my brother, Roderick, who had asthma and could turn so pale he was almost invisible. According to our local psychiatrist, Leo Frommlecker, Roderick was the Lost Child. I was the Clown, perhaps because of my ears, which were unusually large and also pointed. Neither Henry nor Florida cared to be diagnosed. All the same, as Florida pointed out, Roderick was regular white because albino's have pink eyes.

None of us has brown eyes or big noses or kinky hair. Originally, we all had straight, thin, mouse-brown hair, but Henry has lost most of his worrying about everybody, Florida has her coif dyed a different color every month, and Roderick's hair sprang into nervous curls when he entered the Middle School at Bridgewater Academy. Then, by an act of will, he went so blonde that it was difficult to spot him in the sun.

"The boy got the hair," Florida would say whenever she introduced me. Then, straightening my collar and tucking a few strands of hair over my pointed ears, she would sigh and admit, "She looks just like Henry." If the other person said "I see the spittin' image of her mother," the introduction had been successful.

Florida was a Deleuth before she was a Peppers, so she is not exactly like the rest of us, but she has a knack for imitation, and after she had been married to Henry for a couple of decades, you could hardly tell she wasn't the real thing. The biggest difference between the two families is that a Deleuth grew up under the instruction "You're a Deleuth, so you won't amount to much," while the Pepperses constantly remind each other that despite any temporary setbacks, we are Pepperses.

Both families come from the same stock: inbred European royalty with criminal records, weathered and further inbred in the hills of Appalachia. Henry and Florida are the only members of their clans to leave Kentucky without dying first. As soon as they were married, they blazed out of the state in Daddy-Go Deleuth's '58 Ford pick-up, with a black-and-white TV, a Kirby Lady Deluxe vacuum cleaner, and a salted ham strapped down in the back. Florida wore a pillbox hat and gloves; Henry wore wing tips and smoked a Louisville cigar. They were headed for Georgia.

"Mark my words," said Grandmother Deleuth. "Florida will git above her raisin's."

IF YOU'VE EVER heard of Counterpoint, Georgia, you probably read somewhere that it consumes more Coca-Cola per capita than any other town in the world, or that a member of the band KISS attended Bridgewater Academy. Someone might have mentioned that the freshman class at Maude Wilson College for Women boasts a virginity rate of 73 percent. None of it is true.

Counterpoint, governed by the local chapter of the Daughters of the American Revolution, is indistinguishable from any other Southern gothic town: oversized magnolia trees line the streets, a dinky mall attracts wayward youth, and on every other block, the statue of a Caucasian male on horseback scowls at the enemy. Some locals swear they've seen an alligator in the New Hope River, grown to a ponderous length of six feet on Moon Pies and light beer, but the water is too cold for gators. All the same, her name is Earnestine.

The New Hope River divides Counterpoint into the beautiful and the ugly. On the beautiful side, there is the Maude Wilson College for Women, founded in 1876 by the former plantation owner, Colonel P. Wilson. Wilson's real name was Tony Ritto—a lowbrow thief who was run out of Italy with a donkey's tail pinned to his pants. Upon his arrival in Counterpoint with a hundred slaves handpicked on Goree Island in West Africa, the colonel donated a statue of a howling wolf to the courthouse on Front Street. Inscribed on a gold plaque at the wolf's feet is the inscription IN BOCCA AL LUPI, CREPI! which literally translates "In the mouth of the wolf, eat it!" It means "Good luck."

In the summer, Officer Fitzpatrick patrols Front Street on a bay mare with a braided tail. The hooves strike bricks handmade by the colonel's slaves, klop klop. Officer Fitzpatrick patrols the street from Wanda's Wig Shoppe down to Spivey's Drugs—both run by an all-female, white-trash family—and back again, looking at his horse's reflection in the windows. The odor of sizzling hush puppies fills the air, and sometimes, as the sun sets on the muddy river, a ray of light flashes onto the golden wolf at the courthouse, lighting up her emerald eyes. Cats stand sentry on the porches of millhouses painted in lemon, cherry, and vanilla, iced with gingerbread trim. Down by the river, an old black man wearing a suit raises his face to the blue sky and sings in a deep, sonorous voice, "Jesus is tenderly calling thee home. Call-ing to-day."

Turning onto Mansion Street, a broad avenue lined with dazzling white monstrosities vying for our annual DAR Most Beautiful Home Award, you can still hear the old man singing "Call-ing to-day . . ."

OUR HOME SITS on the beautiful side of the New Hope River, but not in the Historic District, atop a hill called Mount Zion, so high that clouds pass beneath our windows. From the roof of our house, we can see across the river to the virulent spawn of Frenchie Smartt's empire: the glaring tin roofs of Smartt's Gas Station, Smartt's Liquor Store, and Frenchie's Bar; the gash of Smartt's Junkyard. Over this skyline rises the purple smoke plumes of Southern Board, the corrugated board plant where Henry has been general manager for nearly half a century. Most people think that Southern Board stinks, but as Henry will patiently explain, it's the paper mill next door to his plant that has an unpleasant odor. This situation exemplifies his theory that a lady's reputation is formed by the company she keeps, but Henry does not himself make that connection. In any case, it's just paper, and if the wind was right, it smelled like money to me.

With Henry's money, the help of a succession of hare-brained architects, and the counsel our local interior decorator, Shirley Frommlecker, Florida created a house unlike anything ever seen in Counterpoint. It had no front or back, that anyone could locate, and the ceilings were painted while the walls were left bare. Since no one ever helped her carry groceries into the house, Florida designed an electric dumbwaiter, which never worked right and finally had to be dismantled, leaving Henry with the constant fear that one of the children would fall down the thirty-six-foot shaft, break his neck, and become a paraplegic. It was Henry who tactfully suggested the intercom, in hopes that Florida would not need to holler at the top of her lungs to someone in another room, but after lightning struck the house twice, the intercom only functioned on LISTEN — allowing unlimited eavesdropping. There was an alarm system that was not connected to anything and could not be heard by the neighbors because there were none. About once a month a bird would set off the alarm, driving us all into the same room in a frenzy of adrenaline-powered family feeling whose aftermath left us sheepish and surly.

Owl Aerie, Florida named the house. When the last shingle had been nailed down, she sent a photo of Owl Aerie to Grandmother Deleuth in Red Cavern, Kentucky. Grandmother was seventy that year and attending a funeral every other week. At the Farley Brothers Funeral Home, she unsnapped her musty, black pocketbook and with trembling, spotted hands, passed around the photo. Everyone agreed that it looked just like a barn. Uncle Lyle, the evangelist, said, "It's a wonder with all that money Henry's making, he can't buy him a coat of paint."

The house was built in the seventies, when Shirley

Frommlecker was reaching her peak as an interior decorator. Henry, conservative by nature, kept a tight reign on her in the upper regions of the house, where he slept, ate his cereal, and read the *Wall Street Journal* in the bathroom, but in the basement, she and Florida went wild. No one in Georgia really had a basement, being mostly Baptists and avoiding the underground. Instead, on the lowest levels of our houses, we built small dank bedrooms for boys and assigned the rest of the space to recreation rooms, called rec rooms for short.

Our rec room, where I had my first religious experience, had orange indoor/outdoor carpet, a billiard table, and some furniture Henry would not allow upstairs: a pair of black-and-white vinyl hassocks designed to look like dice, a lime-green bean bag, and a white vinyl couch accented with leopard print pillows. To create the illusion of light, Shirley covered one wall in mirrored tiles. For added interest, she mirrored the ceiling, and hung psychedelic suns that twirled in the steady draft of the air-conditioning.

Henry never could get used to the strings of aqua beads that replaced a perfectly good door. In the doorway, he'd hesitate, as if trying to decide exactly where to part the beads, and after he entered, he'd wipe his arms. He called the room "your mother's love den."

Shirley insisted that Florida hang her acrylic copy of *Femme au Miroir* over the couch, and Florida obliged, even though she didn't think it was her best work. "I want to do something original," she said. "But I'm not creative enough."

"Oh listen to you! Florida, yes you are," said Shirley.

Shaking her head, Florida straightened the canvas on the wall. "I guess you can't really tell that's a bosom."

"Not unless you're looking for one," said Shirley. She urged her to replace the gray La-Z-Boy recliner with a Jacuzzi, but Henry put his foot down.

"You could wear your bathing suit," argued Florida. "You just don't want to get wet."

"Shirley likes to play with other people's money," said Henry. "Let Leo Frommlecker read a soggy paper. I haven't noticed a Jacuzzi in their house."

"What's wrong with the Frommleckers?"

Henry mumbled something behind the stock page.

"What did you say?" demanded Florida.

"I said, he's a nut, and she's showy."

"You are prejudiced against the Jews, Henry. Tell the truth."

In reply, Henry crackled the paper.

"You're as repressed as you can be," said Florida, but she couldn't get another word out of him.

OUTSIDE THE HOUSE, Henry was nice to everybody. That was his job. Besides being the best general manager Southern Board ever had, he was chairman of the Counterpoint Chamber of Commerce, president of the Elks Club, chairman of the board at the Counterpoint Bank, treasurer of the Rotary Club, deacon at the Bellamy Baptist Church, a Mason, a Boy Scout leader, and a member of the board at the Three Bears Country Club. "I don't *enjoy* any of this," he explained to Florida when she complained that he was inattentive at home. "It's how I make my living."

Florida did her work out of pure love for her family, even if no one appreciated it. She did a lot. Aside from her regular janitorial duties, KP, and a weekly wash, dry, and fold, she ran a twenty-four-hour on-call taxi service for Roderick and me. She chauffeured us to and from Bridgewater Academy, Boy Scouts, Brownies, the Royal Ambassadors for Christ, Girls in Action, ballet, tap, trampolining, soccer, Junior Thespians, Bible School, Beginning Wilderness Survival, Hooked on Books, Intermediate Macramé, and anywhere else we needed to go to enrich our lives or pass the time. She was never late.

She wrote notes to our teachers, ran security checks on our friends, typed our papers, watched our language, and disposed of our dead pets. She decorated the house for every holiday, baked a cake for each birthday, and got Henry to take his socks off when he went on vacation.

Henry was a good provider, once he got kicking, but Florida was convinced he would sleep all day if she wasn't there to get him out of bed. Usually, she had to call him three times. Her work wasn't over when he wandered into the kitchen in his bathrobe, smiling sleepily at the box of cereal she had set at his place at the table. Throughout the day, she urged him to stop dilly-dallying and procrastinating. She picked out his secretary's Christmas gift, tolerated his boss's dumb jokes, and turned the news off at night when he fell asleep in his chair. She wore lipstick and a good bra for him every day of her married life.

On the rare occasion that Florida went out of town, even for a day, our lives came to a halt. We'd sit around in silent, unlit rooms, with glazed eyes, as if we'd been unplugged from our current. Eventually, Henry would offer to open a can of tomato soup, but we were usually too apathetic to eat.

Florida did not limit her activities to Earth. Although Jesus said, "In my Father's house there are many mansions: if it were not so, I would have told you. I go to prepare a place for you," Florida was a stickler for making reservations. At least once a day, twice on Sundays, she prayed for our salvation. On Saturday night, she pressed our clothes for church and set our shoes on a piece of newspaper by the back door for Henry to polish. In the morning, she curled my hair and made sure that I did not leave the house without a slip on under my dress. "We want to look nice for the Lord," she said.

In her spare time, Florida painted. She used acrylic paint because oil takes too long to dry and is hard to clean up. Once, Henry suggested that she wear rubber gloves while painting, to keep her hands unstained.

"Artists don't wear gloves," she answered tartly.

"Well I didn't know," he answered. He had never paid much attention to art, but he considered her renditions of *Starry Night, The Last Supper,* and *Femme au Miroir,* almost as good as the originals, and of course, much less expensive.

Florida performed her jobs so well that no one really noticed them, but three times a week we followed her into the beige interior of Bellamy Baptist Church because Henry told us, with a doleful face, "It's the least you can do for your mother."

Although much of the architecture in Counterpoint has enough historic significance to warrant a plaque, Bellamy Baptist Church was built to appear eternally new. It is beige, inside and outside: beige brick, beige trim, beige carpet, beige pew cushions. Since stained-glass windows don't come in beige, we compromised with pastel, which shine weakly in contrast to the brilliantly colored windows of the Catholic church next door. Those windows pour their heathen colors through our pale glass, and sometimes, in bright sun, red and purple light slashed across my hands as I ran them along the beige pew cushion.

I longed to be a Catholic. I wanted to drink wine instead of Welch's grape juice, wear a rosary, and have a huge cross hanging on our living-room wall, bearing a plaster Jesus who looked like he'd been in a motorcycle wreck, his blue eyes rolled up in agony, blood dripping down his flat, white belly. My best friend, Drew St. John, was a Catholic, and she had class. Until the tornadoes hit, and Jesus called me, I was privately planning to join the St. Johns in hell.

Although I had broached the subject of my salvation with Florida and Henry several times, I had never received a satisfactory reply. "If I'm not born again, and I die suddenly, will I go to hell?" I asked. They babbled all sorts of evasive nonsense back at me, but the answer was plain from the worried frown on Florida's face. Sometimes, when Henry wasn't around, she'd hiss, "The devil's got hold of you. Do you want to end up with him in hell?"

To appease her, I'd say, "Oh, no. I want to go to heaven," but I could only envision endless beige carpet.

EVERY YEAR IN Counterpoint, the Daughters of the American Revolution sponsor a tour of homes. Each year they traipse through half the choice new residences in town, noting pet stains on stair treads, unappealing shower curtains, odors of diapers, whiskey, or take-out food. Then they return to Mansion Avenue, where they select the same five white mansions they put on tour every year.

Still fuming from Red Cavern's dismissal of her house,

which Grandmother Deleuth had dutifully shared over the phone, Florida was determined to present Owl Aerie to the DAR. Henry balked, but he lost like a gentleman, and after locking up his financial records and personal correspondence, hiding the contraceptives, and polishing the forty-one plaques of recognition on his study walls, he left the enterprise alone. He was at work when Lacy Dalton, Regina Bloodworth, and Shirley Frommlecker arrived. Although Shirley was not in the DAR, she was rich, and as our official decorator, she took the privilege of showing the house—"To drum up business," Henry said.

From my vantage point on the roof, I watched the Frommlecker's tank roll up our steep driveway and disappear behind a bend of crepe myrtle, where it stalled out. For a few minutes, the sound of birds was drowned in Lacy Dalton's shriek, punctuated by Shirley's exclamation, "Isn't this the most original thing you've ever seen!"

In a low voice that carried straight up to the roof, Regina said, "Indeed." Regina had been legally blind in both eyes for a decade. When relatives urged her to have corrective eye surgery, she turned up her nose. "Hospitals stink," she said. "Besides, I've seen everything. None of it is as interesting as what I can imagine." A pillar of the DAR, Regina accompanies her friend Lacy to each of the residences seeking admission to the Tour of Homes, and Lacy considers her input invaluable.

"Hold on to your hats, ladies!" cried Shirley, as she gunned the machine back into gear and brought it to a screeching halt at the back door. She drove the only Tracked Troop Carrier in town, given to her by Dr. Frommlecker after she had wrecked two Lincolns. Sliding across the roof on my belly, I dipped my head over the edge to watch as Shirley, wearing a paisley skirt and a turban, directed the women away from our garage door and onto the raised walkway that crosses a cactus garden and eventually leads to the disguised front door. Lacy Dalton, who is shaped like a watermelon, wore a wraparound kelly-green skirt covered with watermelons, a watermelon-pink blouse and matching espadrilles. She tottered along with one hand on her hip so that Regina could hook her long thin arm through Lucy's short fat one.

Regina always wore black, so that she could dress herself. She kept her silver hair cut short above her ears, like a man, and despite everyone's warnings that one day she'd be knocked down and robbed, she adorned her person with half a million dollar's worth of jewels. Even her cane glittered with diamonds as it tapped along the planks. She smelled faintly of rum and vanilla. With their arms linked, the two women walked in practiced synchronicity behind the turbaned Shirley, who was talking a mile a minute. From the corner of my eye, I saw the white flash of Roderick's hair in the sun. He was hunting lizards beneath the trampoline. Silently, I descended the dogwood tree.

"I kid you not," Shirley was saying over her shoulder. "There she stood, in the middle of Front Street, at ten o'clock in the morning, naked as a jaybird. Agnes had just done her hair."

"Frenchie Smartt's girlfriend?"

"Live-in. I can't recall her name."

"I know I've seen her. The one with the bosoms?"

"Of course I didn't stop the car, but I can tell you that she wears an underwire bra."

"What goes up . . ." said Regina.

"Lawdee," said Lacy, turning serious. "Someone really ought to do something about her. I mean, having a cocktail is one thing . . ."

Shirley halted and turned to face the women. In a hushed voice, she said, "Alcoholic."

Just then, Florida opened the front door. All three women beamed back at her and began to talk at once. The high slippery waves of their voices filled the yard, then the door shut behind them, and all was quiet except for the buzzing of insects in the noonday sun.

Roderick approached me carrying a Japanese cricket box in his hand. Shirley had found the box in Atlanta, a purely ornamental piece to set on the living-room coffee table beside the Chinese vase, but Roderick soon discovered that it served as a fine cage for crickets, worms, and lizards.

"Here," he said, handing me the box. "I got two of them. If they get rowdy, just thump their heads."

Once inside, I removed my go-go boots and sidled along the walls so I could spy on the DAR, but they saw me.

"Isn't she precious."

"The boy got the hair. She's the spittin' image of Henry."

"Oh Florida, I disagree, honey. She's you all over again."

Florida opened the front door and hollered, "Roderick! Are you out there in the weeds!"

He yelled back that he was fine.

"Come in here and get your inhaler! I don't want you having an attack tonight." She marched outside with the small green inhaler in her palm.

• • •

"THESE ARE MY WORKS," Florida was saying in her studio while Lacy made *ooh* and *aah* sounds.

"You are so talented. I could just kill you. Regina, they are out of this world. Is that a Matisse, honey? It's just gorgeous."

"It's supposed to be Van Gogh," said Florida. "I flubbed up on the stars. The children were fussing that day."

"Well, I learned all that in college, but I get them mixed up now. I guess it's old age."

"Lacy! You're not old!" said Shirley, laying a ringed hand on her round pink shoulder.

"Oh yes I am! Did I tell you that Bill offered to loan me his razor, to shave my chin?"

"Shame on him!"

"Did you wring his neck?" Their perfumes mixed and filled the air. Regina did not laugh when other people laughed. She stood tall, leaning slightly on her cane, facing the canvas in her black sunglasses.

"Getting old is the best thing that ever happened to me," she said loudly. Then she added, "*Starry Night*. I love that painting."

"Isn't it great!" said Shirley. "I made her put these out when I was doing the house. She had them in a closet—"

"Henry doesn't like to put too many nails in the walls," said Florida.

"Men!" exclaimed Lacy. "I tell you what."

As the women rustled out of the room, trailing their scents behind them, Florida spotted me in the corner.

"Where are your shoes? Is that my cricket box? I've been looking all over for that thing. Put it back where it belongs, right now. Never mind, give it here. You'll knock the vase over." She didn't add "And it cost a fortune" because we had company.

When company came, they used my bathroom. Florida shut the sliding door to my bedroom, opened the hall door, and whipped out the four guest towels and six tiny shell-shaped soaps that no guest had ever dared to touch—until Regina arrived.

While she waited for Lacy to finish her business in the adjoining toilet, Regina stood at my sink, scrubbing her hands with a delicate lavender clamshell. Through the sliding door, which I had cracked open, I watched with delight as she snapped an ironed linen guest towel from the rack. Her back was ramrod straight, and through the mirrored wall facing us, I could see her sharp gray face in the dark glasses. Pressed against the door, I trembled, wondering if she would take them off. Roderick said that her eyes had been plucked out, leaving two holes through which you could probably see her brain. Florida said that was foolish; she'd have glass eyes, like marbles, and Henry said that surely someone would have shut the eyelids. Although I was taking shallow, quiet breaths, and standing so still that my feet had gone to sleep, I felt sure that she was looking back at me through the mirror. *Half a million dollars,* I thought, watching her rings glint as she roughly dried her hands, then tossed the wadded guest towel onto the counter.

Suddenly, she spoke. Her voice was loud, a habit she'd acquired from responding to people who raised their voices to talk to blind people, and it startled me so much that at first I thought she was talking to me.

"Who are they?" she asked.

From the toilet, Lacy grunted, "Who?"

"The Pepperses," repeated Regina. "Who are they?"

"Oh," said Lacy. "They're nobody."

I waited, but no explanation followed. Regina took her cane and went out into the hall; Lacy rinsed her hands at the sink, drying her hands on a Kleenex, and then carefully folded the towel Regina had used and replaced it on the rack.

I sat down on my bedroom floor, on the purple shag carpet that still showed the vacuum cleaner tracks and looked at the iron bed from Grandmother Deleuth's attic, which Florida had painted to look like brass, and the white laminate dresser from Sears. On the wall behind my mamason chair, Henry had carefully hung the John Denver poster that Roderick gave me for my seventh birthday. My heart felt the way it did when I'd eaten too much peanut butter too fast. *Nobody*.

What happened next seemed like fate. I walked into the living room, where I found Regina sitting alone on the couch, sipping a hot toddy from the thermos she carried in her large black pocketbook, thumbing through a copy of *Southern Living*. As she turned the slick pages, her mouth softened, and a dreamy expression came over her face. What was she seeing? The voices of the women downstairs drifted through the intercom.

"Now this is just darling—a fur bedspread. Cute, cute, cute."

"He picked the wallpaper out by himself. I could kick myself for letting him, but I did. Bugs on the wall! He wants to be a doctor; every time I turn around, he's dissecting—"

"Shirley, could you do a ceiling like this in my house, or would that be too much? Go on, Florida, I'm listening."

Although I made no attempt to disguise my presence, Regina and I didn't speak to each other. When I heard the lizards jumping in the cricket box, I took them out to thump them into submission as if there were no company in the room. Inside the box, they had turned from gray to gold. I looked around for Roderick, to show him, but he had disappeared. Regina burped, then crossed her ankles, which were as thick as the trunk of the dogwood tree.

Nobody, I thought, and then I stepped forward and placed one golden lizard on each of her legs. Slowly, the chameleons, with their noses pointed up, gulping air, turned gray. Then they darted beneath the hem of her skirt.

Regina screamed. It was a wild call, released from the deepest, darkest jungle of her heart, and when its chill reached the back of my neck, I wailed with her. Our cries reached an ear-splitting crescendo that sent Florida and the DAR up the stairs at breakneck speed, but it was too late.

With her skinny arms raised over her head, her mouth drawn into a murderous grimace, Regina thrashed her cane into the Chinese vase.

THAT AFTERNOON, AFTER the Daughters of the American Revolution had left with fluttering waves and tense smiles, Roderick said, "Who wants to live in a museum? Not me."

"Well they didn't pick us for the tour, so hush," said Florida. She removed a cookie sheet from his hands. "Oh honey, not my good pan. You don't have to do that today, do you?"

Roderick took the cookie sheet back and covered it with tin foil, spreading Crisco in a rectangle for each lizard he intended to cook. "All I know," he said sternly, "is that I don't want a bunch of ladies poking around in my room, getting goop all over my stuff."

"They like fine furniture," said Florida. "Knickknacks. Junk. I don't think Lacy even got a good look at the vase before it was broken. That Regina is nuts. I don't know what got into her. She's not right. I'm going to submit Owl Aerie to *Southern Living* anyway. The DAR doesn't have the last word on everything. Owl Aerie is original. They like the same old, same old. Old money. They probably want you to have a black maid."

Roderick opened the cricket box.

"I told you they were gold," I said.

"If you have to cook your lizards," Florida said with her back turned, "I am going to ask you to kill them first."

"It's probably a good thing we don't have a maid," said Florida, sitting down at the table with the Chinese vase, now a box of shattered china, and a bottle of glue. "She wouldn't last a minute in this house." With her brow furrowed, she began working the jagged edges of porcelain together like a jigsaw puzzle. Wheezing from his afternoon in the weeds, Roderick turned on the oven and removed an envelope of sterilized surgical instruments from his pocket. "Son," she said, without looking up, "don't you use my manicure set on those lizards. I'll tan your hide. You hear?"

THE SOUND OF a tornado begins with a low whistle. Something is calling you, not coming for you yet, but calling. It is hard to sit still, impossible not to listen. This is how most people die in tornadoes; they run to them. On the day Owl Aerie was hit, the patch of sky outside the kitchen window turned a yellowish, lake-water green, and five pieces of hail the size of golf balls struck the glass in rapid succession, like a knock.

"Henry, don't you go out there," said Florida. "I'm telling you." With his face deep in his cereal bowl, Henry pretended not to hear. He had never missed a day of work at Southern Board, and he saw no reason to lay out now. "A national tornado isn't a good reason to stay home?" cried Florida. Henry didn't think so.

He did not, however, ignore the risks of inclement weather. THE BEST WAY IS THE SAFE WAY was the motto at Southern Board, and the guiding principle of Henry's life. That morning, after his shower, Henry stepped into the walk-in closet he shared with Florida to find his tornado hat.

On the left side of the closet, above a row of polished shoes packed with shoe horns, twelve gray suits hung a hand's width apart on wooden hangers. The suits were followed by starched white shirts. At the end of the shirts, there was a burst of color —a banner of maroon and navy ties. The last tie in the line-up was banana yellow. Florida had given him that one after she received yet another kitchen appliance for her birthday, and Henry didn't have the heart to get rid of it. This was Henry's side of the closet, emerging like a regiment of well-heeled soldiers against Florida's side, which can only be described as savage.

Here, hangers made of wire, yarn, and catgut disappeared under blinding wheels of color. In a dizzying sweep of plaid, check, and polka dot, Florida's wardrobe appeared to be caught in flight. Turquoise and chartreuse sequins flashed beneath something pink and bulbous, covered in feathers. A flame-orange spike heel dangled from the strap of a white patent-leather bag. A pair of padded, cone-shaped falsies from an ocher bathing suit teetered on the top shelf, and a stocking hung between them like a tail. Red was splashed around like blood.

Henry had trained himself not to look over there. Reaching up to the top shelf on his side of the closet, he removed his tornado hat. It was shaped like a motorcycle helmet, covered in a tasteful plaid merino, and trimmed with coyote fur. Coyote earmuffs swiveled up or down. He turned the hat in his hands, inspecting it for lint, then fitted it on his head without messing up his hair.

When he returned to the kitchen with his briefcase, Florida was ready for him. She was wearing what she always wore in the morning: a slinky zebra-print housecoat that zipped to the floor and a pair of sparkling gold spandex house shoes with hard soles that clacked on the tiles. A quilted green scarf covered her head, to keep her hair from going flat when she slept. Even though it was still dark outside, she wore lipstick. "I know you don't want to listen to me," she said, "but I'd like to make a suggestion. May I make one suggestion?" Henry smiled behind his coyote fur.

"I don't know why you're risking your life for a bunch of cardboard," Florida said. "That bridge is probably out. You'll go straight into the New Hope River. What about your family? Your children? Don't you want to share our lives? Aren't we more important to you than money, money, money? You'd stay home this morning from the plant if you had any sense."

No one in our family said *cardboard*. Again and again, Henry has instructed us to never, never say *cardboard* in reference to the Southern Board product. That's ignorant. Did we want

people to think we were ignorant? Of course not. Roderick and
I could rattle off *corrugated board* before we were two.

Henry kissed her cheek and headed for the door. Like all
Southern Board employees, he is steadily losing his hearing.
Florida thinks he is doing it on purpose.

When he kissed her, she lifted one earmuff and said, "Good-
bye, dear. I don't know if we'll ever see you alive again or not."
Henry hesitated. "Go on if you're going," she said, clacking her
heels across the floor as she crossed the kitchen to swipe the
table with a dishrag. "Have a nice day." She swept some crumbs
into her palm. "Go on before it gets worse. I love you."

Chapter Two

GRANDMOTHER DELEUTH CALLED that morning. We knew it
was her because Florida was shouting back into the phone.

"Mother, I can hear you!"

Unconvinced that anybody in Georgia could hear someone
talking in Kentucky in a normal tone of voice, Grandmother
called out so that we all could hear, "The TV says you all are
getting a twister down there! I commenced to worrying!"

"It's only a tornado watch, Mother. It's not a warning.
Henry went on to work as usual. Don't start fretting."

"Well, I am! Watch the chirren, Florida. Don't let 'em out."

"How are you and Daddy?"

"We're settin' here worrying about you all."

"You said that, Mother. Let's talk about something else. Can
you think of something else to say? How about something
positive."

"I don't reckon I can."

"How's Uncle Lyle?"

"Last month one came up this way and took the roof off his barn. Jimmy Simmons, his sister's husband's half brother, don't recollect his name, she said it would have come off anyway. That barn was older than I am, reckon. 'Twas his sister's husband's half brother told him to get up there and fix it, but he don't listen to people."

"What came?"

"Honey, I told you! A twister! Evange Lyle—that's your Daddy's brother—"

"I heard you, Mother. Please don't shout."

"Well y'all don't want to talk to us. Busy."

"Hush that, Mother. I'm talking to you. I just want you to say something positive, stop fretting and worrying. Get out of the house once in a while."

"Daddy-Go won't get in the car, you know that. Says it makes him want to upchuck."

"Be sweet to him, Mother."

"Pshaw. Y'all don't know. Y'all don't know how we do up here, honey. We just set and worry."

"I'd feel bad if that's what I did all day long, too. Pick up the Bible. Read what Jesus tells you. That's the part in red. Look at the *Reader's Digest* I sent you. Get your mind off yourself."

"I reckon."

"Do you want to talk to your grandchildren? They're right here, waiting to talk to you if you'll stop that crying."

"I can't hep it."

"Hush. Here's Roderick." Roderick pushed me toward the phone.

"Hello?" I whispered.

"Speak up," said Florida. "She's old."

"Y'all are sweet chirren," said Grandmother Deleuth, crying softly. "Y'all be good to your mama. I guess I'll be dead and gone before I see you again."

Florida took the phone. "Mother. I'm sending you a Billy Graham tape of positive thinking. Mother?" She shook the receiver, but it was Grandmother Deleuth's habit to hang up a telephone when she had nothing left to say.

FLORIDA DECIDED WE should pray for Henry.

"Don't get contrary on me this morning," she said when Roderick and I made long faces. "It will only take a minute of your time. Grandmother is worrying me to death, and Henry is out in that tornado. Get down on your knees and say a prayer with me before I lose my ever-loving mind."

On my knees, with my hands folded and my head parallel to the kitchen floor, I could not help but notice the pink tail of our hamster, America the Beautiful, poking through the refrigerator grate. While Florida prayed, I kept one eye open, watching the tail twitch, disappear, and reappear. It was all I could do not to shout. However, for the sake of Henry, who was driving straight into a tornado, I kept quiet and squeezed both eyes shut.

Florida prayed, "Lord, we need your help. Guide Henry to pull over on the side of the road. Don't let him be too proud to stop. Let him obey you and do your will and not act stubborn." She paused as she mentally lifted the Ford Galaxie 500 and turned it around to face home. Then she said, "In Jesus Christ's name we pray. Amen."

When we opened our eyes, the sky had darkened, filling the kitchen with an eerie green glow.

"America the Beautiful is under the refrigerator," I said importantly.

"Oh shoot," said Florida. "I guess he got out when I cleaned his cage this morning." She glanced away from Roderick's stricken face. "No. We don't have time to fool with that mouse this morning. The storm is coming." When Roderick whimpered she drew her mouth into a firm line that made her look as old and fierce as Grandmother Deleuth. "I said no, and that is final."

A few minutes later, while Roderick and I waited at the top of the basement stairs with the picnic basket, Florida was on her knees in front of the refrigerator, holding a slice of American cheese and calling out the hamster's name.

By the time she returned with America the Beautiful captured in his exercise ball, Roderick pinned me against the wall by my hair. I could smell the cold, medicinal odor of the inhaler on his breath and feel his wheezing as if it were in my own chest. He punched me in the stomach.

"Say it again!" he breathed into my face.

"Children!"

"Albino," I whispered, wincing as his fist sank into my belly.

"Children, stop it! I'm going to take a switch to you both!"

"I didn't do anything," said Roderick. "She's an alcoholic."

"I'm going out there to cut me a switch. Who's an alcoholic?"

"I am not."

"She drinks a bottle of vanilla extract a week," he told Florida, gingerly taking the exercise ball she thrust into his hands.

"Do you want me to flush that mouse down the toilet?"

asked Florida. "Because I will. I have had it up to here this morning." She adjusted the scarf on her head and added in pianissimo, as if she were just discovering a truth, "I can't take anymore from you children. Or your father. I have *had* it." Outside, the weird green sky was perfectly still, as if God were holding His breath. I sniffled, once. A Muzak version of "Delta Dawn" played softly on the intercom.

Florida shook her head and looked away. "I am through with you all," she said. "I have tried and tried. I can't do it anymore. Henry may be lying in a ditch right this minute—in pain." She grimaced. "While you two fuss and fight and bicker. Act ugly to your mother." Tears welled up in her eyes. The tip of her nose turned pink.

"I'm sorry, Mom," said Roderick, but it was too late; Florida was past her boiling point.

"Ugly, ugly, ugly," she said, describing us to God. "Ungrateful." She took the vanilla extract from my hand and shoved it into the picnic basket. "You all will just have to fend for yourselves." With that, she straightened her shoulders so that her zebra-print housecoat fell smoothly around her body, lifted her chin, and with a gaze that suggested she had never borne children and never intended to, she descended the stairs.

Suddenly, the lights went out. The intercom made a sound like a zipper, and the music stopped.

"Lord!" called Florida, and I cringed, knowing that He had found me.

Back on the stairs, Florida cried out to us—the Lord gave her the strength to reclaim us. "Children," she said sharply. "We are having a tornado. For once in your lives, cooperate with your mother and get down in this basement."

CROUCHED ON A die hassock, the white one with black dots, in the corner of the rec room, Florida whispered, "Hush," even though no one had said anything. In the distance, we heard the faint whistle of a train flying through the tops of the pines. Roderick put his inhaler to his mouth and sucked in a cold breath. "Here it is," Florida said. In the green light washing through the small window, she and Roderick looked like fish underwater. Under the pool table, America the Beautiful ran madly, turning the exercise ball in slow, hypnotic circles.

The wind blew in a long, soft moan, then sharpened into a shriek that hurt the backs of my eyes. Florida gripped Roderick with one hand just above his elbow and tightened her arm around my waist until I could barely breath. *Whoo, whoo* went the wind, hollowing out again, and I began to hear the music inside the tornado, faint strains of Barbara Groche's organ playing "A Closer Walk with Thee."

Reverend Waller was saying into his microphone, "Won't you come? Jesus is calling you." His thick, wet lips drew close to the wire mesh, bubbling the words on the electric current. "He wants you to come to Him, today, right now. Surrender your life to Him, welcome Him into your heart this minute. He wants to live inside you. Children, won't you come home to Jesus? Come on down the aisle." He stretched his arm out, holding his hand open for anyone to take. "There's still time. Come on down and say, 'Yes, Lord, yes! I surrender all!'" As I leaned against Florida, watching America the Beautiful spin in circles, the organ music faded, and from deep within the moaning sky I could hear the softest strains of Muzak.

The tornado hit our backyard with a scream. The sound was so human that Florida hollered, "Lawd! Somebody is out there! Henry?" She stood up, as if she intended to go outside and look, but Roderick stopped her. He did exactly what Henry would have done. He said, "Sit right back down. Everything is going to be all right." To keep me quiet, he passed over the vanilla extract.

Regaining her composure, Florida ordered, "Everybody cool your jets. Your mother lost her mind for a minute. I'm sorry."

The scream subsided. In its place came more hail and the sound of a vacuum cleaner, a big one, roaring across the sky. Then the hail began to swirl up in the air, faster and faster. Things flew past the window: leaves, pine cones, a red tennis shoe that no one recognized, and finally, clinging to the frayed webbing of a lawn chair, the neighbor's yellow cat. All around us, branches snapped, and then, with a crack like a rifle shot, the hickory tree crashed into the deck. As we stared at all this through the small window on the opposite wall, there was a sudden Pop! and the glass plane flew out into the wind. Right behind it came America the Beautiful, still in his exercise ball, a spinning wheel of fur that sailed into the whorling green sky.

"Mama!" cried Roderick. Florida held him fast; her face swirled between the psychedelic suns in the mirror, eyes flashing, red mouth open wide. I couldn't get close enough to them. No matter how hard Florida squeezed me against her ribs, or how tightly I clutched Roderick's sleeve, I felt as if I had already been sucked out the window and hurled into the cold, howling, madness of the sky.

Then I knew what hell was. It wasn't so bad to be in it, but it was hell for the people who loved you, who had to look at you burning in the flames, out of their reach. With cold panic, I realized that if we died in this storm, the Devil would snatch me down to hell while Florida, Henry, and Roderick wafted up to heaven. I had not been saved. They had been born again to have life everlasting. It was too late for me. Why hadn't Florida listened to me when I told her I had to be baptized? "Wait until you get some maturity," she'd said. I knew plenty of immature Christians. How were the Pepperses going to enjoy their mansion in heaven if I was in hell? They'd worry about me for eternity. For eternity, they'd sit around their swimming pool, licking ice creams without tasting them, smiling and waving at the angels who floated by so people wouldn't think they were ungrateful, but the whole time they would be worried sick about me.

Florida would probably try to sneak out to rescue me, but God has eyes in the back of His head. "Sister, you get right back here," He'd say as she sidled up to the golden gate. She'd nag until the angels shrank back into their wings, but God would not budge, not even if she cried. He'd shake His head, unfold the ironed white handkerchief from His back pocket, hold it under her red nose, and say, "Blow." God was all-powerful.

Henry would get so down in the heart he'd put on a zip-up coverall and sit in a lumpy chair in the corner of a darkened room chain smoking like his brother Earl who had been hooked on Thorazine for twenty-one years, ever since his wife had his brain electrified to make him quit drinking.

Poor old Roderick. He'd kick around in the pool by himself, wheezing, thinking about every time he'd broken into my room with a bobby pin. He'd remember the time he socked me in the stomach for no reason except to show off to a boy neither one of us liked. All those times he called me Dr. Spock. If Jesus tried to talk to him, he'd mumble something polite, then go underwater. All day long he'd mope around in the baby pool, leaving his ice-cream cones to melt. At night, sleeping alone in his star, he'd cry.

No one was killed in that tornado, except perhaps for America the Beautiful, who was never seen again. The neighbor's yellow cat turned up in the dogwood tree with a broken leg, and Henry walked in the door at suppertime.

"—right out the window," Florida was saying as she slapped his plate on the table. "Roderick nearly had a fit. We'll get you another hamster, honey. If you have to have one. I hate those things. Sit down, Henry. Your soup will get cold. Here's your tea. It doesn't have enough ice." She was wearing her tornado outfit, a brilliant orange and pink paisley skirt that swirled around her legs as she hurried to and from the stove. The quilted cups of her Jane Russell Living Bra poked through a tomato-red leotard. Gypsy earrings swung from her ears. The ringlet curler she had forgotten to remove dangled against the nape of her neck.

From the doorway, Henry admired her.

Florida said, "Roderick, I am not going to tell you again. Get that chair off its hind legs before you break your neck. Well, Henry? Did you see anything on the road? We thought you were a goner. Louise, no ma'am. I worked hard on this meal. You put that cupcake right back in the box. Sit. If your father would take off his coat and sit—dad-blame, I burned the rolls. I do it every time. There's too much commotion in here. I guess you didn't close the plant. Honey! Not with your hands. The radio said there were trees all over the road. Roof of the Texaco flew into the duck pond. Give me that burned roll—that one's mine. I'm putting some more in the oven. Henry, what happened to your hat?"

"Gone with the tornado," he said, sitting down at the table.

"You're kidding." She stopped suddenly, looking him over to see if anything else had been lost.

"Did it lift you off the ground?" asked Roderick.

"I don't want to know," said Florida. She lifted the bifocals that hung on a chain a round her neck and set them on her nose.

Slowly, Henry sipped his iced tea, then leaned back in his chair and began. "I was driving down the mountain when the sky turned green."

"Here, too."

"Everything was so still, you could have a heard a pin drop. Right then, I knew that sucker was coming. And there was nothing I could do about it, not a thing."

"I told you to stay home," said Florida, leaning closer.

"All the sudden—" Henry looked around the table to make sure everyone was paying attention—"all the sudden I saw a fire hydrant, that one right in front of the radio tower, you know, I saw the fire hydrant shoot straight up in the air!"

Florida covered her face. Then she got up to put a tub of margarine on the table.

"Now the craziest thing was the water under the fire hydrant."

"I'm listening," said Florida, as she dropped some more ice cubes into his tea. "Excuse my fingers. Roderick, if you keep leaning back in that chair you're going to fall through the window. I'm just telling you. For your information."

Henry cleared his throat.

"Did you crawl into a ditch?" she asked.

He frowned at her. "I'm trying to tell you about the fire hydrant."

"Well go on. The water was shooting straight up in the air . . ."

"About thirty feet. Then it began to swirl." With his hand, he showed us how the water swirled high above his head. "I never saw anything like it in my life. Louise, you should have seen that yellow fire hydrant sitting on top of the water. It looked just like an upside down ice-cream cone."

"You're exaggerating," said Florida. "Did you get in the ditch?"

Ignoring her, he looked sternly at Roderick and me. "If you ever get caught in a tornado, and I hope you never do—"

"I was just in one," said Roderick.

"I mean outside, in a tornado, always remember to get in a ditch. That's the first thing you should do. Jump in the ditch, lie face down—make sure there's no broken glass or anything first—and cover your head. That just might save your life."

"I didn't think you'd get in a ditch," said Florida. "You wouldn't get your good suit dirty for the world. Put some butter on that roll before it gets cold. This soup is terrible. Don't eat it. I'm sorry." She buttered Henry's roll, then began to clear the table.

"I'm trying to teach you all something," said Henry, wrapping his hand around the iced tea glass so she wouldn't take it away. "They need to know what to do in a tornado."

"They did fine today. Their mother got in a dither. I'm pooped. Louise, are you through with that? Then eat it and stop playing with it. I don't want to be in this kitchen all night."

"They should teach you all about tornadoes at Bridgewater," Henry said. "With all that tuition they charge, you'd think somebody would teach a class in safety. Water safety, fire safety, CPR, what to do in a tornado. Around here, your biggest danger is snakes. These woods are crawling with them. Rattlers, copperheads . . . You step over a log, and wham! That snake thinks he's caught him a rabbit." He shook his head, seeing Roderick and me the way a snake would, as rabbits. "Down in those woods, we'd never be able to find you. You just lie there beside the log, for days and nights—"

"That's enough, Henry."

He paused. "I don't know how many children die every year from gunshot wounds. Why a parent would leave a loaded gun in the house, I don't know, but they do. Firecrackers are almost as bad. I've seen children with their hands blown clean off."

"Where?" asked Roderick.

"Why, at the wrists. Sometimes the elbow."

"He means where did you see them," said Florida, making another attempt to take Henry's iced tea glass off the table.

"Then there's poison," said Henry. "No matter how smart you are, if you accidentally swallow rat poison, you're in big trouble. You start bleeding from your nose, your mouth, even your eyes—all the orifices."

"I bet you were standing right beside a ditch when that tornado blew your hat off," said Florida.

Henry bit into his roll. "At the plant, we have mandatory safety classes for every employee."

"Your father would not sit in a ditch and get his good suit dirty to save his life," said Florida, sitting back down at the table with a dishrag in her hand. She touched his arm. "Would you?"

"I was ready to get in the ditch. Then my hat blew off."

"I knew it! You chased after it, didn't you?"

"Well it was just across the road. There were no cars coming. I went over there, and it blew a little further, so I went around the curve, and then you won't believe what I saw."

"America the Beautiful?" I suggested.

"I saw Leo Frommlecker's Tracked Troop Carrier coming right down the road. You know that one he bought from the Army Reserve? Of course, that's illegal. But he had it out this morning, driving around in the tornado. That thing cost him a pretty penny, so I guess he tries to get some use out of it whenever he can. He gave me a ride to work."

Florida shook her head slowly back and forth. "My goodness. Leo saved your life, honey. Maybe you'll like him better now."

Henry shook the empty catsup bottle. Then he screwed the cap on tightly and set it upside down on the table because there is always something at the bottom of the bottle.

"Nooo," said Florida into the kitchen phone that evening. "Louise did not tell me she had called you." She motioned wildly to Henry. Then she put her palm over the receiver and said in a stage whisper, "It's Reverend Waller." Pursing her lips, she nodded in my direction. "Well, thank you," she said into the phone. "She can be sweet sometimes, but not always. Yes, we think so, too. Yes, that's what Henry said. Who told you about it? Shirley? Not a scratch on him, thank the Lord. He answered our prayers. We're so grateful to Leo. And you all made it through all right? Good. *Mmmm, hmmm.*" She scowled. "No, Louise is not twelve. She must have misinformed you. She turned seven last December. Yes, she is a bird." She shook her head at Henry. Then she smiled into the phone and said, "We think so, too. We'll see you in church on Sunday. Bye now."

After she hung up the phone, Florida sat down at the table and put her head in her hands. As she rubbed her hand across the back of her neck, the ringlet curler clattered to the floor. Henry picked it up. "She did it again, Henry. She called Reverend Waller and asked to be saved. Told him we forbade her. I don't know what all else."

Roderick walked into the room and asked for a Saint Bernard.

"I have tried and tried," said Florida. "She does this to spite me."

"They have small ones," said Roderick. "I'll feed him. I promise."

"I just can't take it anymore." She patted the skunk stripe in her hair, then rose swiftly from the table and began to make school lunches for the next day. Without looking at Roderick, she said, "Not in Georgia, honey. A Saint Bernard would burn right up. You've got to be practical."

"He'll stay in the air-conditioning." Pale freckles stood out on his nose. He crossed his arms over his chest, licked his chapped lips, and stared hard at Florida, concentrating his will on her. "Please."

I climbed up on the counter to get some vanilla extract, knocking a box of powdered sugar to the floor.

"I've had it!" screamed Florida. "You all can just fend for yourselves tonight. I am through!" With ten sharp taps across the tile floor, she was gone. The three of us looked at each other for a minute, listening to the overhead light buzz. Then Henry got the broom and began to sweep.

The next day, the white Princess phone was removed from my bedroom, until I could learn not to call the preacher up and lie about my age, or anything else.

EXCEPT FOR FALLEN trees and telephone poles, one uprooted fire hydrant, and several broken windows, Counterpoint did not suffer any serious damage from the tornadoes. Apparently, God struck the town not with the intention to destroy but to reorganize.

ONE WAY street signs now pointed in the direction of heaven. On the playground at Pruitt Elementary, which sat adjacent to the city dump, a commode and a rusted television set balanced on a teeter-totter. Yard animals had traveled from the Meshack Trailer Court to the Mansion District. A fifty-thousand-dollar reproduction of *Venus di Milo* sailed out of Lacy Dalton's garden, across the New Hope River, and into Frenchie Smartt's yard. Frenchie fixed the broken arms and put it up for sale.

On the Sunday after the tornadoes, Henry drove us to church early so we could survey the wreckage. He steered the

Ford Galaxie 500 down Mount Zion at a speed even slower than his usual Sunday crawl, commenting on every fallen limb in the neighborhood. "Would you look at that!" he cried. "Old Richardson sure does have a mess to clean up in his yard. Take him a week."

It was a warm day, with a cloudless blue sky, but we kept the windows up. If anyone asked for air, Henry turned on the vent. He obliged requests for music by turning on the AM radio that came with the car, turning the volume so low that a person had to more or less imagine the music being played. When Elvis Presley came on the radio, however, Florida took charge. She turned up the volume and hushed anyone who spoke. "Shhh," she said in the voice she reserved for Elvis. "Here he is." The King's tenor broke through the wheeze of AM radio, boldly striking the first notes of "Rock of Ages."

Florida leaned forward, as if the King might emerge from the dashboard, then she fell back against her seat, let her head sink into the headrest without messing up her hair, and with her eyes closed, began to hum. On her face was pure rapture.

Henry sped the car up to a devil-may-care thirty-five miles an hour, but Florida didn't even notice. "No honey, I'm listening to him," she said sweetly when he tried to turn the volume down.

"That ole mama's boy," Henry said. "I don't know why you get so shook up over him."

"Hush," she said. Elvis crooned,

> Rock of ages cleft for me, Let me hide myself in
>   Thee;
> Let the water and the blood, From thy wounded
>   side which flowed,

Be of sin the double cure, Save from wrath and
make me pure.

"I don't know when he got religion," said Henry. He
laughed to himself as he looked over at her.

"You're jealous," she said. Love had smoothed the worry
lines on her brow and taken the pinch from her mouth; she was
beautiful.

"Ha," he said. "Jealous of that hillbilly? Ha." With one hand
rolling over the steering wheel, he turned the car onto Shad-
drack Street. He was about to point out a bicycle wedged in a
tree when I rolled my window down and stuck out my head.
Florida put a hand up to protect her hair. Henry cried, "Get
your head back in the car before someone drives by and knocks
it clean off. Shut that window!"

I pretended not to hear him. The wind roared in my ears as
I twisted around to get another look at the redhead on the corner. The woman's hair was everywhere, falling over her shoulders, draped down her back. A flattened ball of hair rolled
down the sidewalk; she held a long braid in one hand. With the
other hand, she knocked on the window of the Shamrock
Liquor Store. A large sign in the window read CLOSED. Beside
her, a man in a cowboy hat pulled at her arm, shouting. Suddenly, she swung at him, clipping his ear, knocking his hat off.
He hit her back. Blood squirted from her nose, just like on TV.
Then he hit her again, and she crumpled to ground.

"Stop!" I screamed.

"Stop the car!" said Florida.

"What is it?" asked Henry. "Roderick, pull her in right now."

"What happened, honey? Henry, don't have a wreck. Just pull over. Roderick, is she hurt?"

"She's just trying to get attention," said Roderick, but he was looking out the window, too.

Henry skillfully maneuvered the car onto a grassy patch of Calvary Cemetery without hitting a tombstone.

"What happened?" asked Florida, who had unfastened her seat belt to twist around and get a better look at me. "Did a rock fly up and hit your head?"

"You shouldn't open the car windows while we're driving," said Henry. "I've told you a thousand times."

"A man hit that lady, and she fell down."

"What lady?" Florida frowned. Then she looked back at the parking lot of the Shamrock Liquor Store, where the man and woman were walking off together. "Oh, *that* lady. Go on, Henry. Start the car. We're going to be late for the service."

"Was she in the road?" asked Henry.

"No, honey." Florida shook her head. "In the parking lot of the liquor store."

"She was bleeding," added Roderick.

"Lock your doors," said Henry.

"Hush that sniveling, Louise," said Florida. "We don't need that this morning."

"Why can't we help her?"

No one said anything as the car pulled smoothly off the grass and dipped into the road.

Finally, Florida said, "Say something to her."

"What?"

"You don't listen, dear. She wants to know why we don't help those people."

"Why didn't we stop?"

Henry sighed. "Honey." He sighed again. "We just don't get involved in that. Don't you ever go near a liquor store parking lot. Roderick, that means you, too. All kinds of things happen in those places. They attract an element."

"Someone was shot there last year," added Florida.

"That's what you get when you hang around those places," said Henry. "People shouldn't expect anything else."

Florida reached into her pocketbook, pulled out a compact, and began to apply her lipstick in the mirror. From the depths of the bag, she retrieved a wadded-up Kleenex and added another kiss to it. Then she snapped the compact shut, cleared her throat, and said, "It's time to get your mind on church now."

God and Jesus were the furthest things from my mind. All I could think about was that woman in the parking lot of the Shamrock Liquor Store, with all that fake red hair falling off her head, how, even with a bloody nose and no glasses, she looked like Regina Bloodworth.

THROUGHOUT THE ENTIRE church service, I sat on the edge of the pew, gripping the Children's Holy Bible and praying for another tornado to hit so I wouldn't have to be born again. Now that I knew I was really going to walk down the aisle, I wasn't sure I wanted anybody living in my heart. What if I wanted to be alone sometimes? What if Jesus and I didn't get along with each other? When I stood up next to Henry and lip-synched "I am weak, but Thou are strong," my knees wobbled.

Then there was the whole question of heaven. Hell might actually be more fun. I had never really enjoyed traveling with my family: Niagara Falls, Disney World, Rock City, Grandmother Deleuth's farm in Red Cavern, Kentucky—after the first day, we got in each other's hair.

When Henry put his arm around me, mouthing "Thro' this world of toil and snares, If I falter, Lord, who cares?" I almost wished he would hold me in place, but he only patted my back.

The hymn ended, and I was not saved. No one was saved. Reverend Waller looked at the congregation the way my teacher, Miss Fitzpatrick, looked at the class when something had been stolen. Then we all had to put our heads down on our desks, with our eyes closed, and wait for the thief to tiptoe up to the front of the room and hand the goods over to her. Even though I had never stolen anything, I always felt guilty with my head down on my desk, and had to struggle not to turn myself in. I felt the same way now, looking back at Reverend Waller. He looked straight back at me, with deep sorrow in his face. Jesus was calling, and I wasn't coming. He was glad to take whoever came to the altar, of course; we weren't short of sinners, but it was me He really wanted. He had His eyes on Louise Peppers.

Reverend Waller hung his head for a minute, so that we could all see he was praying, and then he motioned to Barbara Groche, who raised her hands and hit the chords of "A Closer Walk with Thee" one more time. Again, we opened our mouths to sing.

At the beginning of the last stanza, I shot out of the pew. I was wearing my white vinyl go-go boots and had to be careful because the zippers came undone sometimes. It was a long hike down the beige-carpeted aisle to Reverend Waller's outstretched arm, with every eye in the congregation turned on me. I walked for what seemed like a couple of hours, and during that time, a miracle happened.

Up until then, a small part of me had suspected that there was no God, that Reverend Waller, and Florida, and all the Baptists, were making this up as they went along. The apostles were just trying to convince each other that we weren't out here on Earth all by ourselves, making a big mess. They were lonesome, that was all. Baby Jesus, Bethsemene, the Tower of Babel, Jezebel, the lions, water into wine, creating the world in six days then taking Sunday off and making all the stores close—sometimes it was hard to swallow the whole story, especially when people tried to *make* you believe, the way people do when they're lying.

I had other worries. What if Barbara Groche stopped playing the organ before I reached the altar—what if she didn't see me? If that happened, I would be the only person left standing up in church, like the loser in musical chairs. Or what if I got to the altar and kept walking, right past Reverend Waller, out the door? Florida would kill me when we got home.

What happened to me was this: My chest began to hurt. Then I felt warm all over, and light, the way I did when I had had the chicken pox. Everything in the sanctuary at Bellamy Baptist Church began to glow. The sun hit the pastel stained glass in a new way, as if someone had just cleaned the windows. The plain wooden cross over the baptismal, which I had never admired because it didn't have a dead body on it, suddenly looked important. Inside, I felt clean and bright and new. As I passed by Mrs. Gubbel, my Wednesday night Girls in Action leader, I didn't think, *Gobble gobble gobble.* I wasn't afraid of anybody. I didn't worry about the zippers on my boots. I didn't feel like beating anybody up. I felt fine. I felt the way Florida looked when she was listening to Elvis.

By the time I reached the altar and took Reverend Waller's sweaty hand in mine, I knew that it was all true somehow, that you could really close your eyes and talk to God. God and Jesus listened to you and loved you like crazy.

Smoothing the cord of the microphone with his free hand, Reverend Waller smiled and said, "Brothers and sisters in Christ, Frances Louise Peppers comes to us this morning with a decision to surrender her life to Jesus." We beamed at each other. He had bad breath, but I didn't care.

While Barbara Groche played softly "My Redeemer," the church body filed out of the pews and snaked down to the altar to shake my hand, to say they were happy for me, I had made a good decision, and they loved me. I shook hands the way Henry had taught me: two short, firm strokes and look 'em in the eye.

An old, stooped-over lady, smelling strongly of gardenias, wouldn't shake hands. Instead, she pressed my hands inside her gloved ones, and held them. She wore a stiff navy blue hat with a short blue veil, a dress in the pattern Florida called Swiss dot, and two long strands of fake blue pearls. Leaning in close, she said in a raspy voice, "You have shed that old life like a snake skin." Her eyes were milky blue. "Reborn."

"So fresh," she said, running one gloved finger down my cheek. I nodded. I felt so new I was afraid I would squeak if I opened my mouth. Reborn! I couldn't wait to do it again.

Chapter hree

ALL BAPTISTS LIVE for doomsday, but the Pepperses are down-right morbid. Henry is the least embarrassed about it. If he saw a wreck on the highway, he'd change lanes and slow down to see the victims up close. Florida always closes her eyes, so he narrates the scene in gruesome detail, filling in the blanks with his imagination.

"That eighteen-wheeler creamed right into him," he'd say, craning his neck to get a better view. "Cut his arm clean off."

Without opening her eyes, Florida would say, "Henry, you're telling a story."

"No I'm not! I saw the fingers sticking right out of the honeysuckle. Saw his wedding band." Such a scene, real or imagined, brought to Henry's mind other tragedies, which he related in the form of lectures on safety.

He once told about the time he saw the back door of a Pontiac pop open on I-75. "That baby flew right onto the shoulder of the road. Couldn't have been more than two. Luckily, it was all right. I hope that mother learned her lesson."

"That's enough Henry," said Florida, covering her face with her hand, but he went on.

The tornado he'd witnessed on Mount Zion grew bigger with each telling. Twister, he called it.

"Why, there I was lying in the ditch, when that sucker hit the ground inches from my face. It untied my shoelaces."

"You wouldn't get in a ditch in your good suit to save your life," corrected Florida, but he continued, his eyes glowing.

I loved the story about the businessman in Bloomingdale's who fell down an escalator and was strangled by his tie. "People just don't think ahead," Henry would conclude with a frown.

For a long time, Roderick and I thought every family traveled with funeral clothes—church clothes in dark colors, without undue decoration, just in case.

"It's a good practice," Henry said. "What if you got out there and someone died and the store was closed, or they didn't have your size? What if all you had to wear were tennis shoes? Then you'd be up the creek."

Florida backed him up 100 percent. "We're going to see old people," she reminded us of the summer we tried to ditch the funeral clothes for our trip to the Deleuth farm. "You have to be practical. The shops in Red Cavern don't have anything you'd like."

"I refuse to participate in this panic mentality," declared Roderick, removing the clip-on tie that Florida had stuffed in a corner of his suitcase. He was at the rebellious stage: He'd begun to lock his bedroom door, blow-dry his hair, and snicker on the telephone. On his chin regularly sat a bright red pimple that we were all supposed to ignore. He was thirteen. Because of his asthma, he was smaller than other eighth graders: skinny and bluish-white, with delicate wrists like a girl and a head of those soft, swirling, golden curls. After a few valiant attempts to play football, which failed because he was allergic to grass, he resigned himself to an intellectual life of Dungeons and Dragons, Thoreau, and an occasional joint.

"Am I a bison," he cried, blushing as his voice cracked, "running off the cliff with the herd, or am I human being, free to think and act as I choose?"

"He wants a real tie," said Florida, "like yours, Henry. This one is for little boys." She glanced at Roderick's angry face, worrying over his pimple. "Do you need to go to the bathroom before we get in the car?"

"I do not want a tie," said Roderick, glaring. "I want to live unhampered by the conventionalities of this bourgeois, fear-based society. I want to breathe!"

Henry told him to get a job. To avoid a fuss, Florida slipped the tie into her dress bag, along with my Mary Janes.

We spent an hour in the garage, watching Henry pack the car. Roderick had already checked the oil and cleaned the windshield, but Henry had to pack the trunk himself. If anyone put a bag inside the trunk, Henry shook his head, declared "There is a place for everything in this life," and took it out again.

"Slow poke," said Florida. "We go through this every time. Did you pack my knitting? Give me that. I need that in the front seat." She stepped boldly between Henry and the trunk to snatch her knitting bag from the elaborate puzzle he was creating in the trunk.

Henry mumbled something.

"What did you say?"

"I didn't say anything."

"You look like you want to murder me. I'm not going. I'm going to stay here. You all go. Everything is such an ordeal with you!"

"Don't start a commotion." Henry turned his back to her and with one last surveillance of his work, closed the lid on the trunk.

"Commotion? Without me to push you, you'd never get out of this house. Dawdle, dawdle, dawdle. I suwaan! You've got a problem—an obsession. Sometimes you need to just pick up and go. Move your feet!"

Henry removed the handkerchief from his back pocket and polished the lock of the trunk, a sign that we could all board.

Roderick stretched out in the back seat with his inhaler and worn copy of *Civil Disobedience,* while I sat in the front, squeezed between Henry, Florida, and the white toy poodle, Puff LeBlanc, so that Roderick and I wouldn't fight.

Legally, Puff was Roderick's dog. Roderick was allergic to most dogs, including his favorite breed, the Saint Bernard, for which Florida thanked God. She tried to talk Roderick into a Venus's-flytrap, a plant that eats hamburger, and then a koi fish, but in the end, she gave in because at least poodles don't shed.

Roderick swore she would never have to lift a finger. He read several books on dog training and cleaned out a corner of his room for Puff's dog bed, food bowl, and toys. When Puff arrived, he devoted himself to its happiness and well-being, following the pup around with a faint furrow in his brow and looking very much like Henry. Was his water clean enough? Did the collar fit? Why were we holding him wrong?

Puff, however, had his own ideas. Within forty-eight hours of his arrival, he had scoped out the situation and bonded firmly with Florida. All over Owl Aerie, you could hear the tap tap tap of Florida's heels followed by the tippety tap, tippety tap of Puff's painted blue toenails. Up and down the stairs they went, in and out of rooms, tap tap tap, tippety tap, tippety tap. On the rare occasion that Florida sat down, Puff collapsed, exhausted, in her lap. Often he awoke from these naps entangled in knitting yarn, and she would scold him, pushing him roughly to the floor. She spoke no endearments, and did not rub him behind his well-brushed ears. Still, at the sound of her, "Shoo. Git!" he wagged his puff of a tail with delight. Daily, she fed him, walked him, and jerked the tangles from his hair with a cold metal comb. When he had diarrhea, she cleaned it up and fed him teaspoons of Pepto-Bismol, bracing his mouth open with her fingers. Once, she knitted him a sweater.

"He worships me," she admitted. The dog only tolerated the rest of us, who ultimately had a low opinion of poodles and were disappointed that Puff acted so much like one. "You can't change a personality," Florida reminded us. "I have tried and tried with Henry. You take the good with the bad. When I married Henry, I thought he was perfect, but he's not." She poked him in the arm. "Are you?"

ALTHOUGH HENRY HAD never in his life exceeded the speed limit or turned without signaling or blown his car horn, he did have one bad driving habit, and it drove Florida up the wall. Sometimes he let the car run out of gas. It was an addiction, like gambling, an insane obsession to pit himself against chance. He did it that Sunday on the way to Red Cavern, Kentucky.

At two o'clock that afternoon, when the needle of the gas gauge rested delicately on the inner edge of the bright orange E, Henry slowed down in front of a Texaco station in Murfreesboro, Tennessee. Then he read the price sign and drove on.

"Dadgonit," said Florida. She glared at him. "It's on empty."

Henry looked straight ahead. He wore his driving sweater, a soft cotton cardigan with leather patches on the sleeves, and a pair of sunglasses from Kmart. Outside, it was too warm for a sweater, but we all needed one in the car, with the air-conditioning on high. With one hand on the steering wheel, leaning back in his seat as if it were a recliner, he said, "There's at least three gallons left."

"Then why does it say empty?" demanded Florida.

"Oh, that's not accurate. They set these gauges up for the general public. To give them plenty of warning."

"That's why the general public doesn't run out of gas," said Roderick from the back seat. We passed another gas station. Henry made a snide remark about the price, lit a fresh cigar, and drove on.

"Oh boy," said Florida. "Here we go. You do this every time, and it burns me up. You're cheap. Tight. Refuse to pay two pennies more so we won't all be sitting on the side of the road while Mother's dinner gets cold."

Henry looked into the rearview mirror and frowned. "Son,"

he said, severely. "I don't want to have to tell you again to get
your feet off that window. If we hit a bump, your feet will go
right through the glass. Another car might come by and cut
your legs off. How would you like to be sitting in a wheelchair
for the rest of your life?" Roderick sucked on his inhaler, filling
the car with its faint medicinal odor, and without looking
up, turned a page in his book. "That wouldn't be much fun,"
Henry continued. "I can tell you that right now." In response,
Roderick coughed loudly.

"Your cigar smoke is making him sick," said Florida. "He's
wheezing."

Henry turned the air vent to the back seat. "Why, if a big ole
eighteen-wheeler came by, and you broke the glass, that wind
could suck you right out of the car. You'd blow out of here like
a paper bag."

"Mom," said Roderick. "Don't let her open that nail polish;
I'll throw up," but I had already twisted off the lid of Good
Morning Peach and was applying the first coat.

"She's almost finished," said Florida. "Henry, let him crack
his window. Did you pack my book in the trunk? Darn it,
Henry!"

"What was the name of it?"

"*Temptation.*"

"You didn't tell me not to."

"You know better than that. How I can read my book if it's
in the trunk?"

"Where there's a will, there's a way," said Henry.

"You did that on purpose." She cracked her window and let
Puff stick his nose out. Roderick offered her some Thoreau.

"Oh that's too hard. I'm not as smart as you. I can't read

that. Maybe with the CliffsNotes. What did you bring to read, Louise?" Shoving Puff aside, she rummaged through my stack of books: *Very Special People,* an illustrated text about circus people. She flipped to a picture of Adolpho the Two-Headed Man, showing a handsome man in a suit lighting a cigarette for another man, the size of an infant, dressed in an identical suit and emerging from his own chest. From the expression on her face, I could see that she found the book in poor taste. *Paradise Lost,* which I was pretending to read to impress my English teacher, Samuel Rutherford III, did not hold her attention, even after I told her it was about God.

"I read the Bible," she said. "That tells the story of Jesus." She added, "Your savior," and I closed my eyes, pretending to fall asleep. Jesus was her back-up man. Together, the two of them created a superhuman SWAT team; Florida sniffed out the intransigence and Jesus crushed it with his Word.

"You don't want me to talk about Jesus, do you? Why does the Word of the Lord upset you?"

"There's a gas station," said Roderick.

"He won't stop," said Florida, and with a look of long-suffering resignation, she elbowed Puff onto my lap and pulled out her knitting bag.

I DECIDED THAT I didn't like anybody in the car. Mentally, I threw each family member onto the shoulder of the road and replaced them with my friends. An imaginary Drew St. John was riding beside me in the front seat, smoking a cigar.

Once, I had taken the real Drew St. John to Red Cavern. Three and a half hours into the trip, Drew announced calmly that she couldn't remember what her mother looked like. Both of us found this interesting, but Florida was upset.

"You're kidding," she said.

"No ma'am," said Drew firmly. "I can't picture her."

"That happens to me all the time," I said. "It's really weird. I think *Mom,* and nothing happens. I don't get a picture."

"I can see my dad," said Drew. "Unless I try too hard."

"Your mother is very attractive," said Florida, determined to forge this broken link. "She's tall and slender and has short brown hair. She's kind of quiet. She plays golf, and she . . . she drives a blue car."

"Eldorado," said Henry.

"Do you see her now, Drew?" Drew squeezed her eyes shut, then opened them.

"No ma'am."

"Her name is Katherine," Florida said urgently. "She's . . . she's . . . oh, shoot! You can't forget your own mother. You've only been gone one day. You're playing."

To close this discussion, she picked up her novel; from the glossy cover, I gathered it was about a man and a woman who couldn't keep their clothes on. After she'd read a couple of pages, she said, "If I had a picture of her, I'd show you."

That was the beginning of Drew's breakdown in Kentucky. Drew was not a delicate child. Her hair, the color of honey, was cropped short and springing with cowlicks. She had three freckles on her nose; in the summer she had a farmer's tan. A thin silver scar, incurred while jumping down a chimney, circled one sturdy wrist like a bracelet. She was a lefty, and she threw a mean, sneaky punch with her devil's paw. She did not, under any circumstances, touch dolls. Once I saw her eat a worm. Dr. Frommlecker claimed, with his characteristic lack of enthusiasm, that she was a genius.

All the same, Red Cavern did her in. Was it the landscape—mile after mile of monotonous tobacco, corn, and hay—everything growing to the same height inside rusty barbed-wire fences? Even in the middle of summer a gray pallor hung over the sky; nothing was bright and new. Dully painted trucks with dirty windshields rattled down the dusty roads. In the truck beds, cows stared morosely through weathered wooden slats as we sped by in the Galaxie 500, which Henry spritzed and wiped down at every gas station. In this part of the country, the gas pumps were antiques: big clunky things, once painted white, now dented and streaked with rust. These gas pumps had round heads; Henry stared into the glass face to watch the numbers creep by; it was like watching the hand of a clock. Everybody drank RC—there wasn't any Coca-Cola.

At the farm, Drew and I jumped from haystacks in the barn and taunted a bull in the field with a red tablecloth. We collected spearmint from the spring, locked Roderick in the chicken coop, and dissected the skeleton of a dog we found on top of a hill, but I knew she wasn't having a good time. Grandmother Deleuth gave us stained plastic coffee cups filled to the brim with cheerful M&Ms, but still, the gloom settled on us. Grandmother would cry, not so that you'd notice if you weren't looking right at her, but the rims of her eyes turned red, and small tears filled the creases of her skin like dew.

"You all don't know what goes on here after y'all go," she'd say. "How he curses me."

"Hush," my mother would say, while Henry looked on with the face he wore at church. "Let's have a good time."

Then Daddy-Go, sunk deep into his old chair, with his cane leaning against the wall, would lift his stubbled chin and look around with his bleary eyes, blue with cataracts, seeking sympathy for his life.

Both of them went through a litany of death; it was their main source of conversation. Sally Long—she was a Cartwright before she married—she fell on the front step and broke her hip for the third time, and her youngest stepsister, Mabel Brown, fell into the river, caught her hair on a branch, and drowned. Uncle Evange Lyle lost two cows in the electric fence when lightning hit, and the chickens all died of the feed.

"Reckon I'll be next," Grandmother would say, and Daddy-Go would say, "Lord willing."

I saw nothing odd in any of this, but Drew was uncomfortable. During that entire week, she couldn't conjure up her mother's face. Finally, the ghost in the upstairs bedroom got her.

The ghost was Frances Deleuth, Florida's little sister. Frances was killed, I explained to Drew, on the night of her high school graduation, after she'd been voted Most Popular and Best Looking. Florida had been salutatorian of her class, but Frances was valedictorian of hers, which was a shame because whereas Florida applied herself, Frances spent most of her time looking in the mirror. When her suitors came to call, she'd play the piano and laugh until the cows came home. On graduation night, Frances fell off the back of a pick-up truck. She'd been drinking, with boys.

"Her dress got caught in the tailgate," I whispered to Drew. We were sitting on the sinking edge of the high feather bed in the musty, darkened room, our bare feet dangling. "She kept rolling back under the wheel, until she was dead."

Drew put on her poker face while checking the facts. "Why didn't the boys in the truck bed tell the driver that she fell?"

"They did," I whispered. "They kept banging on the window, yelling, 'Frances fell off!' but the driver thought they were kidding."

We sat quietly, swinging our tanned legs, breathing softly. We faced two long windows, drawn with yellowed shades. Motes of dust hung in the narrow band of light beneath the door.

"Do you want to know what else?" I asked. "My father dated Frances before he dated my mother." Suddenly I jumped to the floor and padded across the scratchy wool rug to the cedar chest, where I rummaged through stiff black dresses and an assortment of black hats—some decorated with artificial fruit and flowers—until I found a pair of black elbow-length gloves.

"These belonged to Frances," I said, trying one on. There were no tips to the fingers of the gloves; I poked my hand through to show her. I put on the other glove and pulled them both all the way up to my shoulders. Then, feeling like a black widow spider, I waved my arms slowly back and forth.

A few minutes later, during a game of hide-and-seek, I pulled the crocheted tab of the window shade and found Drew flattened against the glass like a moth. Tears ran silently down her cheeks. Afraid to touch her, and not knowing what else to do, I pulled the shade back down. At suppertime, she was still there.

"She'll fall right through that thin old glass!" cried Henry, hurrying up the stairs to the bedroom. "You all know better than to play in windows!" Florida and Roderick ran outside, as if they meant to catch her. Grandmother Deleuth, dusted with flour, shuffled out of the kitchen and hung by the foot of the stairs saying "Lawd a mercy!" and leaving her mouth hanging open so that a thin stream of spittle dribbled down her chin. In the parlor, Daddy-Go slowly brought his cane around to the front of the chair. Then, bracing himself with both hands on the cane, he stood up. He was a tall man.

Henry stayed up there with Drew for a long time. No one would let me go upstairs, but we could hear him through the vent in the ceiling by the parlor woodstove. Roderick and I sat as close to the woodstove as we could, on the love seat. It was a cruel piece of furniture, too large for one person, and too small for two, without arm rests or pillows, designed to shift its occupants onto the floor. The only way to stay seated was to continually press oneself into the back of the love seat, which was upholstered in horsehair. There we sat, staring up at the dusty grate in the ceiling. Through the grate, Henry's voice rumbled down over our heads, singing "Home on the Range."

Being tone-deaf, I had no idea if Henry was hitting the right notes, but I knew it was music. It was Henry's one song, and he sang it beautifully. Squinting up into the black squares of the grate, I arched my back against the stiff, scratchy love seat, careful not to touch Roderick, who was cranky when his asthma kicked in and liable to strike. As Henry sang, I felt the familiar vibration of his voice, one wave lapping gently over the next, following the deep, strong current of his heart.

Eventually, still standing in the window, Drew fell asleep and Henry carried her downstairs to bed. She never accepted an invitation to Red Cavern again.

"HENRY," FLORIDA SAID as we passed an Exxon. "What was wrong with that one?"

"Too high," he mumbled.

"How much was it?"

"Eighty-eight cents," said Roderick. "I hope everybody is looking forward to a nice long hike up the Appalachian Trail."

"For law's sake," Florida sighed. "We can afford that. You're looking for eighty-seven cents, aren't you? Yes, you are. You do this every time. It just burns me up."

Abashed, Henry said, "I saw eighty-five cents a gallon just a while back."

"Why didn't you stop then?"

"We didn't need any gas at that time."

Florida blew her top. "Git out of my way!" she hollered at Puff as she reached over him to pull her knitting bag from the floor. Puff sat up, digging his painted nails into her legs as he tried to catch her eye with a woebegone stare. The ribbon in his topknot had worked its way to the end of a curl and hung fetchingly over one big brown eye. "Dad blast it!" she yelled, waving a fist of long, sharp knitting needles, and then with her free hand, she lifted the poodle into the air and sailed him into the back seat, where he landed on top of Roderick with a yelp.

"Mom!" Roderick screamed, "You're crazy!" Tears filled his eyes as he clutched Puff to his chest. With daring ferocity, he hissed, "Don't you ever touch my dog again."

Wedged into the middle of the front seat, I felt the muscles twitch in Henry's arm, but he didn't swing his hand into the back seat. Instead, he looked at Roderick through the rearview mirror. It was a look I knew well. When Henry had that look— it was a long blue stare—I felt the shock of seeing him as someone other than a father. At these times he would have looked perfectly natural holding a machine gun, with bodies littering the ground around him. No other human had ever looked at me that way, but once a German shepherd had given me that same cold, still eye, right before he bit me. Roderick whispered a sweet nothing into Puff's ear, and then shut up.

Henry's arm relaxed as he drew deeply on his cigar. On my other side, in Florida's lap, two metallic pistachio knitting needles, each as long as my arm, shot in and out of a tangle of red yarn until something resembling a sleeve began to emerge. We had started the long, lonesome climb up Lookout Mountain with the needle veering off of E. Florida pursed her lips and said, "Knit, pearl. Knit, pearl."

There was only one gas station on Lookout Mountain, a Mom and Pop grocery that charged an arm and a leg, and Henry, with a defeated half-smile, pulled right up to the tank, but the store was closed, it being Sunday.

Florida's needles went click, click. In the back seat, Roderick held his palm to his mouth and swished the small green inhaler, once, twice, and then a third time. His wheeze sounded like a light snore. Gently, almost tenderly, the Galaxie 500 crested the mountain, and at the top, right before a gravel track posted with the sign RUNAWAY TRUCKS, Henry shifted into low gear and stepped off the gas. Although Henry did not actually speed, he went easy on the brake pads, gathering speed after each hairpin curve, flying down the straightaways. FALLING

ROCK signs and waterfalls flew past our heads. A deer jumped for his life.

Florida prayed, "Oh Lord help us," and I began to compose my obituary.

MY DEATH WAS for my English teacher, Mr. Samuel Rutherford III. I loved him. In my school locker, away from Roderick's prying fingers, I kept a notebook of love letters addressed to My Darling Mr. Rutherford (I couldn't bring myself to call him Samuel). How painful it was, each week when I scribbled out the five-hundred-word essay he required, to erase the concluding sentence, "I love you, Mr. Rutherford."

He did not look like an English teacher. He drove an orange VW bug that seemed comically too small for him, like Charlie Chaplin's hat. When he wasn't teaching, he coached football, and he often came to class in a pair of long tight gym shorts and a jersey, clacking his cleats across the concrete floor. He was short and wide, barrel-chested, with thick hairy arms and legs, and a lion's mane of yellow hair. A scar ran down one side of his face, inciting rumors. He had a booming coach's voice, and when he was angry, he threw chalk so hard against the wall that it shattered into a puff of dust. Once, when Celeste Humphreys tried to hide in the broom closet, he locked the door and left her in there for forty-five minutes. I wished it had been me so that we could have looked at each other when he finally opened the door. When he was happy, he whistled.

He had a fondness for the dingbat and the aardvark. "When the aardvark ate the dingbat's new shoes," he'd write on the board, a stub of chalk clenched in his fist, "she threw her Dan-

ish on the floor and called the fire department." Then he dia-
gramed the sentence, making it look like a rocket ship. He
taught us compound sentences: nose-to-nose rocket ships, and
compound-complex sentences, nose-to-nose rocket ships with
shuttles riding on their wings. Nouns, verbs, and prepositional
phrases became part of a twinkling galaxy filled with blue
moons and shooting stars.

It was Mr. Rutherford's job to introduce us to literature.
He did this simply. "Shakespeare," he informed us, "is a great
writer. You may have another opinion, but that opinion is
wrong. Shakespeare is great." To my embarrassment, he
made us read *Romeo and Juliet* aloud. No one dared to snicker.
Shakespeare was great.

"Poetry," he told us one day, "is not for sissies." Then, sitting
on the edge of his desk, clenching a stub of chalk in his fist,
scowling, he recited, "The Death of the Ball Turret Gunner," by
Randall Jarell.

Under his eyes, I began to blush. It was a violent, spastic
thing, starting in my chest and rushing up to the tips of my
ears. My eyes watered. If anyone spoke to me, if he spoke—
Rhoda, he called me for some reason, lips curving over his
strong white teeth—a strangled laugh-cry sputtered from my
aching mouth, and I'd stop breathing for a few seconds. He enjoyed it. Passing me in the hallway, he'd turn suddenly on one
foot and sing out "Rhoda!" just to watch me go through the
whole gruesome business.

He was not married, but I knew that the chances he'd ask
a seventh-grader for a date were slim. In order to get his
attention, without being obnoxious, I sat about thirteen
inches from his desk and absorbed every word he uttered.

Consequently, I learned English grammar, but being recognized as a good student fell far short of my mark. Then I switched strategies. I wrote papers with my left hand, so that they were illegible, and when called on in class, I gaped, mouth open, eyes wide, as if struck dumb by a sudden brain tumor.

This worked. One day, after a particularly fine performance of amnesia, I was asked to stay after class. As the other students filed out the door, my heart fluttered and thumped like a bird with a broken wing. Already, the blush was beginning. Would he kiss me?

"Well, Rhoda," he said. He kicked his feet up on his desk, leaned back in his chair, and laced his thick fingers behind his head. He looked at me, hard. His eyes were blue. It was just us, in the chalky room, shades drawn, fluorescent lights buzzing. Slowly, the fire in my chest flickered up to my neck, and then my cheeks, spreading out to my ears. Love! How could I tell him? He had to know my scorching agony—it was him! He was in me, burning and burning. The way he stomped to the board with his stub of chalk, how he scratched his neck, the ball turret gunner, and the aardvark . . . "You're slacking off," he said. "Any reason?"

I gazed back at him. This was the moment. I could say, "Mr. Rutherford, I lust for you." My face was on fire; my palms sweated; my loins ached. I opened my mouth. "Kiss me," I wanted to say, and then he would stand up from his swivel chair, lift me onto the broad, battered old desk, and deflower me. He waited. My mouth closed, and then opened again.

At last, my words came out. I said, "I dunno."

"I suggest you get off your butt and get back to work," he

said, and that was the end. His face closed. He was done with me. I was a child.

As Henry swung us around the steep, precarious curves of Lookout Mountain, I envisioned Mr. Rutherford's face as the news of my tragic death reached him. He'd be strong at school, tougher still at football practice, but when he went home to his little stone teacher's cottage at the edge of the Bridgewater campus, he'd crumple. "Rhoda, Rhoda," he'd moan into his wet pillow as his heavy chest shook with sobs. "Oh Rhoda, how I longed for your passionate surrender." A suicide would be even better.

At the bottom of the mountain, Henry pulled into a Sunoco. It was open. They were asking ninety-one cents a gallon. Henry pulled up to a tank and let the car idle for several minutes while he debated with himself. We watched him, waiting. He couldn't do it.

"Oh Lawdee!" cried Florida as we pulled back out on the highway. The gas needle was pressed against the far left corner of the gauge. "We're through!"

"That's a racket," Henry explained softly. "See, he knows that ole Bob up on the mountain is closed on Sunday—the two of them are in cahoots. Bob, you close on Sunday, and I'll close on Monday, and we'll wrap this thing up tight. Why, I wouldn't be surprised if they were first cousins." The engine made a sound like a straw sucking up the last Coca-Cola from a bottle. "There's another service station right up the road," Henry said.

When the Galaxie 500 finally hiccuped to a stop, Florida was the first one out. A string of yarn had gotten wound around her ankle, and it caught in the door, but she whipped the harness off and without looking once behind her, set off down the highway. It was an empty road, the same gray as the sky.

At the wheel, Henry said, "Headstrong!" He rolled his window down and called out angrily, "Florida!" but she didn't even turn her head. In her Jacqueline Kennedy sunglasses and stretch pants, with a red scarf knotted under her chin, she looked just like a divorcée.

"You want me to go get her?" asked Roderick.

"No!" shouted Henry. "You all stay put. This family is loose as a goose. She's going to get killed out there." Again, he called for her out the window, but she was now a silhouette in the distance. He tried to start the engine, but it wouldn't turn over. His face turned purple. Blue veins stood out on his neck and hands. "Loose as a goose!" he repeated, and then stepped out of the car, locking the door behind him. He looked furiously at the disappearing figure of his wife and then issued a curt command to us through the open window. "If either one of you so much as lifts a finger, I will skin you alive," he said.

Two minutes later, an egg truck rattled by. It passed Henry in a cloud of dust but stopped for Florida. Henry picked up his pace, walking in quick, measured strides with a hard frown on his face, but by the time he reached the truck, Florida had already negotiated a gallon of gasoline with the driver. She waved gaily to Henry and signaled to the rest of the family with a sweep of her arm. We were saved.

ONE MILE FROM the Deleuth farm, Florida leaned across me to apply her lipstick in the rearview mirror. Then she looked around the car to see if anyone's hair needed combing.

She told Roderick to tuck his shirt in. She opened her hand, palm up, to me, and said, "Spit out that gum."

We passed cow after cow after cow, chewing cud behind an endless string of barbed wire. The houses were ugly: tight little brick boxes set on empty lawns. Most of the trees had been cleared, and the few that were allowed to remain had been chopped off to the size of large shrubs and painted white. Florida explained that some people thought stubby white trees were pretty.

"Why?" I asked.

"Because it's not natural," she said. "When you live in the country, you get sick of nature."

All around the small brick houses were vast fields. The tobacco plants, already taller than Daddy-Go, bloomed a defiant green. There were fields of hay, and Martian-green corn, and more stolid, staring cows. Occasionally a horse lifted its head, then flicked its tail and galloped away from the fence, but not fast, and not far. Grandmother and Daddy-Go had never gone further than the county fair in Louisville. When we showed them pictures of the ocean, they were unimpressed.

Henry eased the Galaxie 500 around the last curve. The tires crunched along the rutted gravel lane, and suddenly we were all waving to Grandmother and Daddy-Go, who had been waiting in the yard for an hour, watching the road.

As the engine died, Daddy-Go raised himself from the swing with his cane and hobbled forward; Grandmother beat him by five yards. She wore what she always wore: a homemade double-knit polyester dress covered with a cotton apron trimmed in rick-rack, coffee-colored nylon knee-highs, and the pair of Adidas running shoes we had given her last Christmas

to cure her corns. Her thin gray hair was wound up in a bun. A
pair of silver, cat-eyed glasses, studded with rhinestones, hung
from a chain around her neck, and tears ran down the soft,
wrinkled map of her face. Her first name was Cornelia, but
Henry addressed her as Mrs. Deleuth, in the voice TV anchor-
men used when they said Mr. President.

"We thought something had happened to y'all," Grandmother said, holding out her arms as she sobbed and tried to
smile. "Reckoned y'all weren't coming a-tall."

"Hush, Mother" said Florida, embracing her as she watched
Daddy-Go slowly make his way across the lawn. "We're here.
Look at your grandchildren. They came all this way to see you."

Brack, or Daddy-Go, as Roderick and I called him, was a big
tall man in overalls and unlaced brogans. His Stetson was half
his age and matched the burnt leather of his skin. White stubble roughened his cheeks; tobacco stained the creased corners
of his mouth. Several years ago, his brown eyes had disappeared behind the silver clouds of cataracts, and this is how I
knew him: a slow man bent under the weight of himself, moving at the imperceptible speed of the earth, and seeing everything with sightless, silver eyes. He was crying, too. They always
cried when we came.

"Hush that crying, Daddy," said Florida when he grasped her
arm with his free hand. "What are you sad about?"

"Chou chou," he said. That was his pet name for Florida.
Grandmother called her Sister.

She said, "Sister, look at them chirren. They're big! Look at
that girl." But she was still crying, as if we'd all died.

"She'll be in eighth grade next fall, said Florida. "She loves her English teacher. You should see what she reads. Hard words! It's over my head. And Roderick—"

"That boy done run off," said Brack, turning his head to spit a stream of tobacco onto the grass. Roderick was gone.

"He's stretching his legs," said Florida, glancing around until she spotted his white hair flashing in the sunlight as he ascended the propane gas tank. The tank was a white cylinder, bigger than any animal on the farm; it looked like a UFO.

"He'll fall off there and break his neck," said Grandmother.

"Your nasturtiums are looking pretty," said Florida. "I don't know how you do it. I can't get anything to come up." She walked toward the house—it was over a hundred years old—a big, awkward thing with Georgian columns, covered in white siding and bordered with Grandmother's perfect flower beds. Henry was shaking hands, first with Mrs. Deleuth, then with Mr. Deleuth. He wouldn't let anyone help him with the luggage. I wandered around the yard, careful to stay away from the tank so Roderick wouldn't think I was following him. He straddled the tank as if it were a white steed and didn't look like a teenager at all.

I knew yards. Our yard at Owl Aerie was a new yard, with tender young grass that flattened beneath my feet like shag carpet, and something called Japanese rock gardens. Ancient cactus plants grew up around the edges of the new grass, and occasionally, a copperhead wound through the hollow eyes of the sculpted dragon in the rock garden; it was as if we were trespassing. Aside from the boring Georgia pines, which didn't have decent climbing branches and glued your fingers together with sap, we had a frail dogwood that offered a precarious climb to the roof, and an old hickory tree that had been turned into a pretzel by tornado and lightning. The great advantage of the yard at Owl Aerie was the view. From up there, Counterpoint, Georgia, and the rest of the world, was reduced to a string of twinkling lights; it was very pretty. Red Cavern, on the other hand, was in a valley, and from Grandmother's yard, the world rose up all around.

Around the corner of the house I heard Florida exclaim, "Look at that garden, Mother! I declare!"

"It ain't much this year," Grandmother Deleuth answered, as she did every year. She grew snap beans, lima beans, tomatoes, cucumbers, corn, squash, red potatoes, and field peas—enough to can for the winter and feed all her relatives and friends. I didn't care for vegetables, but I liked having them around.

The best part of the Deleuth yard was the swing. It wasn't fast, but it had a good, solid creak, and it hung from the branches of a two-hundred-year-old elm tree whose branches had never been cut. The metal slats of the swing were covered in thick, bumpy layers of paint, interesting to touch. Beneath the swing, the ground was worn by Daddy-Go's brogans, ground into grooves of silken dust that the toes of my sneakers brushed as I swung back and forth.

There were grand things in this yard—a dinner bell, a crooked little gate that led to the rattling chicken coop, the cool, dark springhouse, the tin woodshed, and beyond that, the barn—but what I liked best was the dirt. Patches of it were covered in stringy, stubborn bluegrass; here and there you could uncover the stone of a walkway, and of course, blocked off by rabbit fencing were the rectangles Grandmother had claimed for herself and which turned fecund beneath her gnarled, crabbed fingers and from her fierce will sprouted seeds that shot up into green stalks bending with the weight of their fruit, but the dirt was the main thing. It was old dirt. It had a smell. I liked to lie on my belly on the stiff bluegrass, which was usually yellow, not blue, and press my nose into the dust as soft as sifted flour, feeling good all over. I thought, *This is what God smells like.*

I was taking a big sniff when I felt the toe of Roderick's shoe in my side.

"Get up, whale butt," he said. Immediately, the God smell left. "What are you doing down there? You're mentally unstable; do you realize that? Somebody's going to lock you up one day; I'm not kidding." To prove that I was of sound mind and that I could not be ordered around, I had to stay on my belly in the dirt, pretending to be occupied with something mysterious and important, while he prodded me with the toe of his shoe. This continued until Henry walked by, his arms full of luggage, and ordered us to stop it, whatever we were doing.

Florida and Grandmother came around the corner of the house, with Puff behind them, tugging on his rhinestone leash. He, too, was sniffing the ground, beside himself with the wild new scents. When a cow mooed in the distance, he strained against the leash, pulling himself up to his hind legs and yipping madly. His bow was long gone. Ignoring him, Florida paused again at the nasturtiums.

"Mine dried right up," she said. "Did you have any trouble with the petunias?"

"The tenant's cat got most of 'em. Never seen a cat eat flowers before. She come down here and says I killed it." Brack,

who had made his way back across the lawn and was maneu-
vering up the concrete steps to open the screen door, said
something no one could hear.

"What's that, Daddy?"

"Addled," he said, allowing Henry to get the door for him.

"She had a black eye—that man batters her—says she's married to him, but I don't reckon she is."

"Hush," said Florida. "We don't need to hear all about that."

"Last week she had a fellow up there drinking and carrying
on . . ."

"Addled," said Brack again. "That cat sucked eggs like a dog."

"Is that right?" said Henry. "Watch your step."

"Why don't you evict her and get a new tenant," suggested
Florida.

"Oh honey! They's all just white trash. Carrying on." Her
voice trailed off into despair. "You don't know how we do
when y'all are gone away."

"I guess not," said Florida briskly. She looked at me. "How
did you get so dirty?"

"Wallowing in the dirt, of course." said Roderick. "Oink, oink."

"Come on in, Henry," said Mrs. Deleuth as he held the door
for her. "I'll have dinner directly."

"I hope you didn't go to any trouble."

"Pshaw," she said. Henry continued to hold the screen door,
scrolled with a large D, as we filed into the low dining room. In
the corner sat a diesel stove, and for the occasion, the cherry
table was covered with a pale-blue vinyl cloth. Beside the door
were the section of newspaper where Daddy-Go kept his brogans and the sixteen-penny nail where he hung his hat.

Two steps led up from the dining room into the parlor, where

Grandmother and Daddy-Go slept on a heavy old mahogany bed. The headboard was elaborately carved with birds perched on a winding vine; some of them balanced grapes in their beaks. Brack's mother had purchased the bed for five dollars, and it was too big to carry any further into the house.

Everything in the house was heavy: the cast iron stoves in the parlor and back bedroom bent the floorboards, and the wood that Henry brought in at night clunked down heavily beside them. We were all heavy in the featherbeds, sinking down and down and down. In the summer, Roderick and I slept in cots on the back porch, but even then our quilts weighed down on us, making it difficult to move our arms and legs. I dreamed that I was a hummingbird weighted down with the wings of an eagle. Roderick dreamed that he he was trapped under the hull of a boat.

The doors in this house did swing airily, closing with a gentle, precise click like the doors at Owl Aerie. These doors were made of oak slats, hung on cast iron hinges, and closed with latches. Closing a door at the Deleuth house was a momentous act. Separated by one of these doors, we felt the cool hollow of each other's absence. Likewise, when a door creaked open, and someone entered the room, everything shifted.

At Owl Aerie, since we had no neighbors, Florida left the windows uncovered to take advantage of the view, but on the farm in Red Cavern, even though the nearest neighbor was five miles down the road, Grandmother pulled yellowed shades over the long windows, and at night, drew the dusty velvet drapes across them. The dust in the Deleuth house was thick and permanent. Over the years, it had settled deep into the folds of the wool rugs, the velvet drapes, the quilts, and even the clothing, so that everything became the same heavy, muted, nameless color. I liked the dust; it smelled faintly of the yard, but Roderick suffered in the thick air. After a few hours in the house, he'd begin to wheeze, and after a day or so, he was squirting his inhaler every fifteen minutes, struggling to breathe. If he went into the barn he had an out-and-out asthma attack. Florida hovered over him until he ordered her to leave him alone; then she lectured Grandmother about housekeeping.

Many years back, a clean-shaven young man in a new suit had come by the farm with a Kirby vacuum cleaner, which he demonstrated on the parlor floor. Grandmother, who let anyone in the door—except the tenants—was so embarrassed at the sight of this strange man cleaning her house that she pulled out her worn leather coin purse and bought the Kirby. When he was gone, and she tried the machine herself, it became clear why they'd sent a man to the job. The Kirby was a monster—a gleaming, flashing, screaming ton of lead. When Florida got married, Grandmother gave it to her and let the dust settle in peace.

Time was heavy on the farm. Every half hour, a yellow door sprang open in the cuckoo clock that hung on the parlor wall. A bird sprang out, screeching "Cuckoo!" It was an insane and ponderous cry, heavy with doom, like the crow of the rooster on cold black mornings.

At the side of the house was a cast iron dinner bell that Roderick had to pull with both arms. Then the pendulum swung—dong, dong, dong—loud enough to crack the sky, and it would not stop. That afternoon, even after Henry went outside to stop the noise, the bell rang inside the house, in our ears, dong, dong, dong.

GRANDMOTHER DELEUTH, WHO was eighty-one that year, had the habit of picking up a story wherever she'd last dropped it in her thoughts. As she moved around the kitchen preparing dinner, she suddenly shouted to Florida, "Fell sick and said he never was no account no way."

"Mother," said Florida firmly. "Who, what, when, and where."

Grandmother was impervious to the criticism of her story. She raised her voice, yelling impatiently, "Your cousin Frank's youngest sister! Who married the Thompson boy with the game leg. He run off with Perry Marvin when he was a boy— out to Deer Creek with his Daddy's gun, and they got to fussing and fighting over a gal over in Louisville and the Marvin boy shot him. Franklin D. Deleuth, honey!"

"We can't read your mind," said Florida coolly. "Did you make biscuit?"

"Yes, Sister," she said, flustered now, but determined to finish her story. Moving from cupboard to cupboard, she shouted out, "She said she'd like as not butcher them hogs after the boy fell sick and couldn't tend to them."

"Who got sick? Frank?"

"No, honey, Frank's boy, Moses. Irma Jean's son. The one that drinks. Your uncle Evange Lyle has been out there a time or two to preach to him, but that boy's no account, I was telling you. Never has been." She went to the back porch and came back with a ham. "Irma Jean brought this ham—I carried it out of the springhouse this morning to let it soak. I don't know if y'all will like it or not. I told her not to butcher them hogs afore the frost—they oversalt 'em."

"I just want to eat your biscuit," said Florida. "Nobody makes biscuit like you do."

"Pshaw. I used to cook, but I forgot."

Chapter Four

I WAS IN the final stages of starvation, dying quietly on the musty parlor floor, when Grandmother came out of the kitchen in her flour-covered apron, walked halfway across the dining-room floor, and hollered, "Yoo-hoo! Y'all come on while it's hot!" Florida came right behind her, calling, "Yoo-hoo, Henry! Roderick! Louise! Supper! Somebody get Daddy out of his chair. Y'all come on now."

The dining-room table was laden: fried chicken, sliced ham, creamed potatoes, gravy in a boat, butter beans, corn on the cob, bright red tomatoes, pickles in a dusty mason jar, biscuits steaming under a dish towel, a jar of sorghum, and a pitcher of sweet iced tea with melting ice. The cranberry jelly, still showing the rings of the metal can, quivered on its china dish when Daddy-Go let go of Henry's arm and sat down heavily in his chair.

"—thought y'all weren't coming today," said Grandmother.

"Well, Henry ran out of gas."

"Henry, butter you a biscuit before they get cold. Brack, put that bib on before you spill gravy down your shirt. Like to fell over dead last night when I saw that cow coming around the yard—"

"Mother. What cow?"

"Celestine's cow, honey. I told you. Her Angus broke that fence and—"

"Let me help you, sir," said Henry, unfolding a paper napkin to tuck into Daddy-Go's collar.

"Uncle Lyle went down there to fix it, but she claimed she didn't have no money to pay him. Claimed their tobacco did poorly. Now she's always lived in a brick house. Orders her dresses from Louisville."

"Slow down, Mother. No one can follow you."

"I said, her black Angus."

"Whose black Angus!"

"Honey. Lyle's wife's sister Celestine that fell down that well when she was your age."

"Mother, I'm forty."

"Well, y'all played together. Preacher-man. Your cousin Estelle married his half brother and had a chile that died."

"Oh, you're talking about Evange Lyle. He's a character. I'd like Henry and the children to meet him. He's always been out of town when we visit."

"He goes and goes. I never saw anything like it."

"Roderick, get that dog away from the table."

"Y'all don't set her out?"

"Puff is a boy, Mother. No, he can't go outside by himself. He's an inside dog. A toy poodle."

"I reckon," said Grandmother. She passed the butter beans

then paused to stare down at Puff, who sat up on his hind legs, front paws dipping daintily. Florida had put a fresh bow in his topknot. Frowning, Grandmother nudged him with the toe of her shoe, as if he were a big barn rat whose costume would fall off.

"Oooh, Mother," said Florida. "I sure have missed your biscuit."

"I quit trying to cook," said Grandmother.

"They're as light as angel wings," said Henry, taking another one from the basket.

Daddy-Go, seated at the head of the table and staring blindly down the center, held an angel wing in his big trembling hand. Melted butter and sorghum dripped onto the napkin tucked into his collar.

"Eat that biscuit 'fore it gets all down your shirt," said Grandmother. "He's just like a baby."

The biscuit dripped. Daddy-Go spoke slowly, panting, as if he were lugging each word from a gravel pit.

"I was born in this house, and I aim to die in it."

We all looked at him, startled, except for Grandmother, who said, "Hush that, Brack!" and went to the stove to get more corn. "Y'all don't know how he does me when y'all ain't here," she said, shuffling back into the dining room with a platter of steaming corncobs. "Like to worry me to death."

Daddy-Go continued, "I was born in the parlor bed, and I aim to die in it."

"How he curses me," said Grandmother, beginning to cry. "You all don't know."

"Hush, Mother. Don't start that. We just got here. Let's have a nice dinner."

"Curses the farm and the day I was born," said Grandmother with tears running down her soft, creased cheeks.

Sitting up straighter in her chair, Florida asked Roderick to pass her the ham. Then she said sternly, "Let's talk about something pleasant."

"I can't," said Grandmother.

"Try," said Florida. "You've got two fine grandchildren sitting here. Don't you have something nice to say to them?"

She gave Roderick and me a wan, damp smile then brought up her favorite subject—death.

"We just set up here and fret until the sun goes down, when y'all ain't here. I guess the good Lord is gonna take us away afore long. We ain't no use to nobody."

"Aw," said Henry cheerfully, "I think you've got a few years on you yet."

"Life is strange, but death is certain," she replied.

Daddy-Go reiterated his request to die at home, in the parlor bed where he was born, and then, for a while, no one had anything to say.

I liked Grandmother's corn because into each end of the cob she inserted tiny yellow forks in the shape of corncobs, so we wouldn't burn our fingers. I was turning my cob by the tines, methodically devouring each line of plump yellow kernels while trying to catching the warm, dripping butter with my tongue, when I looked up and caught her eye. Like most country people, she stared. She stared with the frankness of a cow or a dog or a child, having never acquired the complex art of pretending not to look. It had taken me years to master the subtleties of averting my eyes, dipping my chin, lowering my eyelids, and otherwise disguising my intention to see what I wanted to see, and even now, I sometimes blundered, blushing red hot when Florida chastised me. Therefore, Grandmother's stare offended me. She was rude. I looked away and continued eating my corn.

Still staring, she said, "Look at them hands."

"She has pretty hands," Florida said loudly. "I wish I had hands like that. Mine are all beat up from painting and gardening. Henry wants me to wear gloves, but I won't do it."

Self-consciously, I set the corncob down on my plate and wiped my hands on the napkin, hiding my painted fingernails in the folds. Suddenly I was terrified that someone would say aloud, Good Morning Peach. Why had I ever painted my nails? Drew St. John didn't paint her nails. The very thought would disgust her. I hated myself. I hated Grandmother, so I stared back at her with narrowed eyes. Her face was shattered with lines, like a hard-boiled egg that had been tapped against the edge of the sink.

"Look at them white hands," she said.

"She has a name," said Florida. "Don't call her 'she.' Her name is Louise."

"She ain't never worked a day in her life," said Grandmother. "She's a *lady*."

From Henry this was a compliment; from Grandmother, it was not. Either way, I loathed the word. *Young lady, Ladies' Room, Lady Fingers*. I ran from the table, slamming the back door so hard that Daddy-Go's hat fell off the nail.

THERE WAS NOTHING new at the farm, and nothing separate. The news on TV sounded old, caught with rusting rabbit ears and spit out through crackling voices on a fuzzy screen. The telephone was on a party line; when you lifted the heavy black receiver, you had to wait your turn. In the sepia-colored photographs, curling at the edges, even the babies were old, dressed up like miniature adults and staring into the camera with sad, wise eyes. And everybody was kin to everybody; even the cows had cousins up the road.

The oldest thing on the farm was the cave. It ran under the road in a narrow wet tunnel and broke open in the corner of the back pasture. I went there after Grandmother called me a lady, slipping through the barbed-wire fence and sprinting across the rough field to what looked like a pile of rock. When Florida was a girl, the county had blown the cave up with dynamite, to make the road, but there was still a round, dry room with stalactites hanging from the ceiling like light fixtures. On one wall, you could make out the sketch of a tail and a hind leg, carved by Indians. Florida, who had seen the whole wall before it was blown up, said that it was a deer. Every year, for as long as I could remember, Roderick and I had collected arrowheads in the field; we brought home jars of them, but they always got lost. I found one that day, lodged into a crack in the wall, and held it in my fist as I cried. Everything was old but me.

After a while, pressing my thumb into the smooth cuts of the flint, I began to think about Mr. Rutherford, and how we might live here together, as Indians. I'd pour some more sand on the floor, and sweep it smooth every morning. He'd let his hair grow and braid it. Our skin would be dark and smooth, our eyes black and clear and smart. We'd wear short, soft deerskin skirts and cook our venison on sticks. At night, in the blackness that sucks your breath out, we'd kiss.

I looked at the back wall of the cave, into the black hole that led to the tunnel under the road. From far away, out in the pasture, I could hear Florida calling. I rubbed the arrowhead, gunning up my courage, then I tossed it to the floor and went headfirst into the hole.

It was as black as a Kentucky night. I couldn't see the walls or the ceiling or my hands as they slapped against the wet rock. Immediately, I lost my sense of direction. As I crept forward, the ceiling lowered, forcing me down further on my knees until my head scraped, and I had to slide onto my belly. I squirmed along until I hit a wall. Then I panicked. I felt the walls at my elbows slowly squeezing in, felt how they would crush my ribs together. There must be, by now, a road on top of my head, maybe a cattle truck rumbling over it, and my head ached, as if I held it all up. What if I got stuck?

Gingerly, I tapped one hand along the slimy floor, bracing myself for the squish of a snake, or the knock of bones. All I could think was, *No air! No air! No air!* My muscles tightened, ready to spring, but I couldn't move. Gradually, my arm found an opening, and I pulled myself through it. I pulled with my elbows, scraping my knees, and then I turned a corner. Suddenly, there was light. Florida stood in the weeds, clapping.

"There you are, you little bugger. I didn't know how I was going to get you out. Thought for sure a snake had gotten you. Like to scare your poor mother to death. Didn't you hear me calling you?" I stood up. We were on the other side of the road.

THE NEXT DAY Daddy-Go had a stroke. He was sitting in his chair in the parlor, eating from the box of chocolate-covered cherries Florida had brought him, when he suddenly clutched his chest. He called out, "Momma!" which is what he called Grandmother. The fingers of his free hand clawed the air until they caught Roderick's sleeve. Roderick stood, white-faced, while Daddy-Go twisted his shirt back and forth, gasping for air. We thought he'd choked on the candy.

"Spit!" yelled Florida, running to him with a cupped hand. "Spit it out, Daddy!" The old man rocked back and forth, pulling Roderick with him. For almost five minutes, they gripped each other across the chair, struggling with the ghost of death, while the rest of us pressed in, pushing, crying out cacophonic instructions. Finally, Roderick said calmly, "Call a doctor."

On the party line, Florida screamed, "My daddy is dying! Emergency! Emergency!"

Beside her, Henry repeated firmly, "Give me the phone. Florida, give me the telephone."

In the end, someone on the line ran next door to get Dr. Kimball, who told Henry to bring Brack to the emergency room. With Henry on one arm, and Roderick on the other, Daddy-Go could walk to the car, but Grandmother had to be hoisted into the back seat. She was a whirling dervish, screaming and crying, waving her arms everywhere.

"Hush, Mother," Florida cried, "or the doctor will have to put you to sleep!" When the sound of the engine died away, Roderick and I went back into the silent house and stood in the parlor, looking at Daddy-Go's chair. He had spent two-thirds of his life in that chair, and it was completely molded to the form of his body. When other people sat in it, they felt as if they were sitting in his lap. The cuckoo clock struck noon, the door sprang open, and the yellow bird shot out, saying "Cuckoo, cuckoo," but we were outside long before the twelfth cry.

THAT SUMMER DREW had gone to the prestigious Berry Hill Camp for Girls in Virginia. I don't know what it cost to attend Berry Hill for eight weeks, but when I had suggested to Henry that he sign me up, Florida said, "Oh honey, we can't afford that." Henry was never so blunt about money, but when I showed him the brochure featuring a circle of girls in sailor shirts in one photograph, and in another, a girl on a horse jumping a fence, and in yet another, kayaks of Berry Hill girls broaching a waterfall, he glanced at the tuition and snorted. "That's the price of a year at Bridgewater!" he exclaimed, shaking his head over the lineup of tanned girls in striped one-piece suits, perched to dive off a rock. Drew left on a plane.

From her letters, I extracted every detail about camp life: The sailor suits (you purchased three and had them dry-cleaned) were not really stupid; they were a uniform. I had never cared for uniforms before, but now I wanted one. When Drew sent me a photograph of her cabin—five tanned girls in sailor suits—I looked deeply into their eyes and saw that they were better than I was. It wasn't their fault. They were in another class. At the time, I didn't know about trust funds, but I suspected a vague magic in their lives, a delicious exemption from drudgery. I put up a feeble fight: all you get for an evening snack is four saltines and half an orange?

They don't want us to get fat, Drew answered. I saw the girls in their Lanz nightgowns, nibbling at oranges on their cabin porch. Someone was watching their weight. Horses— Red Cavern was full of horses, but they were different from the horses at Berry Hill. A Berry Hill horse was named Maverick on the Run or Apple Blossom Annie. It spent each summer with one camper, teaching her equestrian arts. Our horses, with names like Bob and Star, hung out with cows; they were covered in flies; they bit children. Florida wouldn't let us ride because she said Grandmother would worry herself to death.

Everything we did on the farm worried someone to death. If Roderick and I built forts from bales of hay in the barn loft, jumping from the height of rafters into the roofs of the enemy fort, Florida had a conniption fit over his asthma. Henry wouldn't let us near the tractor, for fear we'd start it, and Grandmother was certain we'd lock each other up in the springhouse and mysteriously fall down the well. Added to these restrictions, and the knowledge that I was missing out on some very important training at Berry Hill, was the fact that Roderick suddenly perceived himself as being too old to play with me.

We were only a year apart in age, but this year, Roderick was out of my league. I'd seen the signs of burgeoning adulthood— a dull glaze over the eyes, a tendency to sit still for long periods of time, an interest in money—but when Daddy-Go went to the hospital, the difference between us was clear. Roderick sat on the swing in the yard. He sat and sat. In the afternoon sun, his hair took on a white glow, shimmering like a halo around his head. When the fireflies came out, he sank into shadow. Finally, I asked him, "What are you doing?"

"I'm waiting," he said.

"For what?"

He looked at me slant-eyed. "For them to get back," he said.

With my head down, I trudged out to the back pasture. Insects buzzed in the dry, course grass; I slapped at a gnat. In the distance, a cow lowed and then a dog began to bark rapidly, snap, snap, snap. The clouds hung in thin gray wisps, like Grandmother's hair. I felt sick to my stomach, as if I'd eaten too many M&Ms, so I sat down on a flat gray stone at the edge of the lily pond. It was a large puddle, really, covered by green scum, and the lilies were disappointing, floating up like soggy sponges left in a bathtub. Once Roderick and I had found a half-empty whiskey bottle, and another time, a turtle who stretched out his wrinkled neck and looked past us with tired, ancient eyes. Stirring the murky water with a stick, I thought about Roderick sitting on the swing. He'd sit there until dark, waiting, growing older every hour.

Suddenly, I saw the snakes. They were the same greenish brown as the water, almost as thin as worms. There must have been a dozen of them, squirming together so that I couldn't tell where one ended and another began. Were they baby snakes, or was it something turned inside out? Shaking violently, I leaned closer to see. The brackish water stank. Then I saw the mother and ran.

I ran as hard as I could, not stopping to open the gate but pushing through the barbed wire, tearing through the tomato plants in the backyard, skidding to a stop in front of the swing where Roderick still sat. He frowned.

"Sit," he said. "What happened? You're bleeding.

"No need for that," he said, when I had told him about the nest of snakes, and begun to snuffle. "You're sure you didn't touch one? Okay, you're fine. They're probably just some harmless water snakes, but you can't be too careful about these things. Now, what are you crying about?"

I didn't know, but I wanted him to keep looking at me, so I told him about Christmas-in-July, an annual event at the Berry

Hill Camp for Girls. "They get a real tree and decorate it. They give each other presents. They have stockings."

When I envisioned the circle of tanned girls around an enormous fir in their crisp white sailor shirts, I imagined giant snowflakes swirling against a hot yellow sun. The rich had the power to change the season.

"Huh," said Roderick, unimpressed. "Drew's over there this summer?"

"She goes every summer. It costs as much as Bridgewater."

"Well, I'll say," he said with a mocking curl of his lip. "Christmas in July."

BRACK'S HEART, DR. KIMBALL concluded, had indeed skipped a few beats and didn't have much mileage left. He did not, however, insist that he spend the night in the hospital.

"He'd die right here out of orneriness," he said.

Brack, unable to speak, pointed a trembling yellow finger in the direction of home.

NEWS OF BRACK'S stroke spread up and down the party line. By sundown the next day, half of Red Cavern had stopped by the house to check on him. Evange Lyle Deleuth, the famous evangelist, arrived after supper with a pineapple upside-down cake and his Bible.

Lyle had read the Bible through, from Genesis to Revelations, every year since he was saved at the age of thirty-one. He knew the big shaggy book by heart but he carried it everywhere he went; it was part of him, the way that Brack's hat, unnecessary and even unsightly, was part of him.

He carried it under his arm as he stepped into the dim parlor, smiling with a band of big white dentures. Though he was older, he looked several years younger than Brack as he took his trembling hand and leaned over him on the bed.

"Well hello, Brother," he said. "I hear you're feeling poorly."

"Set awhile and visit," said Grandmother, pushing him toward Daddy-Go's chair. They were both big men, and Lyle's large square head fit into the indention in the back of the chair.

"My wife sent that cake over. She had to stay home and tend to her mother, but she says howdy to y'all and hopes Brack gets to feeling better."

"We thank you, kindly," said Grandmother, bobbing beside him as she wiped her hands on her apron, then took it off. "This is my young'un here, Florida, her husband, Henry, and their chirren."

"I know that lil' ole gal," said Lyle with a chuckle.

Henry shook hands, but Florida remained glued to the love seat. She was put off by the Bible.

Evange Lyle Deleuth was tough competition for anybody with religious leanings. He was a radio evangelist with his own show and the author of several books and tracts, which he had personally distributed around the world. He had saved the soul of one of Hitler's bodyguards. When people in Red Cavern saw him coming, their sins flashed before their eyes. He could talk the chicken off the bone, and what's more, he could sing. The only person immune to his charm was his little brother, Brack.

"My brother here has never come to hear me preach," he said as he accepted a glass of iced tea from Grandmother. "You come on out, Brack. Once you hear me up at the pulpit, you'll

buy all my books and tapes. Then go out and bury them in the
backyard somewhere."

Brack leaned over and spit a stream of tobacco juice into the
empty coffee can on the bedside table.

"Just like Daddy," said Lyle, leaning back in the chair. Then,
catching my stare, he grinned at me. He didn't look old at all,
except for his white hair. Looking around the room, he said, "I
love people." It sounded like a confession, and we were all
quiet, focused on him. "I never learned to get along with all
people. Most people I don't get along with too good—like my
brother here. I don't know why. Some people say it's my
preachin'; some people say it's the way I act. But I always
thought I was nice." The cuckoo clock ticked loudly.

"You're good people," said Grandmother mournfully.
"You're a good man, honey."

"I'm a loving soul," said Lyle. "I love people. Chirren. Old
people. I see some people I'd like to smack in the face, but I
love 'em, I really do. A few times when I get mad, I think, Man,
I wish I was something besides people. There's times I wish I
was a bullfrog." We sat in silence, as if he'd cast a spell on us.
Looking around the room, I saw bullfrogs.

"That boy there," said Lyle, with an approving nod at
Roderick, "now he's got short hair."

"He attends a private school—Bridgewater. They're very
strict about hair. It has to be above the collar, or they send
them home. They'll make the parents leave work to come out
there and cut it. He'll go into ninth grade this fall."

"My, my," said Grandmother, staring at him with wonder.
She added, "He's right puny for his age."

Roderick quietly lifted a framed photograph from the wall and began to study the back of it. It was a sepia-colored photograph of the USS *Leviathan* — a fierce-looking boat painted with a jaw of sharp, jagged teeth. Daddy-Go, who was a bugler in the Calvary, had written on the back:

> Sunday night 7:30, Feb. 10, 1919, 800 miles out of New York City. "I am now on board this ship with over 9000 soldiers, over 500 officers, crew of 2200. She is 954 ft. long. She is due in NY some time Tuesday. We left Brest, France, Feb. 3, got on board Ground Hog Day, Feb. 2. We are now traveling over 20 miles an hour. 800 more miles and we will see the Statue of Liberty. Will be some old rejoicing, ha."

That was the only time Daddy-Go had left Kentucky. He said the French women were pretty.

"Son," said Lyle, "there's two men in the Bible that had long hair, as I know of. You look in there and find them. See what happened to those two. I ain't telling you today. You go look it up."

"He reads the Bible," said Florida. "I think."

"This all you got?" he asked her. "The boy and the girl?"

"I've got my hands full. I do other things. Things with the church. I teach an art class to retarded adults."

"She's on the go twenty-four hours a day," said Henry, with a smile. "It makes me tired just watching her."

"My mother had nine, seven of 'em boys. My daddy used to say, 'One boy is a boy, two boys is a half a boy, and three boys is no boy at all? I don't know if my daddy is in heaven or not. Now my sweet mother, she is right up there with about 146 old preachers I've known, but Daddy was kind of different. He had something to say about most everything though."

Brack raised his head off the pillows, coughed, and said in a hoarse voice, "He used to say a man was like a snake. You don't know how long he is until you stretch him out." Then, without warning, Daddy-Go began to speak French. I couldn't understand the words because he was so hoarse, and my French was limited to the painful repetition of Mrs. Robichaux's crackling "Où est Jean? Jean est à la piscine" and a few songs on the radio. All the same, it was French. Florida said he had learned it in the war.

For a moment, even Lyle was silent. Then Grandmother began to cry. "He's foolish," she said, wringing her hands. Her hands were red, with swollen knuckles, and covered with small cuts and scratches. She never used Band-Aids. I hid my own hands under the hem of my T-shirt. We all crowded around the big bed, but Daddy-Go said clearly, in English, "Go on now! Git," as if we were a herd of cows, so we backed off.

"I hear you've got a new book out, Lyle," said Florida sadly. With his hands in his pockets, Lyle stared at Brack. Then he jerked his head up and said, "You can't be a big-time evangelist until you write a few books, write a few tracks, and then go into the Holy Land. Now the radio is what I like. The thing I like about the radio is that I can send out a picture of myself taken ten, twenty years ago, when I was still pretty, and that's who people see when they hear me today. Also, you can't play a harmonica in a book."

"Louise, you should talk to him," said Florida. "Maybe he could help you with your essays." She turned to Lyle. "Roderick and Louise both attend Bridgewater Academy. That's a prep school. Ninety-nine percent of Bridgewater graduates go to college, some of them to Ivy League."

"Is that right?"

"They smart chirren," said Grandmother. She shook her head at the wonder of it, but she was still crying.

"Bridgewater stresses writing skills. Louise has to write an essay every week. Her English teacher, Mr. Rutherford, reads hers aloud to the class." She and Henry beamed at me while I worked a hole in the rug with my toe.

Try as I might, I could not conjure up the image of Mr. Rutherford. The same spirit that had erased Drew's memory of her mother was in me now, wiping out the world beyond Red Cavern, Kentucky. *Mr. Rutherford, Mr. Rutherford,* I called inside myself, but he was only a name. I began to wonder if there were really a ghost like the Frances Deleuth one I made up to scare Drew. Glancing over at the big lump of Daddy-Go on the bed, at his white face covered with stubble, the thick white hair sticking out, and his bleary white eyes, I felt the chill touch of smooth fingers on the back of my neck.

"Be still!" said Florida, when I jumped. "Let me fix your hair. It's gone haywire back here. Did you brush it this morning?"

"You published a book in Jerusalem?" Roderick asked Lyle.

"I said in the Holy Land. Now the Holy Land is not where you think it is, over in Jerusalem and Jordan and that area. That's the Bible Land. The Holy Land is over here in Kentucky."

Florida tugged some hair over my ears, sighed, and then looked up at Lyle with admiration.

"And you're ninety years old!" she exclaimed.

"You don't look a day over thirty," said Henry. "I hope I look that good when I'm ninety." He laughed.

"I'm ninety-one," said Lyle proudly.

"I guess you've seen it all," said Florida, stepping closer to Daddy-Go. She touched his hand.

"No ma'am, I haven't. I know one or two things, though. I know you can't make people do right. I know that if you've got a lot of money, you've got a lot of problems. Yessir. And if you've got a lot of education, you're going to smart off somewhere."

Florida stiffened. "I don't know about that."

"You wait," said Lyle, and then from his pocket, he pulled out a tract, which he handed to me.

WARNING. JESUS IS COMING. HERE IS THE STORM. DOESN'T IT MAKE GOOD SENSE TO BRING THE CHILDREN INTO THE HOUSE? PEOPLE ARE SAYING, OH WE HAVE TIME. THAT'S WHAT THEY SAID BEFORE THE FLOOD. IN HELL YOU CRY AND CRY BUT NO ONE HEARS YOU. TOMORROW MAY BE TOO LATE. Luke 17:26, "As it was in the days of Noah, so shall it be in the days of the Son of Man."

Luke 17:29, "But the same day that Lot went out of Sodom it rained fire and brimstone from heaven, and destroyed them all."

Luke 16:23, "And in hell he lifted up his eyes . . ."

After reading it, I offered him a light, fake smile.

"I say to people sometimes, when the Holy Spirit gets to dealing with you, you don't care what people think about you. I get on my knees and just cry and pray. The Lord has blessed me."

He was standing in the center of the crowded room now, and he raised up his arms. "Oh what a day to live in!" he cried. "But one great and wonderful thing about this day we're living in, we're closer to the Coming of Jesus! The Bible says, any day the Trump could sound and the dead in Christ shall rise first and we that remain alive shall rise to meet Him in the air. Oh, we get to go home and be with Jesus! Oh, I tell you no eye has seen nor ear has heard, neither has entered into the heart of man what God has in store for them that love Him. In this day, we ought to love Jesus. Lift up your head and look because He could come today! Wouldn't that be wonderful?"

In the bed, Daddy-Go turned his face to the wall.

"I think I'll have some of that pineapple upside-down cake," said Florida. "Even though I don't need it. Not with this pot belly." She patted her small midriff and stepped down into the dining room where the cake sat on the table. Roderick had already slipped out of the room.

To make up for their absences, Henry focused his gaze on Lyle, encouraging him to go on.

"It wouldn't be so wonderful if you didn't have the seal of the Lord on your forehead," said Lyle. He pointed at me and shook his finger. "Then the locusts would get you. Yessirree. These locusts, the Bible tells us, are as big as horses, wearing golden crowns, with the faces of men, the hair of women, and the teeth of lions. Them tails sting like scorpions."

I gave up trying to picture Mr. Rutherford.

"Yes, if it was me, I'd want to have the seal of the Lord on my forehead when He lets them varmints loose."

In the dining room, Florida said, "I'm just going to have a bite. I really shouldn't."

The cuckoo in the clock crowed four times, and soon the room began to grow dark. Lyle pulled a harmonica out of his shirt pocket, blew a chord to get himself started, and then began to sing.

> There is a fountain filled with blood drawn from
> Immanuel's veins;
> And sinners plunged beneath that flood, Lose all
> their guilty stains:
> Lose all their guilty stains. Lose all their guilty
> stains:
> And sinners plunged beneath that flood, Lose all
> their guilty stains . . .

After Evange Lyle left, Florida said, "Now I thought that was just a little bit rude. If I was sick, I wouldn't want somebody bringing a Bible into the house. We're not having a funeral."

"Won't be as long as it has been," said Grandmother.

"He's showy," said Florida.

"He ought to get him one of those pocket-sized Bibles," said Henry. "A New Testament. He could carry that in his breast pocket and leave it there until he needs it. Nobody reads the Old Testament much anyway."

"Henry, the Old Testament is important. Don't tell the children that."

"I didn't say it wasn't."

"Well, what did you say?"

"Never mind."

"Y'all don't fuss," said Grandmother.

"No one is fussing mother. We're having a discussion. Is that against the rules? Can't we talk about God and Jesus in our home?"

LATE THAT NIGHT, we stood around the bed in the parlor, watching Brack die. "Say good-bye to your grandfather," said Henry. "You may never see him again."

I leaned against the bed, keeping my eyes on a carved bird holding a grape in its beak. When Henry pressed his hand on the back of my neck, pressing his Masonic ring between my shoulder blades, I looked obediently at Daddy-Go. His hair was greasy, and his face had turned gray, the color of dishwater. When he put his cold hand over mine, I felt how hard his body was shaking with the effort to talk. He moved his dry, cracked lips.

"He's trying to say something to her," said Florida. "Daddy, what is it?" He opened his mouth, but no words came out. He let his head fall back on the pillow. Did he think he was in one of those dreams where you can't move, can't speak? Was he trapped under the hull of a boat?

When he finally spoke, his voice was strong and clear. He said, "Voulez-vous couchez avec moi?"

• • •

BRACK DID NOT die that night, but in the morning we found Roderick stiff and cold on his cot. The coroner said he had died of asphyxiation—caused by the small blue pine tree he'd set up in the corner of the porch after I went to bed and decorated for Christmas-in-July.

Chapter Five

IT TOOK ME an hour to decide what a sane person would wear
to see a psychiatrist. In the fourteen months since Roderick's
death, I had gained forty-three pounds on a steady diet of Ho
Ho's, King Dons, and Hershey's Kisses; nothing looked good
on me. There was no uniform at Bridgewater, but I wore one
anyway: a plaid tent dress, a ponytail, and a pea coat. I looked
repressed. My weekend outfit—a pair of oversized army pants
tied with rope and one of Henry's dress shirts—screamed
Electra Complex. If I wore anything that had belonged to
Roderick, Dr. Frommlecker would think I had killed my brother.

Roderick's room had become a museum exhibit, lacking only
a velvet rope across the door. Henry was the official duster; he
didn't trust anyone else to handle the Boy Scout merit badges,
the copperhead snakeskin, the blue sock, and the shell con-
taining a single marble, a pair of toenail clippers, three pennies,
and a burnt match. Each day he smoothed the *Star Wars* bedspread over the pillow. Florida had his sweaters dry-cleaned.

When Roderick didn't come home from Red Cavern, Puff had looked for him all over the house, sniffing in corners, crawling under beds, peering over bathtubs. After several weeks, he gave up the search and became incontinent.

We all needed therapy, but there was only one shrink in town, and Henry couldn't go to Leo because they were in Rotary Club together. Florida wouldn't see anyone who wasn't a Christian. I was the obvious candidate, but Henry stalled with the insurance paperwork because he didn't want a psychiatric diagnosis to go on my permanent record. Henry discussed my permanent record in the same grave voice he used when discussing my permanent teeth. What was lost was lost forever. In the end, he decided to pay cash for the visit, and I wore Florida's ancient full-length mouton, buttoned up to my chin.

In late September in Counterpoint, Georgia, the temperature hits eighty-five in the afternoon, but the air conditioner was on full blast in Dr. Frommlecker's reception room, so I kept my coat on. The receptionist made no comment.

She was one of Alfred Hitchcock's cool blondes—slim and pure white except for an icy blue shadow in her eyes. "Dr. Frommlecker will be with you in a moment, Louise," she said in a sculpted voice. She handed me a clipboard then went back into her glass cubicle.

I hunched down in my fur and set to work on the battery of tests Frommlecker gave all of his patients. Drew St. John, who had been sent here when she was flunking out of the fourth grade, had prepped me for the IQ test. "Most of the answers are C," she said. According to Drew, the results of this test showed that she had one of the highest IQs in the country. Her mathematical skills were equivalent to those of a college soph-

omore, and her reading comprehension was perfect. I chose C
for most of my answers, but occasionally I encountered a question with such an obvious answer that I had to go with my gut.
For instance, in the analogy,

Teeth : chicken :: sentience : _____ .
A. dog
B. grub
C. chicken
D. cabbage
E. human

I chose E, confident in my understanding that people were
fools.

Next, I took the Myers-Briggs personality test. Henry
said I had a good personality, and Florida said I had a lot of
personality, but I was sure Myers-Briggs would ferret out
the truth; I was insane. On this one, I answered C for all the
questions.

Drew had not told me where to sit in Dr. Frommlecker's
office, and I panicked when I entered the room and was told to
sit anywhere. My choices were a straight-backed wooden chair,
a chartreuse beanbag, and a brown couch. I suspected that this
was another test, and I finally chose to lie down on the couch
because that's what I'd seen in the movies. The ceiling above
me was painted bright orange—Mrs. Frommlecker's touch.

Dr. Frommlecker rolled out from behind his desk on a chair
with chrome wheels. He wore running shoes, a pair of brown
Haggar slacks, and a silky shirt unbuttoned at the collar to reveal a gold chain that Henry would have hated. His thin dark

hair was parted in the middle, and he had the smart, beady little eyes of a doctor fresh out of medical school. I could tell right off that he was a Yankee because he didn't smile at me. When I had settled back into my mouton, with my feet resting on a pillow, and my hands folded in my lap, he rolled forward and said, "So who did you fuck?"

It was a shocking question to put to a Peppers. To make matters worse, I was a virgin. I was a virgin by circumstance rather than choice. No one had ever tried to have sex with me unless you counted the Mormon who had put his tongue in my mouth at Bridgewater's Freshman Fling. His tongue was soft and fat and tasted like spit. Afterward, he asked me how much I weighed.

When I didn't answer Dr. Frommlecker, he stared at me until I began to cry. Then, embarrassed, he handed me a box of Kleenex and began to talk about himself.

He was a student of Freud, whose books lined his shelf. He'd written a book titled *The Didactics of the Human Sexual Malady,* which he informed me with a wave of his hand was waiting to be published. Here in Counterpoint, he practiced something called Reality Therapy.

My heart sank. Florida could have told him that Reality Therapy wouldn't work on me. "You don't live in reality," she accused me several times a day. She was right; reality held no attraction for me. Except for the police blotter and the comics, newspapers bored me. I could care less what time of day it was. Facts were like brussels sprouts; I pushed them aside. I liked to think that I could live my way and let other people live their way, but realists wore the world as a tight garment, and like all evangelists, they weren't happy until everyone else was as uncomfortable as they were. Now here I was, in Reality Therapy with Frommlecker.

While he talked, I lay on my back staring up at the orange ceiling, crying silently. The soft fur around my face smelled of Florida and made me think of "The Death of the Ball Turret Gunner"—hunching in my mother's belly with my fur froze.

For months after Roderick died, I couldn't stop laughing. At Bellamy Baptist, I snickered in the pew, and during a French class at Bridgewater, reciting with the class, "Où est Sylvie?" "Elle est au cinema," I laughed so hard that I burst a blood vessel in my eye. In the funeral home, every time I glanced at the coffin—the puffs of pale blue satin, the prom-dress bows, and the glut of cut flowers, I had to press my fist into my mouth to suppress a howl. Lacy Dalton had helped Florida arrange Roderick's trophies and ribbons around the coffin. He was captain of the Bridgewater Debate Team, Third Place Winner of the Bellamy Baptist Go-Cart Race, and two merit badges short of Eagle Scout. Now he was dead. For the occasion, he wore a real tie, not a clip-on.

I covered my snort with a cough, did it again, and then lost all control and let out a hoot. Henry led me out of the room. When hysterics had sucked the breath out of me, the funeral director put a paper bag over my head and made me count backward from ten. He was a dapper little man with a bald, egg-shaped head, wearing a permanent expression of compassion.

When school started, Mr. Rutherford read us "The Hanging" by George Orwell. In the essay, after the executioners hang a prisoner, they can't stop laughing, so I knew he had selected it for me.

"Whatdya think, Rhoda?" he asked after everyone else had left the room.

Looking down at Mr. Rutherford's shoes, I thought back to that day at Grandmother Deleuth's farm in Red Cavern. Roderick sat in the swing in the yard, kicking the toe of his sneaker in the beaten dirt, waiting for Daddy-Go to come home from the hospital. He was too old, too old to play with me, older than Daddy-Go—pale and shimmering in the falling sun. I didn't want to be at the farm where old people were dying; I wanted to be at Camp Berryhill with Drew St. John, and I was babbling to him about Berryhill's Christmas-in-July.

"They get a real tree and decorate it. They give each other presents. They have stockings."

"Huh," said Roderick, unimpressed. "Drew's over there this summer?"

"She goes every summer. It costs as much as a year of Bridgewater."

"Well, I'll say," he said with a mocking curl of his lip. "Christmas in July."

Then Daddy-Go was home in his bed, hollowed-out from his stroke, and Uncle Evange Lyle came to the house to preach to him. While he was playing his harmonica, singing,

> There is a fountain filled with blood drawn from
>   Immanuel's veins;
> And sinners plunged beneath that flood, Lose all
>   their guilty stains:
> Lose all their guilty stains. Lose all their guilty
>   stains:

> And sinners plunged beneath that flood, Lose all
> their guilty stains . . .

Roderick crept outside to cut me a Christmas tree the size of a lamp. He decorated it with the sleeping nasturtiums he'd cut from Grandmother's flower beds. He put it on the screened-in porch where we slept.

"'The Hanging' was cool," I said to Mr. Rutherford, looking down at my topsiders as my cheeks grew hot. They were brand new, but like the topsiders of every single other eighth grader at Bridgewater Middle School, they had been soaked in a hot salty bath and then wrapped with duct tape.

Mr. Rutherford put his arm around me. I felt his thick, warm hand square in the middle of my back, pressed against my bra strap. I smelled his lime aftershave. When I lifted my burning face, I saw his scar up close—a thick red welt that ran up his neck and to his ear. Some said he'd been in a knife fight over a lady he loved; others said he caught someone's cleat during a football game. He looked sad; he always looked sad when he wasn't joking.

"I'm very sorry about your brother," he said.

"He had an asthma attack," I said. "A Christmas tree killed him." A giggle rose up in my throat, and I was about to say "and it wasn't even Christmas yet," but instead I pushed my face against Mr. Rutherford's hard shoulder and began to cry. He kept his back straight, holding me firmly in his arms without pressing me against him, as if I were a tackle. "Hush," he whispered hoarsely. "Hush, now." After that, we avoided each other.

AT THE END of the hour with Dr. Frommlecker, the collar of my mouton was wet with tears, and I had said nothing. In the reception room, Ice Lady made an appointment for me to return at the same time next Thursday.

"Why are you wearing that hot old thing!" Florida cried as I climbed into the front seat of the Ford Country Squire station wagon. "It's seventy degrees outside. I'm perspiring just looking at you. You think you can hide your body in these big clothes, but they make you look even bigger, call attention to your weight. Everyone can see you."

"That's not a very nice way to talk to a crazy person."

"Shoot. You're not crazy. You're just—well, what did the doctor say?"

I mumbled something about reality.

"Honey if you don't take that fur coat off, I'm going to suffocate. I'm sorry. It is just too hot to wear that thing. I hope he didn't see you in it. What do you have on under there?" She turned the air conditioner on full blast and asked if Dr. Frommlecker had any suggestions about my weight.

"Shirley swears by grapefruit, brussels sprouts, and catfish—broiled, not fried. She lost twenty pounds in two weeks, and Lacy Dalton says she lost ten, but you can't tell; she's such a rolly-polly. You've got to stop that snacking at night. Sweets. This morning I pulled an empty package of Oreos out from under your bed. I wasn't snooping; I had to vacuum in there. I'm going to quit buying them. You've been crying. What's the matter? What did he say to you?"

"Nothing!" I shouted.

"What do you mean, nothing? Here you go, shutting me out. We can't communicate."

As we chugged up Mount Zion, I looked out the window, at the view. Beside the narrow gravel road, the earth had broken off and lay far below in an ephemera of civilization: blue rivers curving like the lines of a Magic Marker drawn over green paper, penciled-in roads, and tiny lights flickering like fireflies in the dusk.

"I read somewhere that 2 percent of the corpses buried aren't dead. Isn't that amazing?"

"You're making that up, and I don't want to hear it."

"No, it's true. They find the skeleton on its side, and that silky stuff lining the coffin is ripped—"

"That's enough."

"Ripped to shreds."

"I said that's enough. I'm trying to drive. You're going to make me have a wreck."

"You're right. He's rotted by now. First, his nose rotted off his face, leaving a black, stinking hole, and then his fingers . . ."

"Shut up!"

Heat rushed to my head as I screamed, "Dead! He's dead! I killed him! I killed your son! That's why you hate me!"

Turning a hairpin curve with one hand on the steering wheel, she reached over with her free hand and slapped me.

"Do that again and I'll kill you," I said. We were both crying. "I'll kill myself and everyone else."

"You need help," she said. "You are crazy."

I reached into the pocket of my coat, carefully removed a Virginia Slim Menthol, and without looking to check her expression, lit it.

• • •

EVERY THURSDAY I lay down on the couch, stared at the orange ceiling, and wept for an hour.

The ceiling was like a fire, sparkling in my tears, glinting off Leo's round glasses. Behind the licking flames his eyes were flat and cold. One day he asked, "Why don't you tell me what happened up there at your grandparents' farm—Pennsylvania, was it?" He looked at his clipboard. "Kentucky, I mean." He pushed the box of Kleenex toward me, looking embarrassed.

The rooster crowed. I waited, steeling myself, but when he crowed again, I wasn't ready. I never was. It sounded like the end of the world—that's how country people started their day. Grandmother was already up, shuffling across the kitchen linoleum with heavy sighs. Usually Roderick went with her to gather eggs, but he was asleep, so I went. She carried a pail of seed, and I trailed after her, shivering. My tennis shoes were wet with dew.

"Heh!" she called to the chickens, scattering seed. "Here, heh! Cluck, cluck, cluck, chickee." They stepped stiffly around her, clucking and pecking at the ground. She became like them, stepping and clucking, jerking her head to see.

On the fence post the rooster raised his head to crow again. His throat was exposed. *Cock,* I thought, turning my eyes from the red comb and wattle. When he crowed Cock-a-doodle-doo, I cringed. On the post, he stretched his scaly yellow talons. "Heh!" she called to him, tossing seed, but he ruffled his feathers, flapped his wings, and stared past her shoulder, meeting my gaze with his wet black eyes. I thought, *Scared of a chicken!* and went boldly into the coop after her.

Inside, I blinked. Rays of bloody sun slanted through the cracks in the boards, but the corners were dark.

"Shoo!" she said, kicking at a hen. "Git." The hen squawked, flapping her wings until she rose off the ground and feathers drifted through the air. What was the smell? Like mouton, but stronger. A mother smell.

"Heh." She pulled my arm. With her other hand, she shoved a bird out of her nest. "Stick your hand in there. Git that egg." The egg, crusted with dried shit and feathers, warmed my hand. The bird jumped from her roost. Flap! Flap! Flap! Squawk! Squawk! I ducked my head and stepped back, but my foot landed on another bird; I screamed, and suddenly the dank close air was filled with down and straw, and I couldn't breath, like Roderick. He said I didn't know but I did. I clenched my hands, sucking in more dust, and the thick yolk ran between my fingers.

Suddenly, the door opened, throwing light on Grandmother in her apron, holding the pail in the crook of her elbow and the birds, smaller now. I saw another egg. In the doorway, the shadow of Florida said, "You all come in the house. Something has happened to Roderick." I thought, *I knew that. How long have I known that?*

Frommlecker said, "You had to repress the sexual attraction you felt toward your father, so you transferred it to Roderick. Eventually, you'll transfer it to me. All patients fall in love with their psychiatrists." He looked at me with distaste, as if steeling himself for the day I would fling myself at him.

I spoke my first words to him. "You're overpaid. Henry can't stand you."

"You're a brat." He looked at his watch, signaling that the hour was up.

In the car, Florida pursed her lips and tried not to pry, but she was like a kettle of water boiling on the stove; the whistle had to blow.

"Well, what did he say?" she blurted out. I took my glasses off and cleaned them on the hem of my shirt, pretending to think. "What? Did he say something about me? He thinks I'm a bad mother, doesn't he?" I decided to tell her the truth.

"He said that you are a beautiful woman."

"Pshaw," she said, dismissing the subject.

Frommlecker loved to talk about Florida. He said that she had "a terrific body" and "a sensuous walk."

"That makes you uncomfortable, doesn't it?" he'd say. Then we'd go back to Roderick and Henry. I was sorry I didn't have a sister.

"TELL ME ABOUT your father," Frommlecker said at our next session. "How did he react to Roderick's death?" I stared at the ceiling, imagining that it was the sun, and I was Icarus. Then I cried some more, flying around and around the sun, melting the tips of my wings.

After Roderick's death Henry began to save things. He'd always saved used tin foil, washing it first, and his toothpaste tube was flat from tip to tip before he threw it away, but now he went through trash cans, pulling out things he thought we should have saved.

"Do you want this?" he'd ask, handing me a postcard Drew had sent from Camp Berry Hill. "I didn't read it," he said, when I narrowed my eyes. "I just thought you might want to keep it in your scrapbook." Last fall, when he tried to clean out the garage, he found that he couldn't get rid of a pair of used brake pads, a stained bedspread, a high chair.

"You all might be able to use this one day." He tightened a screw in the high chair. It was only a month after the funeral, and we all made these slips. Sometimes when Florida walked into the house, she hollered "Yoo-hoo! Henry! Roderick! Louise!" as she always had. Afterwards, there was dead silence.

"You were saving this for me and Roderick?"

"Roderick and I," he corrected. "Educated people always put themselves last. "Don't say *me;* say *I.* That's the proper way to speak. You say, 'Judy and I went to the store', not 'Me and Judy went to the store.' *Roderick and I,* not *Me and Roderick.*" He smiled kindly. Me and Roderick. I wanted to cry. Instead, I said tartly, "Objective pronouns are always used after prepositions." He blinked several times, but insisted that educated people never said *me;* that was rude. I was about to tell him that Mr. Rutherford called this Johnny Carson grammar, when I looked up at the garage wall and saw Roderick's handprint.

Lightly, I pressed my hand over it, in case I'd made a mistake, but no—it was his. Oil. He'd checked the oil in the Galaxie 500 before we left for the farm in Red Cavern, where I killed him.

"If I have to tell you one more time not to touch the walls with dirty hands . . ." Henry had said, going behind him with a rag. Now we both looked at the spot he had missed.

"Don't touch it," Henry said. "Don't mess it up. I'm going to tape a piece of plastic over it, to save it." Then he made a hitching noise, and when I turned around, he was sobbing.

Florida turned to God. She joined the Christian Women's Club and began taking her Bible out before breakfast, underlining like mad. She tried to add scripture readings to our blessing at the supper table, but Henry pretended not to hear her when she asked him to read, and I was openly hostile. Then she wanted to know if we loved Jesus, really loved Him. Or did we just say howdy-doo to people at church once a week, leave, and forget all about Him? Had we turned our backs on Christ? Whenever Christians talked about Jesus like this, as if he were a shut-in deeply offended by our infrequent visits, I wanted out of the relationship. I wanted my heart back. I wanted my life back. I wanted to sin on wheels, or at least a Catholic.

For the second Christmas in a row, we had a fake tree. "Don't you find that neurotic?" I asked Frommlecker. I was sitting in the straight-backed chair these days, talking.

"What does that word mean?" When I didn't answer, he said, just as Roderick would have, "Don't use words you don't understand."

I sighed. "The point I'm trying to make is that my dysfunction is the predictable outcome of a family neurosis. Roderick served as a buffer for our madness . . ." Losing my train of thought, I asked, "Do you want to hear a dream I've had about my mother since I was five years old?"

"I don't do dreams," said Frommlecker. "I practice Reality Therapy. Louise, your brother is dead. He's been dead for two and a half years; it's time for you to get a life. Look at yourself. You're smoking cigarettes; I smell it when you enter the room. How much do you weigh?"

"One thirty."

"Don't lie to me. One sixty, minimum. You're fat, Louise. You bombed your finals last semester. You'll never get into college. You don't have a boyfriend. You buy liquor on a fake ID. Don't lie to me. You smoke pot. You'd do heroin right now if I offered it to you. You're making your parents miserable. You make me miserable. What are you going to do about yourself?"

"All shrinks eventually fall in love with their patients," I replied sourly.

Briefly, the pained expression of failure crossed his face, and I thought he might make it as a doctor after all. Then he checked his watch and rolled back to his desk.

"You get out of here," he said, "and don't come back unless you're wearing a pair of running shoes. I run five six-minute miles every morning. You won't be able to make it around the block, but you're going to get your butt out there every day. And quit smoking. It stinks." He handed me a book titled *Looking Out for Number One* and told me to come back next Thursday.

That afternoon, Florida and I went to the mall where I was fitted with a pair of Adidas, just like the ones we had given Grandmother Deleuth.

Won't make it around the block! I thought as I huffed up Mount Zion in my new shoes. What block? I beat off two vicious German shepherds and one rabid poodle, and when I got home, soaked with sweat, I fell to the kitchen floor in a ball of cramps.

"I think you did too much," said Florida, her brows knitted in concern. "You go gung ho. How far did he tell you to run? Did he know you were running on a mountain? I better call him."

"Give me some water," I gasped.

"Henry, did you see how red her face is? I think she might have a stroke. Is your arm numb, Louise?"

"Aw, that was just a warm-up," he said, grinning at the puddle of me on the floor. "She's got another ten, fifteen miles in her."

"Leo will be proud of you," said Florida the next day, when I set off again in my Adidas, shorts, and sweatband. "You be sure and tell him you're running on a mountain."

That weekend Frommlecker ran off with his receptionist. It was a scandal we could have forgiven in Counterpoint; in fact, it probably would have been a boon to Leo's business, but he didn't come back. He divorced Shirley by mail. For that, the town despised him. Doctors, bankers, lawyers, and former patients bonded together to ruin the man.

Every morning, I ran five miles into the rising orange sun on Mount Zion. With my fat thighs rubbing together, my lungs searing, and my eyes stinging, I raced the good doctor.

Chapter Six

IT WAS DANGEROUS for Florida and me to be together in an automobile on the interstate, with no escape from each other, but it was always fun at first. "Well isn't this nice," she said, reaching across the long front seat of the Bonneville to pat my knee. "A mother-daughter day in Atlanta." For the first time since Roderick's death, she looked happy. The autumn sun glinted through the pines along highway. On the radio, the Beach Boys sang, "Do ra ra . . ." Weighing in at a feathery 115, I felt airborne and full of hope.

I was to be made over at Salon di Emilio, recommended by Shirley Frommlecker.

"Louise, you are thin as a rail!" Shirley cried when she came up to Owl Aerie for a Christian Women's Club tea. "Come here and let me look at you. How did you do it?"

"She set her mind to it," said Florida.

"She's an inspiration."

"Now Shirley, you've lost fifteen pounds, at least. I can't get over it." Shirley stirred a pack of Sweet 'N Low into her Red Zinger tea and asked me in a confidential whisper, "Did you starve yourself?"

As I was about to reply, Shirley's attention suddenly swerved to a portrait of Roderick.

"Florida! Don't tell me you did that."

"I tell you what, that thing made me so doggone mad I almost threw it out."

"No! It looks just like him."

"Well I couldn't get the nose right. I can't do noses."

"You are talented. That's all there is to it." She looked back at me.

"Florida, after Emilio gets his hands on this girl, you'll have to beat the boys off her with a stick." Florida pretended to be distressed, but my lack of gentlemen callers had, in fact, been a source of concern for her.

Shirley had been a regular at Emilio's since her divorce; Henry said she was on the prowl, but both Florida and I were impressed with the results. Suddenly, she looked as rich and smooth as chocolate. Henry, who was on the board of Counterpoint Bank, said this was no coincidence. She'd wiped Frommlecker out, but Florida and I firmly believed in style. In the hands of the mysterious and powerful Emilio, Shirley had remade herself. Now I was about to do the same.

"Are you thinking of going long or short?" asked Florida.

"I don't know," I said, sounding like a little girl. "What looks best on me?" I turned the rearview mirror toward myself, and Florida took one hand off the steering wheel to finger a strand of my lank brown hair.

"Well you know what I like," she said. "But you'll do just the opposite."

"No I won't."

"You never looked cuter than when you had that pixie, when you were five. Your features showed up. Of course, that's not glamorous. That may not be what you want. I don't know. You'll have to ask Fernando what he thinks. Speak to him, now. Don't be shy."

"Emilio," I corrected.

"Emilio. Why do I keep thinking of Fernando? Who's that?"

"Ferdinand the Bull."

"That's right. That's a cute story. I used to read that to you and Roderick. You all were so sweet; I sewed you red-and-white-striped nightshirts, with matching nightcaps. For our Christmas card that year." Her eyes misted, then she rolled her window down to signal with her hand, not trusting the blinker.

"Shoot!" she yelled, twisting around in her seat to see if she could get into the left lane. "Dadblame it, I can't get around him." She slowed down to thirty miles an hour.

I remembered the pixie that felt so light on my head, and the nightshirt that wrapped around my knees at night. On Christmas Eve, Roderick and I slept in the same bed, so we could stay awake and see Santa. In the blackest hour of the morning, he leaned over me until I awoke with his thin fingers tugging at my arm, his wheeze, smelling of the cold inhaler, rasping in my ear.

"Your presents are here," he said in an official voice. And we walked solemnly down the dark, cold hall. That was the year I had the bad dream.

"I used to have a dream about you," I said to Florida. "I had it over and over. Do you want to hear it?"

"Why is that man flashing his lights at me? Honey, do you

have your seat belt on? I never! I'm going to flash mine back if he doesn't stop that." Her earrings swung as she shook her head. They were MacMe earrings, created by Mary MacDermott —"My artist friend," Florida called her. When Henry saw the earrings and heard how much she paid for them, he said, "You should have told me you wanted some of those. I could have gotten you a pair out of my tackle box. I'd only have charged you forty-five dollars."

"You're so stodgy!" said Florida. "Boring, boring, boring."

"Of course if you wanted live bait, I could hook some worms, but I'd have to charge you another dollar."

As a preppie, I disapproved of the entire MacDermott line. I was wearing a Harris Tweed sport coat that I had commandeered from Henry.

I'd turned up the collar and slit the sewn pockets open so I could stuff my hands into them and slouch. The jacket had been used as a pillow, a smoke screen, and a flag of surrender. Drew St. John had thrown up on it. Still, the fine wool retained some of the clean, corrugated-board-and-freshly-minted-dollar-bill smell of Henry. He'd given Florida a handful of credit cards to buy me a new wardrobe in Atlanta.

I decided to tell Florida my dream. "The first time I dreamed this, I was five years old, but it keeps coming back. You and I are walking across a big field. There's grass as far as I can see— maybe it's the Badlands. Way off in the horizon sits a tiny shack with smoke curling out of the chimney. It looks like a child's drawing of a house, with gray crayon smoke."

"Is that the exit? Shirley said I could take the bypass and get there faster, but this doesn't look right to me. No, I'm going to turn around if this fellow will let me over. Oh, it's a lady. Move, lady. Come on now."

"I'm trying to tell you my dream! You're not listening."

"Honey, I am trying to drive you to Fernando to get your makeover. If you want me to turn around and go home, I will. I cannot do two things at once. I just cannot!"

"Excuse me for living."

"Okay, she's going to let me in." Florida waved and mouthed "thank you" through the window. "Now go on. Tell me your dream. I'm listening."

"I don't feel like it now."

"Don't be so sensitive."

"Are you listening?"

"I'm listening. Shoot."

"We're walking through this huge field to the little shack, and as we get closer, a man comes out the door. He's a bad man. He's wearing a black stovepipe hat and a black suit; he has a black handlebar mustache and a sharp chin. I think he's a magician."

"This cannot be a one-way street. Who came up with that hare-brained idea? It was two-way last time. Oh, foot. Here we go. Is your seat belt fastened? Henry would wring my neck. I hope we don't get arrested." All around us, horns blew with fury.

I lit a Virginia Slim Menthol, cracked the window, and picked up my tattered copy of the book Florida abhorred, *Looking Out for Number One*. I read to myself:

> If a troublemaker refuses to be ignored, should you
> do nothing about it? You certainly know that doing

nothing is not the answer, because looking out for
number one involves effort; to remain stagnant
makes you a sitting duck, waiting to be controlled
by others.

"We're almost there, Number One," said Florida.

I did not reply.

"Now don't you get in a snit with me. You've been real sweet
up till now. Let's not blow it, okay? You need to be thinking
about your hair and your makeup. Your image. What you want
him to do to you. I guess he's got pictures; I don't know. He'll
have some suggestions. You've got to speak up though. Be
firm. Some of these Atlanta hairdressers, Counterpoint ones,
too, for that matter, will go to town if you let them. Last time
I went to Agnes, she wanted me to go strawberry blonde. I almost let her do it. She was talking my ear off. I guess the price
is the same no matter what Fernando does. We'll ask him."

"I brought a picture," I said, still sulking.

"Think about what you need to wear to school. We're not
going gung ho. I'm telling you that right now. Be sensible.
Don't buy a lot of sloppy clothes—now that you've lost weight
you can show off your figure. Do you want a blazer? Henry's is
too big for you. It looks ridiculous. But you like his clothes;
you don't like mine."

"I wore your mouton."

"That's when you were unstable." She swerved the Bonneville into the parking lot of Morris Plaza and said, "Now,
pray for a space."

Florida believed that one should never pull out a credit card
on an empty stomach, so first we had lunch in a swank little

café on the third floor of the mall, under the skylight. The place was called Le Tigre. It was decorated in the style of a Paris bistro, with a dark wooden floor, red-and-white-checked table-cloths, and oil lamps. Handwoven baskets of French bread sat on every table. There was no evidence of a tiger motif until one encountered the waiters, who tiptoed about on the fine line be-tween haughty and rude. Our waiter was named Henri.

"That means Henry, doesn't it?" Florida asked him.

"I believe so," he said, looking over her head.

"That's my husband's name. What a coincidence." She stud-ied the fellow, dressed in tight black pants, with a white poet's shirt and flowered vest, and added, "He'll be tickled when I tell him." Henri tapped his pencil on the order pad he had whisked out of his pocket while she was talking and began to recite the wine list.

"Oh, no, no," she interrupted. "We don't need alcohol. My goodness. Do you have iced tea?" Here, I broke in, suggesting coffee.

"I didn't know you liked coffee," she said. "That's fine with me."

"The St. Maarten Java," I told the waiter, and quickly closed the menu before Florida could look it up—a rich, dark roast in a Caribbean elixir of dark rum, light rum, brandy, and old-fashioned whiskey.

"A lovely choice." Henri smirked, then ran through the menu at ninety miles an hour, in French. "Our speciality today is bouillabaisse crouton rouille. The chef has made it with fresh tilapia. For appetizers, we offer—"

"Go back to that booled one," said Florida.

"I beg your pardon?"

"Booled. Bilay. I can't pronounce it." They stared at each

other for a moment. He straightened up a fraction of an inch, lifting his chin, and Florida squared her shoulders and lifted her chin. "Go back to it," she said. "Say it in English."

"In Southern English?" offered Henri. Across the room, he received a cool look from one of his superiors and immediately smiled at Florida, showing his dimples. When the head waiter was called to the phone, Henri's smile vanished. Once again, he looked as though he might have to ask Florida and me to leave.

"If you can do it," she said. "If not, regular English will work just fine."

"Soup with Jesus fish," I said. "Tilapia is the fish Jesus multiplied and gave to his followers." I raised one eyebrow at Henri, who was probably the son of a gas-station attendant in Smyrna.

"Bien sûr," he said. He raised his own eyebrow.

"He's a snooty one," Florida said, when he was out of earshot. "Henry would be critical of this place—I can't bring him everywhere I bring you. Men are so conservative. Shirley said the food was out of this world. She said be sure and try the—oh shoot, what was the name of that? It began with an *s* . . . Louise, tell me. Roderick would know. Oh, where is my mind!"

"Look in your purse," I suggested.

"You're hungry, I can tell. Go ahead and smoke a cigarette if you have to. I don't like it, but you have to do it, I guess. I don't know how long it will be before that boy gets back here."

After the first St. Maarten Java, the conversation improved.

"I'm so proud of you for losing your weight," said Florida. "Crystal, she's the girl who works with Agnes at Cuts and Curls, said she saw you walking around the lake at Bridgewater and hardly recognized you, you were so skinny. She was out there to pick up her niece, Laurin, I think her name is. I don't know where they got the money to send her to Bridgewater, but I guess they did. Saved. Last time you came into the shop with me you were heavy. I told them I was taking you to Emilio. Agnes was jealous, but she's like that. She said, 'I could charge twice as much if I had a shop in Atlanta.' She's got a big head. I didn't say anything to her. She could stand to lose ten or twenty pounds herself. I think you'll be much happier, don't you? I want you to be happy."

I lifted my empty coffee mug. "I don't think that was me, the fat girl."

"No, I don't either," said Florida. "You got depressed. Blamed yourself. Roderick always liked slender girls. He'd be proud of you."

"But I don't know if this is me."

"Wait till Fernando fixes your hair. And your makeup. Of course you have to keep at it, what he does today won't last forever. You've got to get out of bed in the morning and apply what he teaches you—"

"That's not what I mean."

"I'm sorry. What do you mean?"

We looked at each other impatiently. Florida offered me the rest of her coffee, seeing that I had already finished mine.

"Thank you," I said, taking a quick swallow of the stinging drink. "Well, what I mean is . . . there's this guy, Lao-tzu or somebody, who said, 'I dreamed I was a butterfly, fluttering hither and thither . . . and now I don't know if I was a man dreaming that I was a butterfly, or if I am a butterfly dreaming that I'm a man.'"

Henri sashayed by and paused to ask if we needed anything. "Two more St. Maarten Javas," I said, and he was off before Florida could finish asking if these drinks had liquor in them.

"No," I said. "It's just strong coffee."

"Well, my toes feel warm. My toes never feel warm." Then she actually laughed. I laughed, too, flushed with love, butterfly or not.

THERE WERE NO ugly people in Morris Plaza. It wasn't like Magnolia Mall in Counterpoint, where you'd see a man bobbing along with an enormous belly bouncing over his belt, or a woman wearing a really hideous pair of corrective shoes, or a gaggle of teenage girls in tight, cheap clothes with their hair all gooped up and their faces painted into bad art. If you were a bearded lady, you'd feel comfortable at Magnolia Mall, but not in Morris Plaza. The interior of the plaza was all glass and soft lights and shine, like a mirror. Here walked some of the most beautiful people on earth.

"Money," said Florida flatly as we descended an escalator, looking down into the crowd.

I was not so cynical. All shot up with St. Maarten Java, I breathed in the essences of white rose oil, frangipani, and musk. Passing by a mannequin in Saks Fifth Avenue designer formal wear, I dipped my hand into the sea-green folds of a mermaid's gown. Everywhere, I saw gold, diamonds, pearls, sapphires, rubies, and emeralds, irreverently pressed against human flesh. But what flesh! Even the old people looked somehow new, and the babies, gliding along in their carriages, wrapped in gossamer threads, seemed powerful and important. I saw girls my age, bejeweled and coiffed, clad in suede, cashmere, and Egyptian cotton, who looked like walking sculptures, and men so handsome it hurt my eyes to look at them. While Florida went into Cutlery for Kings to look for a bread knife sharpener, I sat on a bench, gazing into the crowd, sniffing the rich delicacy of their perfumes as they passed me by.

I wanted to be beautiful. If you were beautiful, you didn't need to be nice to people. If you were really gorgeous, you didn't even have to be clean. Policemen were always disarmed by beauty—had a beautiful woman ever been sent to the electric chair?

Then Florida was standing before me, talking a mile a minute and looking very provincial in her wool/acrylic blend blazer. Her MacMe earrings swung as she talked. "Remember to be practical. Try on before you buy. I don't want you doing what you did last time. I'm trusting you now. Those size 4 clothes are still hanging in your closet, never worn. Get something that fits you right now, not in the future. You don't need to lose any more weight anyway. Black, white, and beige wash you right out. Short people need color, or they don't get noticed. You need some socks, and a good bra. Stay out of Victoria's Secret. Try Sears." While she rattled on about underwire and adjustable straps, she dug into her pocketbook and pulled out Henry's credit cards. She dropped the Sears card, which I didn't want anyway, and when she bent over to pick it up, the heavy bag fell off her shoulder, spilling its contents all over the floor: a pink comb with broken teeth, several wads of Kleenex imprinted with lipstick, a pair of knee-highs, a half-eaten package of crackers, last year's Christmas card: JESUS IS THE REASON FOR THE SEASON, FROM THE PEPPERS, a chrysanthemum bulb, two pairs of broken sunglasses, and to my horror, slipping out of a wrinkled paper bag, a pair of my own panties.

"Mom!" I screamed as I snatched up the bag.

"Shoot," she said. "Louise, help me. I just knew I would do that. There's a penny. Get that. Is my lipstick broken?"

"What is this?" I demanded in a low voice, shielding my underwear from the sight of the beautiful people.

"Oh honey, don't start fussing at me. I just brought that in case you forgot your size. The store won't let you try them on. It's a federal law. Here, give me the panties. You don't have to take them into the store. Don't be so self-conscious for goodness sake. There's no sense in getting a makeover at Fernando's if you're going to act little."

I wanted to hit her.

Instead, I took some credit cards and spent the next hour shopping for the person I wished I was. A few hours later, I entered the waiting room of Salon di Emilio, carrying several shopping bags of clothes that would have looked wonderful on someone else.

Florida was already there. "Did you get lost? I had to come in and sit down because these shoes are killing me. Never buy uncomfortable shoes, Louise. Don't put your bags there; someone might steal them." A silver-haired woman in a fox fur sniffed and looked away.

"Remind me to make an appointment for Puff at Styles for Pets when we get home," said Florida. "I am not paying for the pedicure this time. He almost took my head off when he found out what they charge to paint that dog's nails. Roderick never liked that anyway—said it was sissy." I sighed. Would all my wishes come true after I was dead, too?

Everything in Salon di Emilio was black and white. The floor was made of black-and-white tile, shooting out in diagonal lines that made my head swim. Track lighting ran around a chrome maze on the ceiling, casting no shadow on the boys di Emilio, blondes in black turtlenecks who floated like the swans on the lake at Bridgewater, craning their necks now and then to catch glimpses of themselves in the mirrored walls. Jazz played from hidden speakers, and I smelled incense.

At Cuts and Curls, Agnes' beauty shop in Counterpoint, there was no waiting room. You stepped right into the scene, into the drone of hair dryers and high-pitched voices rattling off confessions: "I ate the whole pie. I couldn't stop myself, Agnes. Tiffany said she thought I'd like to choke before I was done."

"I told him, 'Well, you may be my only son, but I will be damned if I'm going to let you bring that girl into this house.' Just between us, I think he was relieved. She had her claws in him good."

"Five thousand three hundred and eighteen dollars. I'm not kidding you. I said, 'Darling, that's too much to spend on me!' Of course it wasn't."

"Ain't it the truth!" Agnes would say, moving from one customer to another with a curling iron or a bottle of spritz. "You're telling me." Most of the women had satisfied looks on their faces, as if Agnes had solved some compelling dilemma. Once or twice, I tried to join in with a confession of my own, but I never quite got the hang of it. As soon as I walked into Cuts and Curls, the gases from permanents and industrial hair spray assuaged my senses and glued my thoughts fast to my brain. I did well to muster a "yes ma'am."

Now, at Salon di Emilio, I sniffed the delicate incense, sank back into a white Naugahyde armchair, and began to worry about what people thought of us.

If Florida recognized any snootiness on the part of the woman in the fox fur, she did not care. She was looking for Emilio. She stood at the carved ebony reception desk, tangling with an uppity young man who had invented a European accent all his own.

"I'd like to see Fernan . . . I mean, Emilio," she said. "We have an appointment."

The receptionist studied his manicure. "Someone will be with you in a moment," he said. "Please have a seat."

"Is that him?" She started toward a fat man who passed quickly through the room with a can of diet Fresca.

"No," the boy lied. Florida stared him down.

"We are scheduled for a three o'clock appointment," she informed him. With Emilio. He's doing my daughter's makeover: cut, color, perm, makeup, manicure, and pedicure."

On the white Naugahyde armchair, I prayed that she wouldn't mention Shirley.

"Shirley Frommlecker, from Counterpoint, is one of his regulars. She recommended him to us."

Inclining his head ever so slightly, the receptionist said, "Emilio only does consultations."

"I'd like you to look in your book and see if that's written down anywhere. We don't want to see anyone but Emilio." She added, "If you don't mind."

The woman in the fox fur now watched Florida with interest. I could have told her the outcome. If Florida had gone to

Oz, she would have rooted the Wizard out in five minutes flat. Once, while vacationing in Gettysburg, Pennsylvania, she had stepped over a yellow ribbon surrounding John F. Kennedy, marched forward, and while several Secret Service men aimed their guns at her, she gaily snapped the president's photo. There was no way the receptionist could have known that Mrs. Peppers was not afraid of bullets, but he sensed a problem and went to get his boss.

Emilio was a short, fat little man with a salt-and-pepper goatee, all smiles.

"Delighted," he said, kissing Florida's hand and then mine.

"Louise is fourteen," she told him. "This is her first makeover. She just lost over thirty pounds."

"How charming," he said. He clapped his chubby hands. Breathing loudly and smelling strongly of onions, he snapped his fingers at one of his swan boys. "Justin," he said sharply. "Bring some wine for the ladies."

"God makes mistakes," Emilio was explaining to Florida as he slowly circled me. He lifted a handful of my hair, rubbed it between his fingers, and let it drop.

"The boy got the hair," Florida said, before she could catch herself.

"Ah, you have a son?" Florida pretended not to hear him.

Emilio leaned in close to us and said in a confidential voice, "She's really a redhead."

"Oh, I don't think so," said Florida.

"Not red-red. Not even strawberry. I'm talking a deep, rich auburn. Don't you see it?"

"We were thinking of blonde," said Florida. To me she noted, "Boys like blondes."

"It is certainly up to you," said Emilio. He turned away as if he had suddenly lost all interest in us.

"She has a picture, I think," said Florida. "Louise, show him your picture. It's from a magazine. I know you all don't like to work from those."

"They can be inspiring," said Emilio. He faced me. "Let's see it."

My neck grew warm, then my cheeks, and finally my ears, which turned red hot at the tips and then began to buzz. The more I told myself, *Stop! Stop that right now!* the harder I blushed. With my head down, I dug through my pockets.

"Well, get it out," Florida said. "Hurry now, he doesn't have all day." To Emilio, she whispered, "Big secret. I haven't seen it yet." I was blushing so hard I thought I would bleed.

I handed Emilio a tiny square of glossy paper, which he rapidly unfolded while Florida leaned over his shoulder. For a moment, there was silence. Emilio stroked his goatee.

Finally, Florida spoke. "Honey! That girl is black!" She sighed, looked at the wall, shook her head. Then sat down, holding her pocketbook in her lap like a small dog. "Let me see it again," she said.

"West Indian," said Emilio with authority. "Anyway, doll, I can't see her hair in that shot, so tell me what you want."

"Speak up," said Florida crisply. "She likes the natural look. She thinks her mother wears too much makeup. Louise, there is no sense having him put makeup on you, if you're just going to take it off. What do you want?"

"I don't know." I looked at the black-and-white floor and began to panic. Why had I shown them the picture?

I should have known they wouldn't understand how I wanted to be that woman, lying naked, face down on a boulder. Her long arms were stretched wide, hugging the rock—you couldn't stop yourself from touching the slick paper to feel the difference between skin and stone. Every muscle in her strong back was a rippling thought, and her hair spun wildly out to the sun, a long curling scream. Waves crashed against the rock, spraying across her thighs in an emerald arc. I had looked at the photograph and thought, *This is beauty. This is what I want.*

"You have to be realistic," said Florida. "Tell him if you want long or short, and what color."

"Come with me," Emilio said, waving his hand decisively. "We'll put you in the chair and let it happen. Art needs space sometimes."

"I don't want you to be unhappy," said Florida.

"She'll love it," he said. "And you will, too, Mom. Come, come, let's play!"

"I think she wants me to stay in here," said Florida. "Where I won't interfere." I followed him into the next room, into the familiar hum of hair dryers and the clip, clip, clip of scissors, the engulfing hair spray. In this room, I was handed over to a wiry fellow in a black turtleneck named Mike.

"Shampoo, perm, and set," said Emilio. "Red dye number 31. Have you seen my roast beef sandwich? It was supposed to be delivered half an hour ago. Jesus Christ."

"A fresh prisoner," said Mike. "Hop into the electric chair, short stuff. Woops, take off those earrings before they get hung and we lose an ear. Look, she has points on her ears—little antennae. Loving it."

"I'm going home," said Emilio.

"Kiss, kiss," said Mike, pressing my head under a stream of warm water. It would be worse, I thought, to leave without being changed at all.

Florida sat in the waiting room all throughout the shampoo, color, and perm; it nearly killed her. For all she knew, I was in there becoming a black person. To calm herself, she struck up an acquaintance with the woman in the fox fur, who turned out to be from Kentucky. Finally, curiosity got the best of her, and Florida came into the next room where I was sitting under the dryer, holding a tall glass of wine and a cigarette, giggling with Mike.

"And girlfriend," Mike was saying, "he was a fudge packer if I ever saw one!" He waved his glass at Florida. "Is this Mom? Hello. I just put her under the dryer. Do you want me to turn her off so you can talk?" He lifted the plastic bubble, exposing my curlers. Drunk, I peeped at Florida, then, in a fit of laughter, lowered the bubble back over my face.

"Quit acting silly," said Florida. "What color did you all decide on?"

"Red, honey," said Mike. "Red as sin."

"Oh, dear."

"You'll love it. Can I get you some wine?" Florida shook her head. "I'll just sit under this empty dryer if that's all right. She doesn't like me to interfere."

"Princess!" cried Mike, throwing up his hands.

"Let me tell you," said Florida.

My knee grazed Mike's knee as he pumped me up to eye level, keeping the mirror behind me. I had not seen myself since he washed my hair.

"It's red all right," said Florida, who had pulled up a chair to watch the makeup. "I don't know if you'll like it or not."

"You hush," said Mike, flapping a powder brush at her. "Or I'll have to do you, too."

"No, this is just for Louise. I'm old and ugly; there's nothing you can do with me."

"Shame on you! You're a head turner if I ever saw one. And you know it, too, don't you?" Florida adjusted her earring while Mike admired her. "With your figure and those green eyes—I'd do you blonde in a minute."

"How much would that cost?" asked Florida, and when he told her, she changed the subject. "Emilio must have gone back to his office."

"Mmmm, hmmm," said Mike, bending close to my face with a sharpened pencil. "Hold still, hon. You are going to be gorgeous. Close your eyes, pooh bear. Don't squint. Squinting . . . Don't make me have to beat you with this mascara wand." With my eyes shut, feeling his warm, winy breath on my cheek, I tried to imagine the face he was drawing over mine. "Suck your cheeks in." A short, stiff brush stroked my skin. "Grand." He tweezed one last hair, then said, "Open your eyes, Cinderella," and spun my chair around to face the mirror.

I stared. A new Louise stared back at me. The new Louise was older than I, of average-to-slightly-below-average intelligence. She did lunch, ditched girlfriends for dates, went to church, and read romance novels. She was immune to imagination. She wanted a husband—her own or someone else's.

Nothing extraordinary would ever happen to her. No matter how I moved her mouth, or her eyes, I couldn't change her expression of sultry pique. My own expressions had been buffered out.

Mike stepped back and stood with his head cocked, one hand on his hip, smiling at his creation. Another hairdresser swung by, paused, and said, "Girlish! What have you done to this child!"

"Isn't he fabulous? An artist. Is this her mother? I could tell. Do her, too, Mike. I want to see!"

I touched my hair. "Is it Murfreesboro Red?" I asked Florida quietly.

"Oh for goodness sake, Louise. No!"

"What's Murfreesboro Red?" asked Mike, who was about to get his feelings hurt.

"Murfreesboro, Tennessee," explained Florida. "We pass through there on the way to my home in Red Cavern, Kentucky. A lot of those people have red hair."

"They're inbred," I added. "Whenever you look out the window, you see the same crazy shade of red hair."

"She's exaggerating. Some of them are normal. Anyway, that's not the red he gave you. Now leave Mike alone so he can finish you."

"Inbred Red," said Mike. "Loving it!" He pointed another pencil at me. "Open wide, wide, wide; I have a big surprise!" I winced as he painted on my new mouth.

"How did you do that?" asked Florida, impressed. "Louise, did you see how he did it? That doesn't look like your mouth at all! I don't know if she can do that herself or not, every day. You'll have to keep at it, Louise. You can't just roll out of bed in the morning and go to school. Beauty takes hard work."

A woman in a pink-and-white-striped smock with a head full of orange curlers came by. "Nancy!" said Florida. "I almost didn't recognize you. I want you to meet my daughter, Louise."

"Louise, this is Nancy. We met in the waiting room. Nancy is from Kentucky; she's heard of Red Cavern. She has a daughter your age. Is she fourteen, Nancy?"

Nancy and I smiled blandly at each other. She looked older without her makeup, and less fierce without her fur.

"Sixteen, going on twenty."

"She's an ice skater, Louise. Goes to Westminster. What color is her hair?"

"It's blonde, the same as mine used to be," said Nancy.

"We talked about blonde. Emilio wanted her to go red. I tried to stay out of it."

"Stunning," said Nancy. "Absolutely stunning."

"Louise, tell Nancy what you were telling me earlier today about the butterfly." I feigned ignorance. "You know. What was it? At lunch. Something about this fellow who dreams he's a butterfly. You know."

"I forgot."

Florida turned back to Nancy. "It was a real cute story. Philosophical. Gets that from her father, not from me. Louise, what was that man's name? Chinese?"

Emilio walked in through the back door, carrying a pint of ice cream. "Ah," he said when he saw me. "Fabulous, fabulous. I bet you didn't even know you were pretty."

"Do you two know each other?" he asked Florida and Nancy.

"We're old Kentucky girls. We just found out."

"Oh, Florida," said Nancy, touching her shoulder. "I remembered something after you left the waiting room. I know somebody from your neck of the woods—Regina Bloodworth. I just met her awhile back, and she is the loveliest person. Just as sweet as she can be—cheerful—and a real hoot, too, when she wants to be. Do you know her? She said she was from Counterpoint."

"The blind lady?" asked Florida.

"No, she's not blind. She quilts."

"I knew a Regina Bloodworth who was blind, but it doesn't sound like the same person. She moved away."

"Well, it must be someone else, then. Or maybe she said, Cartersville. I was almost sure she said Counterpoint, though."

Suddenly, loud enough for the whole shop to hear, Florida said, "You don't like it, do you, Louise?" I couldn't bear to look at Mike or Emilio. "It's sexy, and you're not used to that. You don't look like a boy."

Everyone agreed that I certainly did not look like a boy.

In the car, Florida said, "You don't like what he did, do you? I knew you wouldn't. If you go home and wash all that out, I'm going to kill you. I spent almost two hundred dollars on Emilio. What don't you like about it?"

I pulled the rearview mirror toward myself, still trying to find the real Louise behind my face. My eyebrows were gone. "I don't recognize myself," I said.

"That's what we came here for." Florida blew her horn at a

woman across the parking lot. "There goes Nancy. She looks good." I caught a glimpse of fox fur and sweeping red hair; I couldn't bear to look at the rest. I lit a Virginia Slim; my nails were long and tapered, painted in a color called Very Berry.

"You don't appreciate anything I do for you," Florida began as soon as we hit the interstate. "I have tried and tried. It's just 'Me, me, me,' isn't it? Looking out for number one. You take and don't give."

I French inhaled. "Leave me alone."

"Leave me alone. That's all you say. 'Just leave me alone.' What have I done to make you hate me? Just please tell me that. I'd like to know." She started crying.

My head began to hurt from the wine. "I'm not going to wash the permanent out tonight, okay? Stop crying."

"It's not that! I don't give a darn what you do with your hair. If you want to go around the rest of your life looking like a slob, that is fine with me. Next time, I just won't spend two hundred dollars on you. Plus the clothes. How much did you spend on those? Did you get the right size?"

"Yes, Mother," I said haughtily, glancing in the mirror to see if my face had any expression.

"Don't talk to me in that tone of voice! Why are you so hateful to your mother? What have I done to deserve this? You used to be a sweet girl. When you were little, you were my sunshine. Always smiling, agreeable. Loving. Easy to please." A note of coy sympathy crept into her voice; I braced myself for what was coming. "What happened to change you? Was it Roderick's death? I want to know."

"I'm the same," I said feebly.

"Oh no, you're not. You used to have Jesus Christ in your heart. You were a Christian. Now you've shut Him out. Rejected Him."

"I don't want to talk about religion," I said firmly, and this rankled her. What is it about Christians, I wondered, that makes them do the soft shoe and then take out the whip? Frommlecker could never understand my problem with the psychological sadism of evangelicism. "So don't go to church," he said. "Sunday morning is a good time to run."

"I am not talking about religion, young lady," said Florida. "I am talking about your personal savior, Jesus Christ. You don't want to hear what I have to say because you know it's the truth. You don't want to hear the truth. That's why you ate the way you did. And now the smoking." Her voice rose, became hard. "You are going down the wrong path, Frances Louise Peppers. I'm telling you that right now. Jesus is not pleased with you, and you know it. You can change your outside appearance all you like, but no amount of makeup or hair color will solve your problem. The problem is in your heart."

"Shut up!"

"Don't scream like that!" yelled Florida. "Do you want me to have a wreck? I'm going to pull over. I've had it. You can walk home."

"Keep driving," I said quietly, as if she were a hostage I held at gunpoint.

"This is just what I'm talking about. I never in my life told my mother to shut up."

"You should have."

"I'm going to call Henry." She took the next exit and swerved into a gas station.

When Florida returned from the phone booth, her face looked haggard. "He didn't answer the phone. I don't know where he could be. Sleeping. I let the phone ring twelve times. Called twice."

"Maybe he went to the store."

"Your father doesn't go to the store. You know that. Except for the hardware store, and that's closed. I have no idea where that man is. Well, we won't worry about it. Worrying doesn't help."

We worried in silence for a quarter of an hour, then I said, "I'm sorry I upset you."

"I'm not upset. I'm used to the way you treat me."

Even though it was dark and there was nothing to see, I pressed my nose against the window glass. When a car swooshed past, its headlights made a brief arc across the front seat, as if someone were shining a flashlight into the window. I couldn't imagine what the author of *Looking Out for Number One* would do in this situation.

"THE HOUSE IS dark," Florida said as she pulled into the long driveway of Owl Aerie. "Why didn't Henry leave a light on? I bet he won't even recognize you. You don't look like the old Louise, that's for sure. Now you're feminine, sexy, more mature looking. People might even think we're sisters." She kept talking as she unlocked doors and switched on lights. When we entered the dark kitchen, she called out "Henry!" in a frightened voice. "Henry! Puff! Where are you?"

He stood in the doorway of Florida's studio. He reeked of mouthwash, and he was so drunk he could barely talk.

"Well there you are," said Florida. "What you doing with all the lights off? Where's the dog?"

He said, "Paintin'."

"Painting? In the dark? Henry, you don't paint. What's wrong with you?"

His shirt was rumpled and untucked. It was the first time in my life I had seen Henry with his shirttails out; I would have been less embarrassed to see him in his underwear. He took a couple of steps toward me, with his arms outstretched, then he stopped.

"Well," said Florida. "What do you think? Isn't she beautiful?"

He said, "Thasnoher." His eyes grew wide. "You're differin'! Who're you?"

"Where's Puff?" asked Florida.

Henry hung his head. "Awwlgoteem." He flapped his arms like a bird and made his face sinister.

"An owl got him? Oh honey, no! I knew this would happen. What time? Why did you let him out without watching him? Did you see it? Was it—" Her face crinkled. "He was alive, wasn't he? When the bird carried him off? Oh my God. I can't think about it. This makes me sick!"

"Chased him," said Henry sadly. "Gottaway."

"Henry," said Florida. "You are drunk."

He made a sudden turn, flung out his hand. "Yamsnot!" His face turned dark red. Then he said something that sounded like, "You look nice," lurched backward, and fell down.

CROUCHING BEHIND MY bedroom door, I heard Florida's voice over Henry's muffled protests. "She knows you're drunk. Look at you. You ought to be ashamed of your-self. She knows. You've scared her. Disgraceful! You're going to be just like your brother, Earl."

"Yamsnot!"

"Oh, yes you are. Alcoholic. What got into you? Are you worried about the dog? I guess he's gone. There was nothing you could do about it. I've been letting him in the yard with-out watching him, too. Sitting here in the dark drinking like a bum. Is it Roderick? You're dwelling on that, aren't you? We can't live in the past. What's done is done. What's gone is gone."

I touched my stiff, strange new hair, which smelled like diesel oil, and let the tears run down my face, washing off a fifty-dollar paint job. When I had finished crying, I dialed a na-tional help line in the dark.

"Do you want to hear a dream I had about my mother when I was five years old?" I asked the voice.

"In the dream, my mother and I are walking across a field to a shack with smoke coming out of a crooked chimney. A man with a black handlebar mustache, in a black top hat, steps out the door and begins walking toward us. He's a bad man."

"I'm listening," said the volunteer.

"My mother screams, 'Run!' We turn around and run as fast as we can. He chases us. I run as hard as I can, but I fall behind. My mother keeps looking back over her shoulder, yelling, 'Run Louise! Run!' I can feel her panic, then I can feel him at my heels. 'Hurry!' she cries. 'We're almost there! Run faster!' We're trying to cross the invisible line that runs across the field. Once we cross it, he can't get us. My mother gets across, but I don't. She spins around, reaching out for me, but the man already has me.

"Are you there?"

"Go on," said the volunteer. So I did, with my head bowed in prayer.

Chapter Seven

SOMETIMES FLORIDA SAID bitterly, "Henry is married to the plant," and I would imagine him entangled in the embrace of an overgrown kudzu weed. When she was proud of him, she called the plant by its name. "Henry is the general manager of Southern Board," she told strangers in a velvet voice.

Every pen, notepad, and calendar at Owl Aerie bore the name Southern Board. It was printed on windbreakers, pen-knives, and clocks. When Roderick was alive, he told people that Southern Board was stamped on the behind of each family member. During a confused period in my early childhood, I had used Southern Board as my last name. When I turned six-teen, Henry gave me a Southern Board key chain imprinted with the company's motto: THE BEST WAY IS THE SAFE WAY and the keys to a hand-me-down Pontiac Bonneville. The Bonneville, originally a company car, had smelled new for the entire year Henry drove it. When it he gave it to Florida, it picked up the odors of lipstick, Kleenex, and acrylic paint. In my hands, it had acquired the aroma of a saloon and was known about Bridgewater as Partyville.

During the long summers, I cruised Partyville up and down Front Street with all the windows down. I slurped Tanqueray and tonic through a straw while the B-52s crackled from cheap speakers. If Officer Fitzpatrick saw me, he paid no mind. Sometimes I put on a tennis skirt and drove to the Three Bears Country Club where I smoked a joint in the powder room with Drew. When I got really bored, I climbed around on the girders of the Meshack Bridge, daring myself to jump into the muddy waters of the New Hope River. Florida thought I should get a job.

"The clothing stores would want you to fix your hair every morning," she said, "and they don't pay anything anyway. I'd let you help me out with my Special Art class, but you don't like retarded people. They get too personal with you. Henry always meant to put Roderick to work at the factory, during the summers." Tears welled up in her eyes, but she brushed them brusquely away. "Southern Board pays good money, but your father wouldn't let you work out there. With all those men."

"A corrugated board plant is no place for a young lady," Henry said, first looking me in the eye, then bending down to the newspaper in his lap to let me know the discussion was over. I appealed to Florida, but she was in menopause that year, and half mad.

"Oh honey!" She looked stricken, as if I had asked to be a stripper. "Oh baby, no. No, no, no! You're too spoiled to work. You'd have to get out of bed in the morning. You know your father won't put you in that dirty factory."

In the end, Drew St. John paved the way by taking a job at

Sweetheart Bakery, owned by her father. Mr. St. John, who owned a good chunk of North Georgia, was a gentleman and therefore, Henry deduced, must be making a lady out of Drew.

DREW AND I had been best friends since we were five years old, and we were as different from each other as real sisters. When I told her that I planned to have an affair with a factory worker at Southern Board, letting the word *affair* trail off my tongue, she was shocked. She widened her eyes, then narrowed them, letting her lip curl in disdain. She said, "Gross!"

She had had a similar reaction when I began listening to country music. I tried to keep it a secret, but occasionally Drew overheard me singing quietly to myself "Good Hearted Woman" or Johnny Paycheck's hit "Take This Job and Shove It." Once, she found a Merle Haggard tape in my car.

"I don't believe you," she said. She held the tape away from her as though by merely touching it, she might become a redneck. "How could you possibly like this shit?" I rattled off a comparison between rednecks and the pastoral world of Thomas Hardy, but she knew I didn't mean it. How could I explain the warm, happy feeling I got when I listened to Loretta Lynn sing about birth control?

That summer, no one wanted to know what I was thinking. "You don't listen to me!" I screamed at Florida during one of our fights. "You've never listened to me for ten minutes in my entire life."

"All right!" Florida yelled. "I'm listening!" She set the oven timer for ten minutes. The kitchen was silent. "Well, I'm listening. Talk."

I tried to say the things I had wanted to say, but I couldn't, so I threw up my hands and screamed, "Stop it!"

"See," said Florida when the buzzer rang. "You don't have anything to say."

I started a diary. Everything I wrote was stupid, but I forced myself to scratch out the words without stopping for ten minutes a day. It was like trying to dig my way out of the ground with a teaspoon.

IN JUNE, I entered the plant. On that first day, when Raymond Patch, the foreman, led me on a brief tour of the factory, I was terrified. Ceiling lights shot streaks of yellow through the iron rafters while the Georgia sun bore through high green windows. The heat itself was green. Gigantic machines slammed metal against metal, penetrating my soft Styrofoam ear plugs with a rhythmic, churning roar. The hot air was thick with paper dust and smelled like a skunk. As I followed Mr. Patch deeper into the plant, the odor become so intense I thought I would vomit.

Raymond didn't seem to notice the smell. He was a skinny man with a pointed face and small green eyes fringed by pale, almost invisible lashes. He wore a baggy polyester suit the color of tobacco and an unfashionably wide tie of similar material in a lighter shade of nicotine. He smoked so much that he had to fight for every breath. The expression of concentrated will had become permanent on his face. Apparently, women unnerved him.

"This here is the corrugator!" he yelled, stopping in front of a long ream of rolling brown paper. "Stay away from it. Two years ago, a fellow fell on that and burnt like a piece of bacon."

Staring at my new boots, he asked me if I had read the safety booklet. When I said yes, I knew that he knew I was lying. He rubbed his ear, then pointed to a hunk of metal whirring with blades as big as hubcaps. "Slitter!" he shouted.

I nodded. On the wall next to the time clock hung a calendar marking the days of continuous safety in the plant. When I came to work, Southern Board had gone 212 days without an accident.

All of the men, except Jeremiah, looked at my feet. Henry had refused to buy me Red Wing boots. "You won't be working in a factory for the rest of your life, I hope," he told me at Pay Less Shoes. Then he laughed, patting me too hard on the back.

Jeremiah Stokes was a strong, handsome man, smart as a whip, with a great noble heart and plenty of horse sense. Had he been white, he would have been Henry's closest friend. The best Henry could do was promote him every year until he was in charge of all the other black men in the plant and had his own office in the back, next to the bailer. He was the only employee at the factory taller than five foot nine, Henry's height, but like all the other men Henry had hired, his hands were huge.

"Jeremiah has his own place back here," said Raymond Patch, leading me into a small office paneled with pine board. Raymond leaned against his desk, arms crossed, while Jeremiah towered in the doorway. The office was tidier than the one Mr. Patch shared with two other foremen.

"Jeremiah is as neat as a pin," Henry liked to say. On Sundays after church, he sometimes drove us past Jeremiah's small brick house in the black section of Counterpoint. Idling the car in front of the manicured lawn, he would exclaim, "Clean as a whistle!" Then he admired the polished white Cadillac which Jeremiah never drove to work. We never got out of the car, but sometimes Jeremiah came to our house. On these occasions, he wore a coat and tie and parked cars for our guests. "Jeremiah is as honest as the day he was born," Henry told people.

Now, as I stared at the crisp blue curtain Jeremiah's wife had hung on the office wall to make it look like there was a window, I wondered, for the first time since I had set my heart on entering Southern Board, if I could hold a job. Had anyone said "What is this little girl doing here?" I would have run out the door and never come back.

"Well, look what we have here," said Jeremiah, smiling down at me. "I think she favors her daddy."

Raymond, acting as my bodyguard, didn't comment.

"Your daddy is a good man," said Jeremiah. "A fine person. Now, he used to talk about bringing Roderick out to work, but I never heard him mention you." His voice softened. "My wife and I were really sorry when your brother passed away. We lost one of our chirren, when she was just a baby. I ain't been the same since." Raymond coughed. "But now we got you out here with us," said Jeremiah, straightening his broad shoulders. "We're proud to have you." We shook hands.

"Ready to go to work?" barked Raymond. Jeremiah stepped aside to let him pass, reaching down to turn the cap backward on my head when I followed.

Within minutes, I was throwing scrap board into the bailer. I continued to do that for another seven hours.

After I had worked at the plant for several days without any mention of being fired, I began to worry about my popularity.

Besides a twenty-four-minute lunch, Southern Board workers had two twelve-minute breaks a shift. The white people spent these free periods in the break room at the front of the plant. It was a crowded, smoky little room, but whatever table I chose remained empty except for me. The men crammed chairs around the other tables where they sat elbow to elbow with their black lunch boxes open before them, blowing smoke in each other's faces. Occasionally, a Frito hit me in the back of the neck, but when I turned around, all the men had their heads down.

"YOU'RE NOT THERE to socialize," Henry said when I complained to him. He leaned forward in his La-Z-Boy recliner, eyeing me sternly over *Business Week*. "I hope you understand that. Just do your work out there and come straight home."

"Hen-ry!" Florida hollered into the intercom. "Lou-ise! Supper!"

"Dad, they throw things at me."

"Throw things?" He frowned. "What things?"

From the top of the stairs Florida yelled, "Louise! Tell your father to come and eat!"

"Coming!" I yelled back, without moving. "Potato chips. Empty chewing tobacco pouches. Pieces of string."

Henry laughed. "That's just their way of being friendly. They're having fun with you, honey. If they didn't like you, they wouldn't tease you. How's old Drewster doing at her job?"

"She hates it. She—"

Florida stomped into the den, announcing that she was

throwing supper in the garbage can since no one wanted it. She had recently acquired several MacMe jogging suits in alarming colors, designed by Mary MacDermott, and would wear nothing else.

"Women need to express their anger," Mary told her clients. "I've started smashing plates in the garage. I have a special hammer. I've painted the word *kill* on it." Florida could not break a plate on purpose, but she took Mary's ideas seriously because she was a real artist; people drove down from Atlanta to buy MacMe clothing. "Try some 'I feel angry' statements," Mary suggested.

Florida was angry at her hair for going gray on her. She was angry at Henry for not being romantic and for working all the time and for picking lint up off the carpet. She was angry at the owl who had seized Puff LeBlanc. She was angry at the white-trash tenant on the Deleuth farm, who a tossed a cigarette and burned the place down. She was angry at Grandmother and Daddy-Go for digging their heels in when she found them a house in Red Cavern. All afternoon, she'd been angry at Helen Olfinger, who was her own age and the most talented person in Special Art. Helen had drunk the green paint.

Now she was livid because Henry and I would not come to the table before the food got cold. Standing in the center of the den, she announced, "I am not your slave."

When she was gone, Henry blinked, as if coming out of a dream. Then he said, "I think your mother has supper ready," and began to fold his paper.

As SOON AS everyone was seated at the table, Florida bowed her head, squeezed her eyes shut, and prayed, "Lord, thank you for the food you bestowed on us tonight and for giving me the time to prepare it for my family, in my busy day. Teach all of us to be more grateful. Be with Roderick in the mansion you have prepared for him. Guide Louise and help her to make mature decisions as she grows into a Christian young lady and starts dating, if that is your plan for her. Teach her to listen to those who know better and would help her. Be with Mother and Daddy—help them to adjust to their new way of life in town and be grateful for it. Help them not to get negative. Be with Helen Olfinger. Help us all to not get discouraged. Amen."

Embarrassed, I sank my teeth into the cold tuna melt. Lately, Florida had been asking Henry and me if we were ashamed of our Savior. "I am proud to know the Son of God," she would remind us, on the verge of tears. Then she would select one of Henry's faults—his concern with public opinion, for instance —and rail. "I don't go to church because it looks good," she told him. "That's not what it's all about it. If that's why you worship, to see and be seen, then you are going down the wrong path."

Every Thursday morning, Florida put on a suit for her Christian Women's Club meeting. She met with Miriam Gubbel, the organist at Bellamy Baptist Church whose daughter had shot herself in the ear; Lacy Dalton, who had lost a breast; and Shirley Frommlecker, whose husband had divorced her by mail. There were others: Agnes from Cuts and Curls, who had gone bankrupt twice; her niece, Laurin, who laid the entire Bridgewater Boy's Tennis team; and Frenchie Smartt's girlfriend, from the other side of the river, who was just as sweet as she could be. Weekly fellowship with these women—

except for Agnes, who was a pill—gave Florida the courage to go on living.

"Witness," the women said with their waxed lips, holding cups of herbal tea. "Witness," they murmured, making the word soft, alluring, and infinitely feminine.

I was turning into an atheist and a hellcat.

"I can see it coming," Florida would say with her lips stretched into a fierce grimace.

"What?" I asked, taunting her. "See what coming?" Then I laughed with the high whine of a girl brought up in a rusty trailer park on the other side of the river, a girl no one cared about, with no respect for her mother and father. I no longer sent underwear to the laundry room, which told Florida that I had either stopped wearing it or was in something too fancy to be seen.

"You have turned your back on Him," she said. "Mark my word. You'll be sorry." I mimicked her until she wept.

Henry tried to stay out of it, but we wouldn't let him.

"You two stop that fighting," he said one morning, lifting his head from his cereal bowl.

"You two! Who is you two?" cried Florida. "Don't put me on the same level with her. She is a child." I knew she was right. My disrespect was ugly, but I was afraid to give in to her will. I was afraid that Florida and Jesus would take my soul, leaving me lost forever behind a mask like the one that had been created at Salon di Emilio. In my dreams, she came at me with a knife.

She started tucking Bible verses into my lunch bag. One day, I sat at an empty table in the break room at Southern Board and read the note under my peanut butter and jelly sandwich:

Whosoever therefore shall be ashamed of me and of
my words in this adulterous and sinful generation:
of him also shall the Son of man be ashamed when
he cometh in the glory of his Father with the holy
angels. St. Mark 9:38.

A plastic spoon winged past my ear. I ignored it. Then a man
called Polecat, because he was skinny and worked on top of a
ladder, wedged his thick hand into the plastic window of the
Lance's snack machine, pulled out a package of Choco-Fil
cookies, and farted with such an explosion that I jumped. The
men howled.

"'Scuse my language," said Polecat, shuffling back to his seat.

Someone said, "The boss's daughter never heard a fart before."

"What the hell is she doing here anyway?" asked Smiley, a
scar-faced man who never smiled.

"I reckon Henry and Florida are having hard times. I hear
they had to cut back on the champagne and them trips around
the world. So Henry put the girl out to work."

"Ain't that a shame."

"Naw," said Jack. "They ain't having hard times. They're still
sitting pretty up on that mountain. I'll tell you what happened."

"Jack's the maid."

"Naw, he's the pool man on weekends."

"He's their white nigger," said Smiley, and muttered something about Jeremiah under his breath.

"Smiley's so pretty when he's mad," said Polecat. "Ain't he?"

Jack rubbed his chin and leaned back in his chair. I studied
his face: the crow's feet around his blue eyes, the hardened

bitter twist of his lips that could flash into a grin. *He has lived,* I thought. *He is real.* All of the men had that face, and I wanted one.

Jack said, "See, one day up on the hill, Henry says to his wife, 'Let's you and me do an experiment. Let's us put that girl in the plant. What about it? We'll put a cap on her head and some brogans on her feet. Let's see what happens.'"

"Hey Experiment," said T. C. Curtis, winking at me as he shuffled to the Coke machine.

"T. C., don't mess with Experiment now," said Jack. "This here is a scientific operation."

"Just experimenting," said T. C.

T. C. WAS THE one I chose to be my lover, by virtue of the fact that he was under forty and had winked at me. He was only my lover in my imagination, where he entered as a seed and grew wildly, in eight-hour increments, under the hot green lights.

I had used up all my regular daydreams in the first two weeks of work. While I was shoving boards into the bailer, turning boxes in the printer, or slamming away at the M-12, I now thought about T. C. Curtis. With each stack of boards that went down the conveyor belt, his beer belly became smaller. By quitting time each day, when my ankles hurt and my eyes stung from sweat, the man was an inch taller and a year younger. After work, when I drove the Bonneville over the bridge and up the mountain with the windows down, singing along to "Scarlet Fever," T. C. Curtis was intelligent, sincere, and hopelessly in love with me.

On the 245th day of safety, T. C. sidled up behind me at the

Coke machine, standing so close I could feel the heat coming off his chest, and whispered loudly in my ear, "Will you marry me?"

"Never!" I cried out. My face burned. All around us, the men watched, laughing. For a moment, I saw T. C. clearly: a leering, pot-bellied man in a John Deere cap, with a wad of chewing tobacco in his cheek. Then I resented him for destroying the man I had taken such pains to create in my imagination.

Being a Peppers, however, I did not give up. As the days wore on, 247 days of safety, 259 days of safety, I continued to conduct our romance in the privacy of my own mind, taking occasional peeks at the real T. C. as he hummed by in a fork lift. I began to write about him in my diary. On the cover of the notebook, I wrote the words UNCENSORED DO NOT READ.

Florida and Henry had become limp, gray, and predictable.

"Back to the old grindstone," Henry said on Monday mornings.

"Drudge, drudge, drudge," said Florida. "Back in the rut." At the end of the day, she stretched out on the couch in a MacMe suit and said, "Oh, I am weary."

I was determined to have an exciting life. Each morning, when I reported to Raymond Patch, I stared into his lashless green eyes, praying for an assignment to work with T. C. Curtis, but it never happened. Most of the time, Raymond sent me to the back of the plant to work with the black men on machines that paid a dollar less an hour, but when he was in a bad mood, he put me to work with Dopey.

Dopey was a miracle of the company's insurance benefits policy. Taking advantage of full medical coverage, he kept himself stoned on prescription drugs. Several times a year, when he overdosed, he took up residence in a private room at the hospital while his wife cashed in his checks. When he did come to work, he acted as if he might die at any moment.

When Mr. Patch ordered me to help Dopey clean the railroad, my obsession with T. C. Curtis was the only thing that kept me from quitting. Henry was as much of a neatnik at the plant as he was at home, where he irritated Florida by shining sink faucets, and of all the jobs at Southern Board, tidying up the tracks that ran through the interior of the plant to Henry's satisfaction was the most deplored.

"I can't bend my knees!" Dopey hollered as I climbed down the short ladder to the depressed tracks. "So I'll sweep the trash over the wall, and you pick it up!" Gripping the rails of the ladder with his emaciated, blue-veined arms, and staring at me through a pair of foggy glasses whose frames had been wrapped with yards of Scotch tape, he screamed over the roar of the machines, "and I ain't picking up after no niggers! We only go halfway down. I ain't picking up no watermelon rind." He put one hand across his bony chest, as if the thought of touching a black man's trash was giving him a heart attack. He removed a pill from a vial in his shirt pocket. Then, patting a sticky strand of white hair across his skull, he settled himself against his broom handle and watched me work.

I put on my gloves. Mr. Patch had given me a broom, but it was useless, so I crept along the tracks with my back bent, dropping wads of chewing tobacco into my pail. Occasionally, I found a scrap of cardboard or an empty coffee cup, but for the most part, since it was the men's custom to stand at the wall and spit, I was in a field of chewed tobacco.

Dopey followed me along the top of the wall with his broom pointing out trash I had missed, and when someone walked by, he swept dust down on my head. He looked exhausted.

Throughout the afternoon, the men came by to see for themselves that Mr. Peppers's daughter was indeed picking up their spit. Polecat and Jack pushed carts of board along the wall, pretending not to notice me until Jack jerked the cart to a stop, shading his eyes with his hand as he looked down. "Polecat! What's that crawling down there on the tracks?"

Polecat looked. "Why, that's a rat," he said.

"Naw, not the rat. That other thing. The little fellow. The funny looking one with the ponytail and gloves."

"Why, that's Experiment! Experiment, did you fall down there?"

T. C. came by with a big wad of tobacco in his cheek and pretended to spit. Smiley stood beside him and frowned.

When I had worked my way halfway down the tracks and had nearly reached the invisible line that divided the front and back of the plant, Dopey emerged from hiding. Standing with his legs spread, as though a great gust of wind might blow him over, he shouted, "All right! We can stop here. I ain't picking up after no niggers."

I continued to stomp along with my pail, even though there wasn't anything to pick up. The black workers didn't throw things on the tracks the way the white workers did. Growing more and more agitated, Dopey followed me along the edge of the wall. "I said, all right now! Don't go no further!" He took another pill. "I ain't sweeping up no watermelon rinds, you hear?"

Suddenly, a silence fell over the plant. The corrugator still hissed; the M-12 chugged and banged, and the bailer swallowed, chewed, and spit up its scrap board, but the hum of voices had ceased. The floor, which had been crawling with lines of men engaged in a regular path of social intercourse, emptied. As if lifted by some magical hand, each employee now stood, back bent, head down, over his assigned job. Even Dopey managed to get down the ladder and stroke his broom along the clean tracks.

When I raised my head, I was eye-level to Henry's black wing tips, polished to a dull sheen, never a shine. He wore a light gray suit with a navy blue tie. In the green fluorescent light of the plant, his shirt was whiter than paper. His gold watch and ring hung in the murky air like two distant stars.

"How's my little worker?" he asked, smiling down at me.

"Your daddy is a handsome man," Jeremiah had told me once, in the same matter-of-fact voice he used when he said, "Your daddy is a good man." I saw this now, and at the same time, I understood what Florida meant when she said, "Henry, you're turned off. As soon as you get away from the plant, you turn off like a light." Now, he was on.

"Are you doing all right?" he asked.

"Yes sir." I grinned at him and went back to work. For some time, I was aware of his eyes following my gloved hands as they reached for invisible trash, and I tried to do the job perfectly. When he was gone, I knew it without looking up.

Dopey, having decided it was too much trouble to get back up the ladder, and hoping to stop me from cleaning up more of the wrong trash, parked his broom in front of me. Leaning his wizened body on the handle, he adjusted his glasses and began to sing, "Always on My Mind." I listened, amazed. Dopey could sing.

IT WAS A good summer to sing. In the morning bluebirds, cardinals, and chickadees belted out hymns until the heat sent them deep into the green woods. On most afternoons, thunder crashed liked cymbals. All night long, the katydids played in stereo. After work, driving the Bonneville up Mount Zion with the windows rolled down, I lip-synched to all the love songs on WXYB Continuous Country Music.

One hot Saturday night, at Frenchie's Bar across the New Hope River, Drew snatched me back to reality. Frenchie owned most of the property on the other side of the river. His business acumen qualified him to be a member of the Chamber of Commerce, the Georgia Business and Industry Association, and even the Three Bears Country Club, but he did not run in those circles. He had a beard, for one thing—a short beard, but facial hair nonetheless. He went to tractor pulls, followed professional wrestling, and did not conjugate his verbs. He beat his three-hundred-pound wife and openly cavorted with other women. He hated black people and was responsible for the unofficial zoning laws that rocketed them over to our side of the river where we clucked our tongues and gave them a corner. Frenchie was a member of the two organizations that would have him—the NRA and the KKK.

That summer, I loved to venture across the river where country music abounded. With reservations, Drew would accompany me to Frenchie's Bar, the only establishment in Counterpoint that accepted our University of Nebraska swimming pool ID cards, verifying that we were eighteen years old, the legal drinking age in Georgia. She met me in the parking lot. Humming, "Get off my satin sheets," I swung Partyville in beside her Jeep. She was wearing a pressed white polo shirt and rumpled khakis; her hair, like mine, was pulled back into a tight ponytail.

"Well, there you are," she said in a surly voice. "What a relief. Two rednecks have been doing wheelies around my car. Boy, was I impressed." She mimicked them, drawling, "Hey there honey! Wanna come out to the lock and dam with us and get fucked up?" Then she did her redneck laugh, a noise that sounded both sinister and retarded, "Huh-huh." Out of habit, I checked the parking lot for T. C. Curtis's black Monte Carlo.

We climbed through the Harleys parked at the front door and entered the cinder-block shack where red neon lights flashed across tired faces at the bar. Drew selected a small table in the corner, and we ordered a pitcher of beer. We talked about our mothers. I reported that Florida was sneaking Bible verses into my lunch bag; Drew announced that Mrs. St. John had sent her a laundry bill—the nerve. We spoke in the well-modulated voices of Bridgewater girls, flashing the multicolored rubber bands on our braces when we laughed. We got very drunk.

The men leered at us, and a few stumbled over and tried to start a conversation, but Drew was curt. If the gentleman persuaded himself that her cold front was a bluff, Frenchie himself came out and chased him back to the bar. He had no interest in protecting a girl's virtue, but when he saw a dollar, he didn't let it get away. So we sat in our corner, like two Siamese cats in a barnyard, talking about sex.

"You won't believe what happened at work today," Drew said,

flushing pink to her ears. "There's this huge black guy, Gus, who's always flirting with me? He's horrible. He really is. I mean, he's funny, but he's horrible. We were on the dough line. The dough rolls out of a tube, Gus pushes a button that slices it, and I inspect the slices that come down the conveyor belt. That's my job title: inspector. Don't be too impressed. Gus calls me, Inspector Drew. Well, this morning, before I was really awake, I saw this huge roll of dough coming down the assembly line. It kept getting longer and longer; he wasn't pushing the button that slices it. I looked back at him to see what the hell he was doing, and he goes, 'Baby, this is how much I love you!'"

She laughed from her belly, crossing her arms over her chest, pushing her sleeves up over the line that marked her tennis tan, silver braces flashing, rocking back and forth in her chair. She wore no makeup, no socks, and no jewelry except for a pearl necklace that had belonged to her grandmother. She smelled of soap. She was everything I wanted to be.

We were halfway through our third pitcher of beer, arguing the importance of wang length versus wang circumference, when I made a comment about men's balls.

"Stupid!" Drew's blue eyes widened in amazement; her lip curled. "How many balls do you think a man has?"

I took a sip of beer, hiding my face in the mug. In the most nonchalant voice I could muster, I said, "Three."

The look on Drew's face made me wilt. "Louise," she said in a strained voice, clumsily taking a cigarette from her pack, "listen to me. A man has two balls: one, two. Two, okay?"

I shrugged, as if one more or one less ball made no difference to me, but she knew better.

"Jesus," she said softly. "What am I going to do with you?"

WHEN I GOT home that evening, Florida was sitting at the kitchen table with a plastic bag over her head. "Daddy-Go had another stroke. Mother called tonight. She's out of her mind. He's going to go soon. He didn't want to leave the farm. Says we're killing him. Doesn't remember that the place burned down. He was walking out in the yard, lost, trying to go home, when he had the stroke."

"I'm sorry," I said. Her nose was red from crying.

"I'm coloring my hair. Your father is downstairs asleep in his chair. I'm going to be a redhead whether he likes it or not. Like you were when you went to Fernando's in Atlanta. You might want to think about going back to him." She eyed my ponytail, but decided not to criticize. "I refuse to get old and gray. How was your movie?"

Leaning against the wall to balance myself, I shut one eye and said, "Fine." Florida had lost her sense of smell when she was pregnant with Roderick, so she couldn't tell when I was drunk.

"Your father won't go to the movies with me."

"Mom, don't start."

"He just sits in that chair every night. Doesn't communicate. Doesn't have anything to talk about but work, work, work. That plant. That's his life. I don't know why he even comes home." Lightly, she touched her neck, fingering the loose skin. "I've gotten old and ugly, Louise."

"No, you haven't."

"We'll have to go up there soon. Daddy won't last much longer. Henry doesn't think you should go to the funeral. Says it will upset you. You lost it at Roderick's funeral. Just lost it. Mother doesn't need to see that. And we don't have a psychiatrist in Counterpoint right now. You're sensitive, always have been. Roderick used to say, 'She's fragile,' when you were a baby. Tell me not to drop you. You never think your child will die before you do. The Lord giveth and the Lord taketh away."

She began to sob. I edged out of the kitchen, keeping one hand on the wall. Suddenly, she ripped the bag off her head, splattering drops of red dye across the table.

"Go!" She screamed. "Go back to your room to get away from me. Crawl into your hole! You and Henry do the same thing. 'Leave me alone!' you say. 'Don't bother me!' All right! I'll die, too. I'm the one who should go. You all don't need me." The sobs choked her. "Don't want me—this dried-up old hag! Ugly! Ugly! Ugly!"

My body went numb; I couldn't speak. As fast as I could, I stumbled to my room, fell, got up again, and finally managed to get behind the closed door and crawl to my bed. For a while, I kept the walls from spinning by holding on to the mattress, but eventually I had to let go. At 3:00 A.M., when the phone rang, I was still puking.

I knew it was Death. Henry was in charge of Death. His footsteps in the hallway were slow and measured. The knock on the door was certain.

Chapter Eight

GRANDMOTHER DELEUTH HAD never liked her husband, but she'd been joined to him for sixty-five years, and the idea of life without him was unbearable. At the hospital, her heart attack followed his. Some relatives said it was the only thing they'd ever agreed on.

In the dimly lit kitchen, Henry held Florida in his arms. His back was very straight. There was a tautness to his face, drawing the skin tight over his cheekbones. His eyes burned with intensity. For a moment, as he held her that way, and she was still, I saw them as they must have been when they married.

Henry arranged everything. When he saw that I had been sick, he thought it was a violent reaction to my grandparents' deaths, and he decided that I should stay in Counterpoint. He changed the sheets on my bed, went to an all-night grocery store and stocked the house with food, made sure I knew where to find my keys and my credit card, and then counted crisp twenty dollar bills out into my palm. He gave me

Reverend Waller's phone number neatly printed on a card. I was to go to work, as usual, and in my free time, visit Drew. They would call me every day from Red Cavern and be home in a couple of weeks, as soon as they had taken care of things up there.

Several days later, slumped over my ham and rye, I watched T. C. meander into the break room, toss his black lunch box on the table, and to the astonishment of all of us on first shift, sit down next to me. When someone popped the tab off a Fanta grape, it sounded like a gunshot.

"T. C., don't mess with the boss's daughter," said Smiley. "You'll get fired."

T. C. bit into a pecan twirl. I sat stiffly, careful not to brush my arm against his shoulder, afraid to eat lest I offend him. When he had finished, he wiped his mouth with the back of his hand and pushed the wrapper toward me. "How do you say that?" he asked, pointing at the label. I was suddenly terrified that he might be illiterate. Was I in love with someone who couldn't read and write? Drew would be aghast.

"Pecan twirl," I said quietly. Even though I hadn't moved an inch, our shoulders were touching.

"What was that?" He grinned. "I'm a little hard of hearing." He leaned his face in close to mine. "Did you say 'pe-con' or 'pee-can'?"

"Theodore Curtis, you better get back over here on your side of the tracks!" someone called out.

"That's right," said Smiley. "Over on that side of the tracks they got a bad-ass cop on a horse. Real scary dude."

"Y'all think he braids that tail himself?"

T. C. offered me half of his sandwich. It was nearly lost in his big hand, and seeing the shallow indention of his fingers in the soft white bread, I couldn't help but imagine how he would hold my breast.

"Thank you," I said.

Behind me, the men sniggered.

T. C. leaned even closer. He put one hand over his ear.

"Is that a yes or a no?" His arm was as big around as my leg, and as he turned closer to me, the span of his chest hid my face from the other men. He took jagged, heavy breaths, like an old man with a bad heart.

"Yes," I said, trying to keep my hand steady as I removed a cigarette from my pack. His lighter came out in a flash. I had the wrong end of the cigarette in my mouth. He turned it around for me, ignoring the hoots from the back table. "I mean no," I said. My voice sounded fake, the way it did when I showed my ID to a bartender. "I don't want a sandwich."

When it looked like we might not have a conversation, he said, "I'm real sorry about your grandparents. Where did they live?"

Then I did something crazy. In plain view of every hand at Southern Board, in a loud voice, I asked T. C. for a date.

No one was as surprised as Theodore himself. He became suddenly shy. "Sure," he said, "I'll have a beer with you after work." Then he turned away from me to eat his sandwich. While he ate, I watched the white T-shirt stretching over the muscle in his back, the two damp curls swirling above his ear. With a leap of faith, I allowed T. C. Curtis to become the man who loved the woman in every country song I had ever heard.

• • •

"HE SOUNDS LIKE a real fixer-upper," said Drew, when I described T. C. to her over the phone.

"It's like negative capability," I explained. "You know. John Keats, the poet? He said that negative capability is required to read poetry, or write it, or something. It's the willing suspension of disbelief."

"Education is wasted on you," said Drew. "Does he have a big wang?"

"I don't know!" I screamed, still embarrassed about the three balls. "We've only gone to second base." Then more calmly I said, "I want him to fall in love with me."

"Next time you hold his hand," said Drew, "measure the distance between the bottom of his palm and the tip of of his middle finger."

"What if he knows what I'm doing?"

"Louise, it's not supposed to be this hard for a girl to lose her virginity. Just focus."

NO ONE AT the plant said anything to me about T. C., but they discussed me among themselves, shouting over the roar of the machinery whenever I walked by.

"What's that thing sticking out of Experiment's cap?" asked Polecat. "She don't have enough hair to make a ponytail. Smiley, don't you think she should cut that thing off? Now that she's old enough to date and all."

"Hey Polecat," said Smiley, stepping around me with a load of board. "Are you cold?"

"Hell, it ain't but a hundred degrees in here."

"Well, Experiment's wearing gloves."

"How much you think she weighs?"

"What I want to know is how much her daddy pays for her to go to that private school."

They all tested me to see if I was smart enough to go to college. "Now listen, Experiment," Polecat would say, climbing down his ladder. "Say you got a litter of six black pigs, and a litter of seven white pigs, and two of them black pigs gets the cough, but only one dies, and the dog eats four of them white pigs, but somebody trades you three black pigs for a lawn mower, how many pigs you got?"

When I gave the incorrect answer, he wanted to know what I studied at Bridgewater. The men circled me, curious.

"Latin? Who talks that?"

"Now Jack, you tell me what's the point in paying somebody to teach religion when the preacher does it for free."

"Hell, anybody can cut up a cat. Rabbits is harder 'cause you got to catch 'em first."

Jeremiah was the only one who asked serious questions about Bridgewater. He wanted his son to attend. "I've been saving up for eight years now," he told me. "I want that boy to have an education." Dutifully, I answered his questions about entrance exams, course requirements, and dress codes, but I didn't try to encourage him. Rudy Bloom had jumped off the Meshack Bridge at spring break, survived, and developed an ulcer. The other black kid, Franklin Harris, made the honor roll every semester, but he always ate lunch by himself. On the other hand, Gabriella Gubbel had shot herself, and she was white. Sometimes when I was working at the bailer, with my head stuck in the big mouth that chewed scrap board, I'd remember how we used to call out "Gabbygabbygabby! Gobblegobblegobble!" just to watch her cover her ears in pain. I didn't know Jeremiah's son, but I wanted to protect him.

When Henry went to Red Cavern, Jeremiah told him not to worry, he would hold the fort. They called each other sir, shook hands while gripping each other's arms, and patted each other brusquely on the back. It was as close to a hug as they could get.

Although a long line of men stood above Jeremiah in the running of plant, he didn't trust them. For those two weeks, he appointed himself plant watchdog and special guardian to Louise. This was a difficult task because of the unspoken, unwritten rule that blacks had to stay at the back of the plant. He made excuses to tour the factory in a forklift, careful to stay on the circumference, and once he even cleaned the railroad, so he could keep an eye on Dopey, who was likely to fall into the slitter and ruin Southern Board's safety record. Whenever possible, he requested an extra hand on the bailer, certain that Raymond Patch would send me.

Once, I had asked Henry why the blacks worked at the back of the plant. He was driving us home from church, nosing the Buick LeSabre around a hairpin curve on Mount Zion. He slowed down to see if there were any new dents on the guardrail. Florida commented that the county needed to get out here and cut back the kudzu.

"Look at that," Henry said, slowing down in front of a broken mailbox. Those rednecks knocked that sucker right over last night. Now why on earth anybody would get a kick out of driving by with a stick and hitting mailboxes is beyond me."

"Henry," said Florida. "She asked you a question."

"I'm listening. Look! There's another one. The good ole boys had a real time up here last night."

"They make a dollar less an hour," I said. "All the machines at the back of the plant pay a dollar less an hour."

"That's just circumstance, honey. There's no discrimination in it. Each machine requires a different level of skill, and the work pays accordingly."

"Your father is prejudiced," Florida explained.

A hundred yards from our driveway, he scowled and pulled the car over to the side of the road.

"Dad, please don't."

"You can't stop him," said Florida. She pulled the KEEP AMERICA CLEAN sack from under her seat and handed it to him. "Get out and help him," she said, so I tripped along in the weeds in my high heels, holding the sack open while he filled it with empty beer cans.

"Can you imagine the mentality of a person who just drives along and throws a beer can out the window?" he asked when we were back in the car.

"Joy riding," Florida said grimly.

THE NEXT AFTERNOON at Smartt's Gas Station, T. C. bought a six-pack of Miller for himself, a six-pack of Heineken for me, and a bag of popcorn. "Maybe I'll take you to the movies sometime," he said.

I could hear Drew saying "Oh thrill me," but I was thrilled.

T. C. wore black sunglasses and looked slightly dangerous, wheeling the Monte Carlo along back roads. I popped a Kenny Rogers tape into his stereo, unleashed my ponytail, and drank with abandon. Each time I finished a beer, I hung out the window and sailed a bottle through the air.

LATELY AT WORK, Dopey had been singing "Good Hearted Woman." As I threw boxes into the screaming mouth of the bailer, I sang with him.

In my mind, I lived out the seductive tragedy of my life with T. C. Curtis. It had all the appeal of suicide, but it was better because I would be alive to see the looks of shock and regret. I did not mourn the deaths of Daddy-Go and Grandmother Deleuth, not the way I mourned Roderick's death, but they altered my world. If my mind were a house, their deaths were like the removal of two large pieces of furniture. I continually stumbled into these blank spaces. It was unsettling. Where were they? At night, I wandered from room to room in Owl Aerie, feeling the silent space all around me.

Every evening, promptly at 5:00 P.M., Henry and Florida called. They passed the phone back and forth to each other, asking me the same questions: Did I have enough to eat? Did I remember to lock the doors and turn on the alarm? Was I lonely? I wasn't smoking in bed, was I? Was I getting to work on time? It was difficult to be late to work since Florida gave me a quick wake-up call at 6:00 A.M. on weekdays, but I managed a few times. On those days, Raymond Patch would step out of his office, wheezing, and watch me punch my time card. From the look on his face, it was clear that a woman could not do a man's job.

In the back of the plant, Jeremiah loomed like the shadow of Henry, bigger, darker, silent. Then, one day, he called me outside. We stood on a ramp, blinking in the strong sunlight. I had to shield my eyes to look up at him when he spoke.

"You ever seen a cat catch a rat?" he asked. On most men, the suit wears the man, but Jeremiah definitely wore his suit. Although he was a big man, he moved with the grace of a dancer; even his voice was a movement that seemed to throw off the cheap, pressed cloth. There in the sun on the hot metal ramp, he was present. He was himself, open and unafraid. He looked me in the eye. I looked at his polished black shoes.

"Never seen a cat catch a rat!" he cried. "Where you been?"

"Working," I said.

"Uh-huh." He broke a stem from a tall weed growing on the wall and chewed the tip. "Well, it goes like this: The ole cat smells him a rat and gets up real close, sniffing around. Then he starts playing with that ole rat. Course, he don't eat it right off. Naw, he jus' plays with it, chasing it into this corner, that corner yonder. He runs that ole rat back and forth, teasing it, see, until the varmit don't know backwards from forwards. Then you know what happens?"

I shook my head. How could he be this way, so plainly himself and unafraid? Like a king, a real one. It seemed almost rude. I glanced through the darkened doorway, into the humming green fog of the plant.

"Then he eats it," said Jeremiah.

"The cat eats the rat."

"Yes, indeed!"

Still squinting in the sunlight, I looked up at his gray temples. He had six children, and one who had died. He had a curtain over no window. I couldn't do that. I'd have to push the cloth back every day and touch the wall. I felt like an ole rat, scrambling for a way to outsmart him.

"What if I'm the cat?" I said. He chewed on his weed, con-

sidering this. Finally, he said, "Well, wouldn't that be something," and walked away.

NO ONE BELIEVED that I would actually bring T. C. to
the house. The first time I invited him, he said, "Wear your
bikini," and stood me up.

I cried. At work the next day, he told me he was sorry, his
aunt had to use the car. He lost my number.

"I'll make it up to you," he said at the water fountain, standing so close that the toes of our boots touched.

"How about tonight?" I said.

That evening, as the red sun fell behind the pines, I hid behind a Chinese vase in the living-room window, watching the
Monte Carlo curve around Owl Aerie's long driveway. The
shiny black car looked evil parked beneath Roderick's old
basketball goal. Slowly, the door opened. T. C. stepped out,
swigging a fifth of tequila. For a few moments, he stood spraddle-
legged beside his car holding the bottle in one hand, a flower
in the other.

I was worried that he wouldn't be able to find the front door.
Henry insisted that my dates come to the front door. Owl
Aerie had seven doors to the outside, so Florida had helpfully
made signs out of driftwood: FRONT DOOR, with appropriate
arrows. The one boy who had sallied up Mount Zion and followed this maze had never returned. He was a skinny kid with
blue skin and red hair, famous for wearing a bucket around his
neck so he wouldn't throw up on people at parties. When he
finally landed at the front door, Florida said, "You look just like
my son," and began to cry.

I let T. C. ring the doorbell twice. As soon as I opened it, he swooped down and stuck his tongue in my mouth. He reeked of tequila and aftershave, but the biggest disappointment was his outfit. Instead of the faded Levis and white T-shirt he wore to the plant, with a pack of Marlboro Reds rolled up in one sleeve, he had dressed up in a pair of jeans with an elastic waistband, and a two-tone terry-cloth shirt. I smiled and took the rose he offered, which was wrapped in green tissue with a pink ribbon.

"I was going to get you a dozen," he explained, "but I thought one would be more romantic." He bent down to kiss me again, but I slipped through his arms.

"Would you like some champagne?" I offered. The Pepperses were not in the habit of drinking champagne, but I felt obligated to keep up appearances for my coworkers at Southern Board. I would have worn a tiara if I could have gotten my hands on one. The best I could do was a pair of diamond drop earrings, with a matching choker and bracelet, that I'd picked up Kmart that afternoon. Since it was my house, I was barefoot.

"You're beautiful," T. C. said, reaching for my breast. Dodging, I suggested he accompany me into the living room for a cocktail, but he followed me right into the kitchen. When I stood on a chair to get the sorbet glasses, the closest thing we had to champagne glasses, he grabbed my butt. He took the glasses out of my hands and smashed me against his chest. "Let's dance," he said.

We staggered around the kitchen, stepping all over each other's feet. Then he whispered in my ear, "I want to eat your pussy."

I punched him in the gut.

"Sorry." He held up his hands as if he were being arrested then pushed them in his pockets. "Am I going too fast?" He stumbled, regained his balance. "I had a couple of beers before I came." He lit a cigarette for himself and one for me. "I'm sorry I molested you. I guess I got carried away." He looked at my dress. "You are sexy, though." His hand reached between my legs, and I hit him again.

"Stop it!" I yelled.

"I'm sorry. Excuse me. Are those diamonds fake or real?"

"These are zircons," I said with dignity.

In the dining room, he glanced over at the life-sized portrait Florida had done of Roderick. In the painting, Roderick looked like his corpse in the casket. Technically, that was his mouth, his nose, his forehead, but his eyes were hollow and dead.

"That's my brother." For a moment we looked at each other like actors who have forgotten their lines. T. C. breathed heavily, like an old man. I realized that I had made a mistake. I had invented a man; T. C. was not him.

"Do you know how to grill steaks?"

"Yep." He examined the bottle of Moët & Chandon I had set in a plastic bucket of ice. He fingered the steak tongs I had laid on a white linen napkin beside the bucket. Then he filled my sorbet dishes with tequila.

LEANING AGAINST THE deck railing, I shook salt onto the web of skin between my thumb and forefinger, licked it, took a sip of tequila, winced, and bit into a lime.

"Let me try that." T. C. was across the deck before I could turn my head, licking first my hand, then my neck. "What's the matter?" He was pushing his hand between my legs. Without waiting for an answer, he swept one arm behind by back, underneath my jacket, and unfastened my bra. It had taken my other date four tries to get my bra off, and then he was so embarrassed trying to fold it that we didn't go any further. T. C. snapped it off like a piece of tape. This bra was called the Mary Jane, white with pink rosebuds. In his hand it looked ridiculous.

"You're going too fast." I pushed at his chest, but he pressed himself tighter against me, until his wang poked into my leg. It felt like another hand, a baby's fist.

In my ear, he whispered, "I'm going to rape you."

All around us the kudzu and the vines in the trees formed a green fence, a green ceiling. The last little poke of sun in the sky shot through the leaves in a green light—like the light at the plant. It was hard to breathe. A few katydids said, "Katie did," once or twice, like musicians tuning their guitars. I tried to go limp. I had read in a magazine that a man can't rape a woman if she relaxes all of her muscles, but I couldn't relax a single one. He had my jeans unzipped and was trying to stuff his hand inside them when I bit him.

"Shit!" he cried. "What the hell?"

"You can't rape me," I said in a high, strained voice, backing away until the smoking grill was between us. I saw Florida's ashen face the first time she looked at the photo of the burned-out farmhouse in Red Cavern. "My home," she said, touching the photograph. "My home is gone." And Henry at the grill, back turned to us. No one else had ever touched the grill. "This place is wired all over with alarms." I tried to make my words sound official. "All I have to do is push a button, and the police will come."

T. C. scratched his neck. Then he ambled over to the grill and flipped the steaks. "S-7 security system. The main box is buried by the bird feeder. I installed it myself, two years ago. It's the kind that ain't connected to the police station." He salted the meat. "And y'all's neighbor is out fishing with my cousin Charlie. I loaned him my pole, as a matter of fact."

"You're lying." I took another step away from him.

"You scared of me?" He put on the cow-shaped grill glove I had given Henry last Christmas and said, "Moo." Then he made the sound of an alarm, "*Whooee, whooee.*" He thought this was very funny. I considered darting past him, into the house to call the police, but I had invited him to Owl Aerie. He was my guest. The only thing to do was make him uncomfortable; then maybe he would go away on his own.

I corrected my posture, smiled icily, and said, "Come into the dining room and have a seat." I set his place at one end of the long table, and mine at the other. All around the china plates I laid rows of silverware, including salt spoons. From the back of a cabinet, I produced two saucers and filled each one with warm water and a sprig of mint.

"These are finger bowls," I said airily. I searched for an intimidating word. "They were handcrafted by the Ungulates in Indonesia."

Swigging from his tequila bottle, he watched me with bleary eyes.

"Why do we have to sit so far apart?" he asked finally, moving his plate next to mine. "I want to sit next to you." As soon as I sat down and picked up my fork he put his hand between my thighs. I decided not to react.

"Aren't you going to eat?"

"I'm going to eat you," he said. I handed him the champagne to distract him and made a haughty face while he fumbled with the corkscrew.

"You unscrew it. Think you can do that?"

"You're a funny woman. You're—different. Not in a bad way. I guess that's why everybody calls you Experiment. They call me Tiger. That's what the T stands for."

"I thought it was Theodore."

"No, it's Tiger." He growled.

When the cork popped and the champagne bubbled through his nicotine-stained fingers, we laughed. The champagne seemed to cancel out the tequila, and everything else in my head. T. C. began to look attractive with his thick legs spread on the Queen Anne chair, his hair mussed and curly, one big paw around the sorbet dish, lips wet with wine.

"You can't rape me if I want to make love to you," I said. "It's my idea, too. I invited you over." When I leaned over to kiss him, he touched my nipples through my shirt and said, "Let's go over to the couch for a minute."

On the couch, the white curve of my breast surfaced like a fish in his hand. My legs seemed to spread by themselves. *Oh,* I thought, *this is sex.* I hadn't expected it to feel natural. When he kissed me, I didn't taste spit; I tasted champagne and then nothing; all my senses merged together into a single, heady craving. I put my hand on his knee, daring myself to touch his zipper.

On the count of ten, I was going to touch his zipper, but on three he pulled me beneath him so fast I lost count. "I'm going to eat your pussy," he said again, and I went cold. That was a rude thing to say. I wanted him to say something personal: You have the most intriguing eyes. But he probably didn't know that word. I noted that he hadn't told me I was beautiful since he gave me the rose. What if he didn't think I was pretty? He hardly looked at my Mary Jane panties before he jerked them down to my ankles.

"You'll like it," he argued, when I kicked him in the chest. "All the ladies say I eat pussy good. I can make you come. I ain't lying. It's the truth. You'll go wild." He laughed all to himself.

"Gross." Yanking my panties up, I slid into the corner of the couch. We were both panting, and I could still feel the wet spot his lips had left on my labia. "You can sit on the couch. Just don't lick me."

He sighed and lit a cigarette. "You don't have to sit all the way over there. I ain't gonna bite ya. And I ain't gonna lick." Then he grinned. "I swear, you'd like it. Women love that. You never had a man go down on you before?"

"I haven't even had regular sex yet."

"Shit." Drawing on his cigarette, he looked out the window. "What am I doing here?" He rubbed his head, and suddenly I was afraid I had lost his interest.

Florida had told me to encourage boys to talk about themselves, explaining that in some mysterious way this would make them find me interesting. I focused my attention on T. C. What would he like to talk about? I didn't know much about his life, except what I had read on his employee record, which I had pulled while filing papers in Mr. Patch's office. For some reason, the file contained his testimony in a divorce suit. Reading them, I was fascinated by his spelling: "Shee dont lik my skedule but she liks my kash i tole her i wuz triing."

"So, what's it like to be married?" I asked, crossing my legs as I lit a cigarette.

"We're separated." He had his hands flat on his thighs and didn't move them except to pick up his drink. He drank, then added, "It's hard work."

"When you were married, did you live in a trailer?"

"Naw. I built her a real nice home. Washer, dryer, dishwasher, satellite TV. She had everything."

"What's it like to have sex when you're married?"

"With your wife? Well, it's good. I mean, I like sex. Every morning you wake up, and she's right there. What is this? An interview?"

"I just want to know. Is being married like having a roommate?"

"Yeah, when she puts you on the couch."

"Didn't you ever want to sleep by yourself?"

"No, like I said, when you're getting along with a woman, having sex with her is nice. Do you want to turn on the TV or something?"

"I don't watch TV. What's it like when you get along?"

"Well, let me think." He took the cigarette out of his mouth with his thumb and forefinger and stubbed it in the ashtray. Then he lit another one. "Say I get off work at four-thirty and get home around five. She's waiting for me in her housecoat, lying on the bed, like."

"Why is she wearing her housecoat at five o'clock in the afternoon?"

"Maybe I'm working second shift. I'm just saying, okay? Say she's wearing her bathrobe. So I take a shower and come lie down beside her."

"What kind of bathrobe is it? Is it terry cloth?" I hated terry cloth. When T. C. married me, we'd live in a real trailer and I'd wear Victoria's Secret gowns.

"It's a short one or something," he said impatiently. "Anyway, I reach inside it, feeling her titties and all, and say, 'Hey honey.' Then we make love."

For a while, he was so quiet I was afraid he had fallen asleep. I was miffed that he didn't have his arm around me and hoped he wasn't sorry to be here with me instead of with his wife. I decided to touch his zipper on the count of one hundred.

"So have you ever slept with a whore?" I asked him.

"That depends on what you call a whore."

"Do you think I'm a whore?"

"No," he said with an irritated shake of his head that reminded me of Henry.

"I bet you wish I was a whore." I was silently counting, *Seventy-two, seventy-three, seventy-four* . . .

He rubbed his temples and sighed. "Well, we've both got to go to work tomorrow, so I guess I'd better be going."

"Stay."

"I'd like to, but I think I'd better be going." He stood up and began to look around for his shirt.

"We could sleep together without having sex," I offered.

"You think I'm going to sleep beside a naked woman and not have sex with her?"

"We could wear pajamas."

"You ain't doing too good at being a whore. Anyway, I sleep in the raw. Are you sitting on my socks over there?" He stood in front me, scowling. I reached up and touched his zipper. Then we both froze.

Finally, he said, "I don't mean to be crude or nothing, Louise, but if I go to bed with you, I'm going to fuck your brains out."

Then I took him to the only double bed in the house, in Henry and Florida's bedroom.

THE NEXT DAY, even though Florida gave me the usual 6 A.M. wake-up call, I spent forty-five minutes writing in my journal and was late to work. At lunch, I sat alone at my table, eating a steak sandwich while the men discussed my tardiness.

"Her daddy wasn't home to tie that string on her," Polecat said. "Every morning, he's got to tie that string on her so she can find her way out of that big house."

"Florida wasn't there to write 'Louise Peppers' on her lunch bag, so she lost it."

"She looks peaked to me, this morning. Experiment, what did you do last night?"

T. C. sat in the corner with Smiley and didn't even look at me.

"Wink at me," I commanded at the water fountain.

"I can't."

"Do you think everybody knows?"

"You might as well wear a sign."

"Really?" I grinned. "Do I look different?"

"You look like trouble." He shuffled away with his head down, and just when I began to hate him, he turned and winked.

That morning, T. C. cut doors and windows into a Frigidaire box, drew a license plate on the back and a Mercedes symbol on the front, fitted the whole thing over his forklift, and

drove up to the bailer to ask me for a date. He blew the horn
twice.

That's when I saw Jeremiah's temper. It was cold and slow,
like Henry's. His face was frozen in fury. In three quick,
graceful strides, like a Panther, he was on top of the forklift.
There was a blur of arms and legs, a hiss, shriek, and then the
Frigidaire box came off the forklift. Jeremiah wrapped his arms
around it, crushed it flat with one blow, and rammed it into
the bailer. Watching from the forklift, T. C. pretended to be
amused.

"Get out of here," said Jeremiah.

"Whatever you say, nigger-boy," said T. C.

Just as Henry would have done, Jeremiah stood with his
shoulders back, silent, staring at the man until he was gone.
Then he went into his office and made a phone call.

I MADE A note to explain racial equality to T. C., but I
was drunk with sex and couldn't really think about anything.
All I could do was remember sex and dream of more sex. At last
I believed I understood the line from Keats that Mr. Rutherford put on his final exam: "Oh for a Life of Sensations rather
than Thoughts."

"Do you know John Keats?" I asked T. C. that afternoon in
the parking lot at Smartt's Gas Station.

"Does he work at the plant?"

"No, he's dead. He was a poet. He wrote this poem, I forget
the name of it, but the last line is, 'Oh for a Life of Sensations
rather than Thoughts.'"

T. C. opened a Heineken with his fist and handed it to me.
"You know what I like about you? I like it when you bite your

lip, like you did just now. You did last night in bed. That was real cute."

I looked into the rearview mirror to see how I looked when I bit my lip—then I screamed.

"What the hell?" said T. C., slamming on the brakes.

Silently, Henry's LeSabre pulled up beside the Monte Carlo. A hard white ray of sun flashed off the silver paint, throwing a glare over Henry as he stepped out of the car. He was wearing a pair of golf pants and a white polo shirt from Kmart. His face was bright red, and his eyes were wild. He opened T. C.'s door, leaned into the car with his hands clenched on the doorframe, and said, "I will kill you." The tendons in his neck were stretched taut, and his voice was choked, as if he were being strangled. "If you ever," he said slowly, tearing each word off, "ever, ever see my daughter again, I will kill you. If you touch her—if you so much as look at her again—*Do you understand!*"

T. C. said, "Yes sir, I understand."

Then I got out of his car, and T. C. drove away. When I climbed into the LeSabre, I stayed as close to the door as possible. Henry drove to the meager shade of a pine tree at the edge of the lot and turned off the ignition. From inside the gas station, a chain-smoking cashier watched us with one hand on the phone, in case someone pulled out a gun. The car was hot. The backs of my arms stuck to the vinyl seat. Sweat ran down my legs. Henry would not turn on the air. He sat with his arms gripping the steering wheel, staring straight ahead, as if he were driving through a storm.

Finally, he said, "I should fire you. I knew it was a mistake to hire you in the first place, but I didn't listen to my better judgment. I trusted you."

I almost prayed, in case there was a God, but didn't. Then, because I knew that Henry could sit in a hot car ten times longer than I could, without eating or drinking or going to the bathroom, would sit here until the end of the world, I said, "I'm sorry."

Henry turned purple and again began to talk as though there was a rope squeezing around his neck. "Do you realize that it's between baseball and football season and those men have nothing to talk about but you? Every single minute of every single day they have watched every little move you made. Every single one! Did you know that? Do you know what those men were thinking? Do you!" He slammed his fist on the steering wheel. He began to shake it, rocking back and forth in the seat. His knuckles turned white.

"Answer me!" he cried.

"No sir," I said truthfully. "I never thought about that."

He looked at me for the first time. His face was misshapen—mouth stretched out, eyes bulging.

"You never thought about that," he said in a soft, stunned voice. He shook his head in astonishment. "It has taken me twenty-eight years to earn the respect of those men, and in one month, you threw it all away. Twenty-eight years of my life, and you never thought about it. Not once." His eyes grew wide and clear like the eyes of a child. "He isn't even handsome. He isn't even a good worker." Behind the window, the cashier blew smoke through her nose.

"What goes on in your head?" asked Henry. "You don't have good sense, do you?" He sighed. "Maybe I just don't know you."

A tear ran down his cheek, and then another, and another.

They came down hard, breaking over the lines in his face, falling into his open mouth as he made dry, choking sounds. He kept a firm grip on the steering wheel as his body shook.

"I love you," I said. "Please turn on the air conditioner."

"You don't act like you love me."

"I do!" I cried. "I do love you!" When I began to cry, he stopped and pulled an ironed white handkerchief out of his pocket.

"Your mother is torn up," he said. "I took her to the house." Thinking of Florida's pain gave him strength. He let go of the steering wheel, wiped his eyes, blew his nose, and sat up straight in his seat. "She's just sick about this," he said. "And boy, oh boy, did you pick a fine time to pull it off. Both of her parents just died, and now this. You hardly waited until the bodies were cold. Don't you care about anyone? I don't think you even give a darn about yourself." He shook his head back and forth. "I just don't understand you. I really don't. What goes on in your head?"

Then, in a calm, distant voice, Henry began to talk about God. God, Henry said, had given me certain gifts and talents, which I should use for His glory and not in the wrong way, not in a cheap way. Maybe God had made me a little different—I had a different way of looking at things—but that wasn't necessarily a bad thing. God had given me Free Will. I should use my Free Will to make the right choices, good decisions. "I don't want you to be some man's tool," he said. "You have a good heart. You're a good girl, a good . . . woman."

"Can we go home?"

"In a minute. I'm talking to you."

"I don't want to work at the plant anymore."

"Now listen here, young lady. You're a Peppers. We don't quit our jobs. You're going back into that plant on Monday morning. You're going in there with your head up. And if you speak to that man again, he'll lose his job. How would like that on your conscience?"

"I have to go now." I put my hand on the door.

"There's one more thing."

"Dad, please stop!"

"Listen to me."

"What?"

"I forgive you." He leaned over and kissed me on the head.

All they way home, he kept the bumper of the LeSabre on the fender of the Bonneville, even running yellow lights to stay with me, in case I took a wrong turn.

At Owl Aerie, Florida was sitting on a straight-backed chair by the kitchen door, holding my journal in her lap. Her hair was bright orange, but her face was gray and drawn up in wrinkles. As soon as Henry shut the door, she said, "You found her." She looked at me as if I were a big ugly earth worm. "Where was she?"

"She's home now."

"She was with him, wasn't she? Across the river." She spat out his name, "T. C."

"That's enough," said Henry. "I talked to her."

"I showed your diary to your father." In the stark kitchen light, her hands looked like Grandmother Deleuth's hands. The spotted, gnarled fingers with their swollen knuckles and broken nails spread like thin roots over the blue cover of my spiral bound notebook. "Repulsive," she hissed. "In our bed."

I wanted to lose my mind. I wanted to charge through the

window, fall to my knees and bark like a dog, swallow my tongue. I tried, but sanity held me in place like a chain.

"Give me my journal," I said, but she gripped it tighter.

"I pray for you," she said. "I pray you will let Jesus back into your heart. That's what God wants you to do. He saw all of this. He saw you."

Nervously, I laughed. "How do you know what God thinks about me? Does he tell you?"

"Hush," said Henry. "Go to your room now."

"God certainly does speak to me. And I listen."

"Maybe he talks to me, too."

She snorted. "Did God tell you to fornicate with T. C. Curtis?"

"Stop it, both of you," said Henry. "This discussion is over." The buzzer on the dryer went off, and Florida stood up. "I'm washing the sheets," she said.

With my hands shaking, I poured two inches of orange juice into a glass and took it to my room where I filled it with vodka. All night I lay awake on my bed with my vinyl brogans laced tightly around my ankles, planning to run away.

THE NEXT MORNING at the plant, Raymond Patch assigned me to the slitter. I trudged over there with my hands in my pockets, ignoring Polecat when he called out, "Watch you don't trip over that long face, Experiment." When I reached the slitter, I looked up and saw T. C. There he was, in a clean white T-shirt with a fresh pack of Marlboros rolled up in his sleeve, ready to catch slit boards. Never before had we been assigned to the same machine.

My voice fluttered as I said good morning. I wanted to rush into his strong arms, press my face against his chest, hear the now familiar wheeze.

"I have a bad heart," he'd said in bed. "That's why I don't breathe so good." I lay with my head on his chest, listening to the struggle inside him, thinking of Roderick with his inhaler.

We could go away somewhere together. Wyoming, or even Alaska. Somewhere dark and cool. We'd build a log cabin. He'd find another factory; I'd be a waitress. Or maybe we wouldn't work at all; we'd plant a garden and hunt. All night long, we would hold each other.

"Good morning," I said again, thinking he hadn't heard me.

He nodded curtly, looked away.

Stung, I pulled on my gloves and picked up a short stack of boards.

"Ready?" I asked icily. When he nodded, I shot the boards one after another, catty-cornered under the blades, making them fly over his shoulder. He caught each one, threw it away, and instantly resumed his stance: legs spraddled, palms open to catch the next whizzing board.

I bit my lip.

He ignored it.

I was a tool. I stacked fresh boards against the edge of the table, packing them like cards and sent the top one over with a clean shove under the blade, so the corners wouldn't turn. He caught it. He was a tool. I sent another one, and another, and another. We were tools.

In a gray suit, with his hands folded behind his back, Henry walked through the factory. A hush fell over the men. Without their voices, the whirring blades, the rip and slap of hot board, the crunch and grind of the bailer grew into a deafening roar. At the slitter, Henry stopped to watch us.

For the rest of the summer, I was assigned to the slitter with T. C. We grew to hate each other. At a different time each day, Henry would appear and then disappear. Every morning, the numbers on the wall declared another day of safety. All around us in the hot green light, metal slammed against metal, fires burned, forks lifted bales, whistles blew, and buzzing all over with the sad songs of men as small as ants, the plant grew.

Chapter Nine

IF A CIRCUS had come to Counterpoint, not the three-ride gig that went up in the Sears parking lot, forbidden to the Peppers family because of insurance liabilities, but a real cotton-candy-stinking, clown-smirking, two-headed-baby, maiden-stealing, rip-your-last-dollar-off, old-fashioned show, I would have been on the first caravan out of town. I wanted to be a clown.

"What kind of clown?" asked Henry in a steady voice. He had begun saving for his children's college education when he was twenty-one. The share I had inherited from Roderick, combined with my own, would send me to college for fifty years. However, like most rich people, Henry watched his pennies. He was not eager to finance a clown.

"A funny clown," I said. He put on his patient face. We were in the garage. He had been vacuuming Florida's car and was now taking apart the forty-two-year-old Kirby Lady Deluxe vacuum cleaner to see what on earth it had sucked up to make it start smoking. There was no telling what it had swallowed in Florida's car.

Now, as he set his wrench down, I could almost hear him praying. Please Lord, not a clown or a beautician or a floozy. Make her a doctor or a nurse or a news anchorperson.

"You know," I said. "A clown-clown. Like Marcel Marceau."

"A professional," he said, having never heard of this person. Biting his lip, he got down on his knees and peered into the Kirby's innards with the penlight of his Southern Board key chain. Then he stuck his hand in there. Five minutes later, he pulled out a small red plastic monkey whose tail was looped around a piece of dried muscadine vine.

"It's part of her flower arrangement for the Garden Club show," I said. I decided not to mention that another dozen monkeys were involved.

Henry knitted his eyebrows, shook his head, and switched off the penlight. "I guess you get your creativity from your mother," he said sadly. He rubbed his chin. Then, tentatively, he suggested that I could be a clown on the weekends, working at the mall or renting myself out to parties, juggling and whatnot, while studying something practical at college.

"Clowning would make a good hobby," he said, smiling hard.

"I don't have hobbies," I snapped, bristling at the word. I had been ready to tell him my deepest feelings about being a clown.

"Well, you don't have to bite my head off," he said.

That year, when I was seventeen going on eighteen, I realized with a shameful thrill that I had a brain. "Bright," said my teachers at Bridgewater. In Mr. Rutherford's Advanced Placement English class, when we read Plato's The Cave, I burned

in my desk, bright all over. English was easy for me because
there were no correct answers to Mr. Rutherford's questions;
one only had to be Mr. Rutherford—a pleasant task for a girl
in love. It was the same with the authors we studied. I pitied
students who had to read *Light in August* line by line; I somehow drank the pages, and when I looked up, I was William
Faulkner, dead drunk in Mississippi. I sank into the minds of
Flannery O'Connor, James Joyce, William Blake, and wandered there among the ghosts and shadows and patches of dazzling sunlight. There were themes: Man versus Man, Man
versus Nature, Man versus God, and questions at the end of
the chapter, but these were unimportant. How do you get inside another human being? This was the question. I saw signs
everywhere: in the untied lace on Drew's moccasin, the warm
red bricks of wall, the white curve of Mr. Rutherford's hand as
he raised his thumb at me, but still, love eluded me. Then one
day, walking off demerits around the lake, I watched a swan dip
her long neck, raise it, and glide, and a verse from Blake came
to me all in one piece like an egg:

> Never seek to tell thy love,
> Love that never told shall be;
> For the gentle wind does move
> silently, invisibly.

My light did not shine as well in prealgebra, which I had
taken for three years in a row. Mr. Rutherford said not to worry
about it—algebra wasn't part of our religion.

At the same time I discovered my intellectual powers, I
reached the disturbing conclusion that Henry and Florida were

feebleminded. They both had college degrees, but apparently college was easier in those days. Florida's only memory of the experience seemed to be running out in the snow in a bathing suit and high heels with her roommate, at which point she realized Henry loved her because he was afraid she'd get a cold. Henry recalled that when he moved to the front row of the classroom to sit next to Florida, he got better grades.

It was hard to believe that these two could produce a Bridgewater intellectual, but there I was: black turtlenecks, baggy army pants, a tight ponytail, and small, round tortoiseshell glasses. I was an atheist and a communist. Although I never actually read the *Tao Te Ching,* I toted it around with me, which made Florida suspicious. She couldn't get past the first page, but something about it smacked of *Looking Out for Number One.* Luckily, I had friends. My friends, atheists and communists in black turtlenecks, ponytails, and funny glasses were also burdened with dim-witted parents. We discussed them the way people discuss their mentally ill relatives, but without sympathy. Mostly, we tried to escape them. We passed around a copy of Solzhenitsyn's *First Circle* and fancied ourselves imprisoned in Russia. We drank a lot.

I tried to get Henry and Florida to drink—tried to introduce red wine with spaghetti, cognac in coffee, and champagne at New Year's—but they were low-brow and Baptist to boot. So I left on the weekends, carrying the lunch bag Florida had packed with my first and last name written on the paper bag, to the radio tower on top of Mount Zion, or the lock and dam, or a field—someplace where I could get drunk with my friends and be somebody else.

When I announced my acceptance to the Ringling Clown

College in Sarasota, Florida, Henry decided to keep me home for a year.

"Why, that's the same price as a real school!" he exclaimed. "They're just taking your money! Why do you want to associate with riffraff?"

"Gypsies," said Florida.

"They've never had an opportunity in life," explained Henry. "It's not their fault. Most of them aren't even Americans. My goodness. You've been to one of the finest college preparatory schools in the country. I would think you'd want to do better than the circus."

"Maybe I can be a snob. The world needs more snobs."

"Here she goes," said Florida. "That mouth."

Florida, who had grown up without a flush toilet, was appalled that a girl would stick her hand out for that sum of money and smart off at the same time. Although she was not a political person, she had won her mother an electric refrigerator, the first one in Red Cavern, by writing an essay entitled "Why I Am Proud to Be an American." She couldn't put her finger on the connection between communism and clowning, but she smelled a rat. Furthermore, without her there to drag me out of bed on Sunday mornings, I would never go to church.

I argued. Didn't Lao-tzu say

> When taxes are too high,
> people go hungry.
> When the government is too intrusive,
> people lose their spirit.
> Act for the people's benefit.
> Trust them; leave them alone.

They listened, nodded. True, I was not a joy to live with—not by a long shot, but these were the sacrifices one made for one's children. Yes, they agreed, I needed one more year of home training before they set me loose. After that, all they could do was pray.

It was decided that I should stay in Counterpoint for a year and attend the Maude Wilson College for Women, if I got in. One day an application in a lavender envelope printed with magnolias arrived at Owl Aerie. When Ebbie, the postman, tossed it to me from the window of the mail truck, I caught it in midair like a bride's bouquet.

Henry took it to Southern Board and had his secretary, Heather, make four copies of it so I could practice filling it out before I typed it. Florida was not allowed to type it because I didn't want her to read my essay.

"That suits me just fine," she said. "I'm tired of staying up all night typing your papers. Last time I was up until 4:00 A.M. I don't know how you're going to get by in college."

"I can get through Maude Wilson in my sleep."

"We'll see." She touched her hair. "You need to grow up. You've made some poor decisions in the past. Goofed off. Gone wild. I'll type your papers this year. I don't mind. I'd just appreciate some advance notice."

"Your mother works her fingers to the bone for this family," said Henry guiltily. "You ought to hug her neck."

Florida had nothing against Heather, but she couldn't help noticing that Henry's secretaries had always had blonde hair, while she herself was a brunette. Henry claimed this was a coincidence. Florida wondered aloud why Heather had to dress like a showgirl; Henry said it was good for Southern Board's image. Florida didn't reply, but her face clearly suggested that Henry thought he was running a casino instead of a corrugated board plant. Finally, she said, "I don't see how anyone can type with nails that long, but I guess Heather has learned to manage."

Henry said, "I vacuumed your car out this morning." He opened his handkerchief and produced the plastic monkeys that the Kirby had twisted into a gross embrace.

"Throw them away," she said. "You didn't say anything about my hair. I had it done this morning."

"I noticed it," he said, searching for a word. "It looks . . . nice."

She turned her back. Her turquoise MacMe jogging suit had once said I AM FREE across the back, in gold stitching studded with rhinestones and sequins, but over time the message had unraveled. Now it said I AM.

I WAS WRITING suicide notes in chemistry lab at school when Drew, who had received early admission to Harvard, took charge of my educational dilemma.

"I don't envy you, Louise," she said, looking gravely at me through the Coke-bottle lenses of her glasses. "This sucks the big one." She considered various solutions while she typed up our lab reports. Finally, she said, "Fill out the application. Be honest. Tell them who you really are. Reveal your penchant for rednecks and your banana-peel smoking habit. Mention that you were one of Dr. Frommlecker's patients. Suggest that you have a drinking problem." Then Drew did something she had never done in the thirteen years we had been best friends: she hugged me.

That night, lying on my bedroom floor, sucking a White Russian through a straw, I answered the last question on the Maude Wilson application: Who Are You? (in five hundred words or less).

> I'm a tough broad living on the dock. I know how to start a car with a paper clip, open a door with a credit card, and roll a joint in the dark. I can find my way through a strange room in the middle of the night better than most house cats, and I know how to run. In a fight, I keep my back to the wall, and if I'm losing, I lick the bitch's ear, as a surprise, then go for her face. Now that I'm staying with my two-ton sugar daddy, Max, I know all there is to know about men. A lot of tough broads on the dock wear make-up and try to look professional, but my girl Dewana says, "Who wants a tired ole ho with brains?"

I went on to elaborate on my sugar daddy and my girl Dewana, and made a few poignant references to my sordid experiences as a foster child. Using the phone book as a reference point, I did a condensed travelogue of the jails and halfway houses in a hundred-mile radius of Counterpoint. Finally, I edited my work using Mr. Rutherford's bible, *The Elements of Style*. Then I took the final copy to Drew. After she made sure I had checked the black race on the application, she gave it her enthusiastic approval.

"They will never let you in," she assured me. "You have next year off."

Maude Wilson's reply came five days before Christmas.

"Yoo-hoo!" called Florida, striking her heels along the tiled hall. At my bedroom door, she knocked while turning the doorknob with her free hand. When the door opened a crack, she stuck a thin lavender envelope through it. "News for you!" I took the letter and shut the door, but Florida carried on the conversation through the wall. "I wouldn't be surprised if they offered you a scholarship. Something, if not a big one. Agnes's niece, you know Agnes—she's at Shear Heaven now—I quit her, but I might go back because this new girl flubbed my permanent. What did they say?" She tried the door again. "Anyway, I was telling you—Agnes's niece, Laurin, got a scholarship. Need-based. Cute girl." She paused to listen to the envelope rip. "What did they say? Louise, I'm talking to you. Why do you have to shut your mother out like this?"

Behind the door, my tears fell silently on the letter which accepted, with congratulations and a minority scholarship, the application of Frances Louise Peppers to the Maude Wilson College for Women.

THE LIVE OAK trees lining the entrance to the Maude Wilson College for Women had been planted by Colonel Wilson's slaves. According to the engraved plaques screwed along the walls of the bell tower, Mrs. Wilson had a religious experience in which God told her to teach the slaves how to read the Holy Bible. Local legend had it that Maude fell in love with one of these tall Senegalese men, and the Sunday School for One Hundred, as it came to be called, was only an elaborate contrivance for them to meet. In any case, the Sunday School was eventually limited to children, and Maude died from an overdose of laudanum.

I sat under one of these trees on the first day of the fall semester, morosely drinking a warm Bloody Mary in a paper cup.
A gaggle of girls in sundresses and espadrilles trooped by. They
walked close together, talking in low voices until one of them
halted, threw her head back, and screamed modestly. This happened several times. They seemed to be talking about boys.

"I did not say that! Who said that I said that?"

"All I know is that I am not partying with them again."

"Was it Eric?"

"My dog could make a better gin and tonic."

"Did you see Mason? God, he's cute!"

"What was he doing with that girl? I mean, she was nice and
everything, but she was heavy."

"She's a cow. She must be his sister or something."

"If Eric said that about me, I'm going to talk to his roommate. We're very good friends. Do you know Tad?"

"Omigod! You're good friends with Tad? He's gorgeous!"

The bell in the tower rang nine times—Introduction to
Shakespeare—but I didn't move. I sat under the tree, holding
a gnarled root with one hand as I looked high up into the limbs
webbed with Spanish moss. I thought of the seed in the black
man's hand, the hand forming the brick, the espadrilles on the
brick. Then I went across the street and bought a bus ticket to
Myrtle Beach, South Carolina, the last stop on the line.

The Greyhound turned down Front Street and rattled past
the drugstore, Wanda's Wig Shoppe, the howling wolf in front
of the library. Out of habit, I scanned the muddy waters of the
New Hope River for the scaly jaws of Earnestine. As we pulled
out of town, the driver shifted into high gear, and I leaned back
in my seat to think about Florida.

She didn't like me. She had more or less said so. From my backpack I removed my thermos of Bloody Marys, added a few tablespoons of paregoric, and stirred the remaining ice cubes with a stick of celery. I kicked my espadrilles off and threw my bare feet up on the seat so no one would sit next to me. Then, sipping my cocktail, I began to review the tragedy of my life. She had practically said she hated me.

"You twist my words around to suit yourself!" Florida cried. She had just come home from a Christian Women's Club luncheon, and she was still wearing her sunglasses. Her suit was black: Jones of New York, with padded shoulders, and her nails were lacquered in vermilion. Gripping the railing of the deck with both hands, she said, "You don't listen to me because you're afraid to hear the truth. The truth is that you have rejected your mother and the Lord Jesus Christ."

"The combination is too much for me," I said without looking up from the *Tao Te Ching*. Sipping a banana daiquiri, I stretched out on my lawn chair in the yard below her. Even though Henry had cut the kudzu back, thick foliage cloaked the ground and twisted through the trees, choking off the sun save for a small patch of shimmering green sky.

"Too much for you? You haven't done a thing all day. You've been wallowing around in that chair all day, feeling sorry for yourself because we won't send you to the circus for twenty thousand dollars a year. You've got to face reality. And let me tell you, young lady, if Christianity is not part of your reality, you're in for big trouble."

"The Constitution of the United States of America grants every citizen of this country the right to religious freedom. Do you know what Kurt Vonnegut said about religion?"

"I know that you are disrespectful to your mother. You're the most hateful child I have ever seen. Hateful, hateful, hateful."

"'Religion!' snorted Newt. 'See the cat? See the cradle?'"

"Words, words, words! All you have are words. Get up and do something. Help out a little. Don't expect me to go in there and make your lunch. I won't do it! I won't!"

"I'm not hungry," I said. "Let me read you something."

"I don't want to hear any more of your heathen literature."

I read aloud, "Throw away holiness and wisdom, and people will be a hundred times happier. Throw away morality and justice, and people will do the right thing. Throw away industry and profit—"

"You are driving me up the wall!" I raised my eyes. In her shoulder pads and sunglasses, she looked like a giant black hawk. "You're all take and no give," she said, flapping her arms angrily. "It's gimmee, gimmee, gimmee, what can you do for me? Jesus Christ tells us not to be selfish. What does that book say about Jesus?"

"'The world is sacred. It can't be improved.'"

Florida's face turned gray. That's when I knew she hated me, and hated herself for it. She ripped off her jacket and swirled it in the air. For a moment, I thought she might jump. She would rise into the sky with a thunderous clap of wings and swoop down on me. But she remained on the deck. The black jacket fluttered in the air and then sank slowly down until it caught on a low branch of the hickory tree beside my chair. It hung there like a flag.

Despite my resolve not to become entangled with religious people, my heart was pounding. I couldn't remember anything else from the *Tao Te Ching,* so I blurted out a bumper sticker slogan: "Jesus save me from your followers!" The door slammed; she'd gone inside the house to make lunch.

Henry came out of the garage holding the weed eater he'd been repairing. "What's all this fussing out here?" he asked.

"Religion is man's defense against God," I said.

"What?" He looked up at the jacket hanging in the hickory tree. "How did your mother's coat get in the tree?"

"She threw it."

He stared hard at me, then shook his head. "You all have lost your minds. I'll have to get a ladder."

When he went back into the garage, I studied the black flag hanging on the twisted old tree. The hickory was proof that lightning does strike twice. Last year lightning had hit the tree then run down the edge of the roof and zapped the intercom system. To me, this was an explicit request from the universe that the Pepperses stop talking to each other. However, Florida didn't need the intercom. She'd holler through the house, "This family is not communicating!" The first time lightning struck was during the tornado, which led to my salvation and all the trouble I'd had since. Life is hard the first time around; why prolong the agony by being born again? As anyone could see, by looking at the black coat hanging in the hickory tree, Christ did not bring peace to the human heart.

AT THE NEXT stop, a black woman wearing a red wig sat down beside me. "Rain's a-coming," she said. "This ole knee lets me know every time." I offered her a drink.

"Don't mind if I do," she said, taking the thermos cup. "A toddy for the body. Oh, my bones get to aching, honey. Don't you get old—you young and sweet."

"I won't."

"Sure as the devil has horns, we gonna get us some rain." Together we looked out the window at a cloudless blue sky. Any minute now, I expected to see the pouf of Florida's hair and Henry's bald spot inside a blue Ford Taurus pulling up beside us. Somehow, they would stop the bus.

She'd say, "I knew this would happen. I just knew it."

He'd say, "Your mother has been a nervous wreck. Do you have any money?"

I had $48.16 plus the credit card in my name that was billed to Henry. I had a set of gym clothes, a new notebook, a new copy of *King Lear,* an empty thermos, and half a bottle of paregoric. I had a vague plan to kill myself.

"Where you going?" asked my companion.

I shrugged. "I had a fight with my mother."

"Is that right?" She had the face of a warrior, mapped with battles. When she drank from her cup she screwed up her face as if bracing herself against another enemy.

"Yes ma'am," I replied.

"What y'all fuss about?"

I pushed my glasses up on my nose and tightened my ponytail. Then I shrugged again. "People never really fight about what they're fighting about. It's always something else."

"Ain't that the truth. You hear about that man went and shot his wife after forty-five years of marriage? Said she burned the cornbread. Shot her right at the supper table."

"In the face?"

"Lord yes, honey. What make a man go and do that evil thang?"

"I don't know."

With a grimace, she finished off her toddy. "That be the devil," she confirmed. "The devil hisself. Lord have mercy on us."

After my blowout with Florida, Henry called me into his study. Over the years, Florida and Shirley had been gradually redecorating Owl Aerie, stripping hallucinogenic wallpaper, replacing beanbags with Queen Anne chairs, and rolling up shag carpets, but some vestiges remained. Henry's study was still done up in relentless brown with chrome accents and track lighting. Shirley had tried to compensate for the monochromatic color scheme by varying patterns; the result was a dark confusion.

Wearing the orange smoking jacket Florida had given him last Christmas, Henry paced the plaid carpet with his hands clasped behind his back while I struggled to sit up straight in a brown-striped mamason chair.

"You want to be different," he was saying. "You want to go way, way out there." He raised his arms in the bright silk sleeves. Everything she bought for him was orange, to bring him out, and everything he bought for her was blue, to calm her down. "Way out!" he cried, "into . . . into . . . outer space." His eyes widened when he looked at me. "Don't you?"

"It appeals to me," I said.

Shaking his head, Henry dropped his arms. "What do you think is out there?" We tried to stare each other down. "Honey, let me tell you what is out there. Nothing." I blinked. "There is nothing out there. Absolutely nothing. You're going to get out there . . . to . . . Mars, or somewhere"—he waved angrily at Mars—"and you're going to find yourself alone." He smiled sadly. "And what are you going to do then?"

Before I could answer, Florida's house shoes gave a warning

clack, clack, clack in the hallway, and the door clicked open. Her face was smeared with cold cream, and her eyes were swollen from crying.

"What are you all doing in here?" she asked, but she hung back in the doorway as if we might chase her away. Henry and I remained silent. "It's late," she said sharply, taking a determined step forward. "You all need to be getting to bed. What are you talking about?"

As much as I feared Florida in her blaze, I preferred her fury to this. In the thin black nylon robe, with the white cream on her face, she looked scrawny and obscenely naked, like a plucked bird. I wanted to cover her, to hold her. She wasn't much of a hugger, though. She always twisted away, leaving me with my arms hanging, feeling foolish. Henry hugged. He held me until my blood ran smooth and warm, and once more, I belonged to the single body of the human race. So I didn't touch Florida. I saw her hovering there by the door, white-faced, plucked, and scared, and I lashed out with my tongue.

"We're plotting your death."

She jerked as if she'd been hit; then she began to bawl. I mumbled an apology, but it was too late. Turning to Henry, she said flatly, "Either she goes, or I go. Choose."

When she had gone to her room, weeping, Henry paced the floor. "If I had to choose," he said with a sigh, looking as if he were already drifting behind the gently rustling pages of the *Wall Street Journal,* into the relative calm of the stock market, "I would choose your mother."

• • •

WHEN THE BUS pulled into Myrtle Beach, South Carolina, my friend was sleeping. Her wig had shifted, revealing a gray braid beneath the red wig.

Outside the bus station, the rain beat down on my head. Water splashed across my espadrilles, bleeding red dye into my new white socks. A sign with a neon palm tree advertised a room for all the money in my pocket. I was dizzy with hunger. In the window of a bar, a neon lady in a bikini flashed back and forth, swinging her hips. What Henry said about me was true: "You just don't think!" I was not good at thinking. Before I reached the logical conclusion to an argument, an obstacle always appeared: something fast and dazzling, something so wild it made my heart jump, made me want to live!

This time it was a Ferris wheel. I saw it at the edge of the strip—a ring of colored lights rolling majestically through the gray sky like a wheel on Ezekiel's chariot. I stepped to the edge of the road and, for the first time in my life, raised my thumb. A red truck with an umbrella opened over the roof, spoke hubcaps, and the head of a baby doll stuck on the bumper screeched to a stop and backed up. One of the back lights was missing, but the other one shimmered over my path as I splashed across the wet pavement.

"Jim," said the swarthy, toothless little man behind the wheel. "Which way?"

"Louise Peppers. Forward." Between us, a chimpanzee strapped into a child carrier held the umbrella that opened through a hole in the roof. "Hi," I said.

For a moment, she gawked; then in a flash, she reached a long arm over my lap and pulled my shoe off my foot, waving the wet espadrille and hooting. She herself was smartly dressed in striped overalls and yellow rain boots.

"That there is Daisy. Apple of my eye. Daisy, reach in the back and get her my flannel shirt." Daisy crossed her arms and stuck her lip out. "Don't give me none of your sass, girl. Get that shirt." Turning her small, elegant head away from him, the chimp bared her teeth at me in an enormous leer. Then she spit. "Don't make me stop this car," said Jim. "Shit. Rain's really coming down now. Louise Peppers, open your window there and reach for that string. When I pull my wiper, you wait a second, then pull yours." I was glad to open the window because the car smelled rank, as if Daisy had needed a diaper change for some time, but I had some trouble pulling my wiper in synchronicity with the other one. Jim didn't seem to mind. He steered with one hand and pulled his wiper with the other, talking all the while. He was missing some fingers and teeth, but he didn't seem dangerous.

"My Christian name is Jungle Jim. Mother named me that 'cause I kept her house filled with strays. Down in Louisiana we had alligators in the bathtub, snakes in the potty, and a panther in the parlor. Not to mention the cats and dogs—had up to thirty-seven at one time. Once I got me a black bear cub— cutest damn thing you ever saw. He'd eat a whole jar of peanut butter at a time. Then one day his paw got too big—he couldn't get that jar off to save his life! Tore the house up, trying to— Daisy, get a shirt for the lady 'fore I have to take your head off. Ain't she cute? She's got a little brother back at the house. Spencer. Now he's shy. Ain't like her. But smart! Personally, I think he's ready to read. I'd teach him myself, but I never went past the third grade. Tried to get him a tutor back in Mississippi, but they were all too stuck up. I'll tell you one thing—a chimp, and most animals for that matter, is smarter than most people I know. And a hell of a lot nicer. But I pick up strays, can't help it. Saw you standing there wet to the bone and said to Daisy, 'We got to pick her up.'"

Afraid that he was going to offer me a warm bowl of milk, I smiled and said, "I'm not really a stray. I'm traveling."

"You a carnie?"

I had some vague notion that *carnie* meant carnivore, and feeling that meat eaters might be repugnant to this die-hard animal lover, I said I was not. He looked disappointed. Daisy chose that moment to hand me the filthiest, smelliest rag I had ever touched in my life. "You put that shirt on over your dress," said Jungle Jim generously. "Don't want you to catch a chill." Miserably, breathing through my mouth, I jerked my arm back and forth in the rain, trying to see out the window. I was about to ask the driver to let me out when I saw the Ferris wheel in front of us.

"This is us," said Jungle Jim. "You want I should carry you on down the road some, or you want out here?" I hugged his dirty shirt closer around my shoulders, shivered perceptibly, and gave him my best sad eyes.

"Aw, hell," he said. "My show ain't for another hour, and this rain will keep most of the rubes at home tonight. Come on over to the trailer and let me get you a cup of hot chocolate."

I jumped out of the truck into the back lot of the Arthur Reese Traveling Show. Hoarse shouts broke through a rollicking circus tune: "Three rings for a dollar, whose the next winner! Step right up! Step right up! Popcorn! Hot popcorn!"

"You know that song?" asked Jungle Jim. "That's the carnie

song, 'Le Sabre.'" In the rain, Daisy did a brief dance. A clown walked by, holding an umbrella over his head. On his heels walked a dog with a wet cat perched on its back. A faint strain of Frank Sinatra crooned beneath the lighted Ferris wheel.

"Party tonight, Warren?" Jungle Jim asked the clown.

"If you say so. Who's the new addition to your menagerie?"

"This here is Louise Peppers. Louise, this is Lollibells."

"Lord have mercy on us," said the black man in white face. He waved a white-gloved hand at me. "Watch out for hair balls," he said.

"You ain't funny," said Jungle Jim.

"You, however, are a gas," said the clown, and walked off with the dog and cat behind him.

Slogging through the mud, I pondered what a remarkable thing a college education was turning out to be, and then, with a cramp in my heart, I thought about poor Florida and Henry, worrying themselves to death.

Chapter Ten

IN THE MORNING I woke up beside a snoring man. I tried to recall his name by going through the alphabet, but this gave me a headache. Afraid that I would throw up on him, I got out of the narrow, rumpled bed and found a bathroom. The water from the faucet made me gag and the orange juice I found in a battered refrigerator scorched my throat, but at last I found a single can of beer hidden behind a rotting lump of lettuce. The drink cleared my head; when I looked around again, I saw that I was in a trailer.

In Counterpoint, trailers sprouted like weeds in forgotten corners of town. Henry liked to drive by them, frowning at the trash in the barren yards, the cardboard on the windows, the grubby barefoot children gaping back at us.

"How can people live like that?" he'd wonder aloud, and Florida would answer, "Riffraff."

I'd always liked the sound of the word.

Although most of my sexual fantasies about T. C. Curtis had taken place in trailers, until now I'd never been inside of one. This was an old trailer with warped walls, torn linoleum, and a rusty bucket sitting in the middle of the kitchen floor to catch the rain. It smelled of mold, cigarettes, and stale whiskey.

Posters of the Arthur Reese Traveling Show covered the stained walls, introducing circus wonders: POPEYE—THE MAN WITH ELASTIC EYEBALLS; DEVIL BABY—BORN WITH REAL HORNS AND A TAIL—ATE HIS OWN MOTHER; and FIFI THE HEADLESS WOMAN, picturing the decapitated gal holding her head under one arm. I recognized Lollibells, grinning down at me from a poster plastered across the ceiling, and Jungle Jim, featured with Daisy and Spencer on his lap, a gorilla standing by his side like a wife, and a parrot on his head. There was a middle-aged woman wrapped in a python, a pissed-off midget, and a Gorilla Girl—a bikini-clad chick in a gorilla mask. She signed her poster "With Love" right on the crotch. Hanging next to Gorilla Girl, a banner announced ZANE WILDER— THE HUMAN DRAGON! A collage of photos showed the dragon swallowing fire, swallowing a sword, and biting into a light bulb. He was tall and lean and buff, with a flat belly, bronze skin, long red hair, and big, crazy green eyes. His teeth were as bright as ice.

In the dim bedroom, I looked at the snoring hump under the sheet. Red hair fanned out over the pillow. I tiptoed closer and examined a freckled shoulder and the shapely hand resting on his his smooth golden chest—a wedding ring. In my head, I heard Florida's voice: "Well, I hope you're proud of yourself now!"

Outside, I sat down on the concrete block steps in front of the door, and not knowing what else to do, opened *King Lear.* I skimmed the introduction, then closed the book again.

I wandered out along the chain-linked fence, staring glumly at the empty midway. There were the shells of hankypanks. They taught me the word last night, and I laughed at the sound of it, laughed as we staggered through the crowd of rubes waving hot dollars in their fists, shouting winning numbers for teddy bears. The song "Le Sabre" blared through a speaker at the carousel. It made me want to throw my money away, do cartwheels, kiss strangers. A cop on duty picked up the play rifle and, with a cruel squint, tried to shoot the piano player in the back. "Aim again, Officer!" cried the carnie. "One more try, just one more try." The policeman was there for the rest of the night, passing dollars over the counter, squinting into the toy gun. This morning the abandoned hankypanks looked like chicken coops.

Circling the carousel that had spun in a ring of pretty lights, up, down, and around—a tiny galaxy of stars and ponies, "Step right up, step right up, put your darlin' on a pony, step right up"—I stared ruefully at the scarred horses with lopsided stirrups, a chipped hoof, a tail lopped off in midcurl. The whip that had snapped through the glowing black sky like a biting snake now lay dead on the ground. At last I came to the Ferris wheel I'd seen from the bus station. Chaise volonte, they called it. Up close, it had been even more fantastic, a wheel of colored light turning through the sky in a concert of Sinatra tunes: "Fly Me to the Moon," "Come Fly with Me," "That's Life"—and the night rushed back to me.

Rufus Swaziek, the operator, had confided that he hated Sinatra, but the owner of the carnival, Arthur Reese, would allow no other music on the chaise volonte.

"Means 'flying chairs' in Spanish," said Rufus. He shook his head. "Arthur is a tragic man. Don't tell nobody I told you, but he is a tragic man. I'd like to play a little disco, a little country music, but he won't have it. He's got to have a sad song, see? Tragic. Puts the damn thing over here in the corner with me. I ain't complaining, but now and then I'd like to hear something a little more upbeat, more modern. It affects your brain rythmns to hear this shit all night long. I go to bed depressed, wake up depressed. Now I ain't blaming him—he's just playing the hand the Lord dealt him, and all the money in the world don't change that, but it affects my brain rhythms. You put me over on the merry-go-round, and I might be dancing to 'Le Sabre.' That's the carnie tune."

Rufus didn't look like he'd ever danced in his life. He was a wiry little guy of no particular age: bowlegged, pockmarked, tattooed, also missing some teeth and a heart valve. The other carnies called him Tic Toc because his artificial heart valve sounded like a clock. Over his scraggly ponytail, dyed the color of summer squash, he wore a greasy cap. "Now git down," he said after I'd been riding for half an hour. "Arthur will kick my butt for giving free rides." Then I passed him my small amber bottle. "Shit!" he cried. "Where did you get this shit? What did you call it? Parachute?"

"Paregoric. It's for menstrual cramps."

"Goddamn!" He ducked his head as my chair swung up for another round on the chaise volonte. "I wished I was a girl."

Above me, painted onto the gilded ceiling of the ride, were

portraits of ladies—old-fashioned ladies with piled hair, pink cheeks, milky white necks, and lips painted into bows. There was a green-eyed redhead, a blue-eyed brunette, and a brown-eyed blonde. Chugging my paregoric, I began to feel about these ladies the way Catholics feel about the Virgin Mary. While Frank Sinatra crooned that this was life, or that was life, or there was life on the moon, or something wonderful, Rufus switched the spotlight from green to violet, and my chair swooped up to the stars. I was flying.

In the mean light of day, the chaise volonte was a piece of junk. A hot breeze came up, smelling of dead fish, melting asphalt, cocoa butter, and salt. The lot was still empty, save for a skinny stray dog poking through an empty red-and-white popcorn box in the weeds. The flaps were down on the dingy tents, and the metal roofs of the trailers glared.

"Reality," Florida called this. I needed a drink. I needed to get my gym clothes and Shakespeare books and go back home. I headed toward the glare of metal roofs.

Pushing the warped door open with my shoulder, I stumbled inside, blinking in the darkness. It took me a moment to realize I was in the wrong trailer. Suddenly, a light switched on, and a woman shot out the corner with a broom.

"Hold it right there!" she shouted, raising the broom.

"Okay," I whispered.

"Who are ya?" she demanded. "What are ya doing here?" She was a big-boned woman with a round Slavic face and bright blue eyes. She had pale hair, very fine and straight, that fell past her strong shoulders. She wore a powder-blue bathrobe.

Gingerly, I backed away from her. It was the right thing to do. I had run into another animal lover, partial to strays.

"Easy now. Don't be scared. It's just me. Just old Madge." She took a better look at me. "Are ya lost, honey?"

"I slept with somebody in a different trailer. I think."

"Well fuck me running! Wrong trailer!" She slapped her knee. "*Whoeee!* Girl, you need a map!"

I stood stiffly in the tiny hallway, shifting in my muddy espadrilles. With a grip like a welder, she took my hand and shook it heartily. "Madge Olinick," she said. "You're a girl after my own heart. Wrong trailer! Wait till Arthur hears this one. I heard yous guys whooping it up last night, and I would have joined yous, but I'm Percy's old lady now. He wraps hisself around me so tight in that bed, I have to fight him off to go to the john."

"Louise Peppers. Nice to meet you."

"Louise Peppers, I don't know where you spent the night, honey, but it sure wasn't here. Percy—he don't miss a beat. If he could bark, he'd be a regular watchdog. You want some coffee?"

"Yes, thank you," I said, taking a furtive look around for a man as I followed her into the kitchen. Percy must still be sleeping.

"Excuse the mess. Sink's stopped up. Tic Toc was supposed to get in here last night and look at it, that goddamned drunk." She laughed again and handed me a mug of thick sweet coffee swirling with cream. "Go ahead and pour some of that rum in there; yous shaking like a wet rat. If ya puke, ya clean it up. That's my rule. I keep a clean house. Clean as a snake myself. Always have been. But goddamn, I married some pigs! Now why would I go and do that?" She put some bacon in a frying pan and lit the stove. "You're not with it, are ya? Never mind.

We get rubes—that's people not in the carnie business—wandering in here all the time. Some of 'em never leave. Take Lollibells."

Sitting at the fold-out table with my rum coffee, I tried to focus on the wallpaper to keep myself from throwing up. It was a mind-altering plaid: avocado green, gold, and orange. One of the stripes seemed to be waving. Madge was leaning over me with a cigarette in her mouth, so I pulled out my Southern Board lighter and lit it. "Lollibells," she said, blowing smoke from her nostrils, "he was doctor material. Did ya meet him? Black fellow. Clown. Fudgepacker. Without his makeup on, looks just like a doctor. Got that serious eye. Always thinking, thinking, thinking. Probably thinks in his sleep, poor bastard. His real name is Warren Tucker, from Rocky Mount, North Carolina—a medical doctor, bless his heart. You got an act, darlin'?"

The stripe in the wallpaper was definitely moving.

"Actually, I'm a clown."

Madge poured some rum into her own coffee. "Yep. Ya got that serious look. Just like Warren when he come around the back lot and says to Arthur Reese, 'You all need any clowns today?' Sound just like him, too. You all. I'm from Chicago, East Side. My old man was a cop. And me in a ragbag. Go figure. We're all family here, darlin'. We may not look it, but when push comes to shove, we take care of each other. Now Arthur, he'll pay ya in kewpie dolls and hot dogs if ya let 'em, but that's just human nature. Yous gotta speak up to him. Real nice, like. Sunny, that's our Gorilla Girl, she'll spit right in his face, but she ain't got no hometrainin'. I ain't saying anything against her, but if I was her mother I'd of washed her mouth out with soap at least twice a day. Till bubbles come out of her butt. It ain't what she says so much as how she puts it, if ya know what I mean. Now where'd I put them pliers?"

She found them attached to the sink faucet, serving as a faucet knob, and palmed them. She rolled her bathrobe sleeve up a muscular forearm and set to work. The lines on the wallpaper slid in and out.

"Ah, them good ole days," she said, giving the pipe two hard taps with her pliers. "Back then we had ten shows in the ten-in-one, not three. We had us two clowns, and a kootch show —you'd see yours truly in a bikini, and darlin', you wouldn't know it to look at me now, but when that thing come off, it rained money, whooee! We had us a ballyman, and a baby with a tail, and a tiger. Larry was his name. He was just a little ole mountain lion from Pigeon Forge, in the Smoky Mountains. Arthur run over him one day, caught his tail is all, and picked him up. We dyed stripes on him, and darlin', when he jumped those hoops, he looked just like a jungle cat. Larry had sawdust in his blood. I seen him catch his tail on fire and go right on with the act. They say dogs is loyal, but that cat was ready to go down with the ship. Then one night he run off, Arthur says. You tell me how a cat that works with his tail on fire gets it up his butt to run off? In Arkansas? We had everybody looking for him—cops, fire department, boy scouts. I says to Arthur, 'Ain't it strange that we can't turn up one little ole mountain lion with dyed stripes?' It ain't like Larry blended in. Of course a rube stole him. Arthur don't admit that kind of thing cause it's bad for business. Right now, poor Larry is a striped rug on some redneck's floor. I sure do miss him."

All this time, I'd been trying to figure out what Madge did in the carnival, but I was afraid to ask in case she was a freak. She didn't look like she had anything wrong with her, but what if she was a hermaphrodite, or some kind of anatomical wonder who could pull herself through a coat hanger? It wasn't something I wanted to see on a queasy stomach. On the other hand, was it rude not to ask? I steeled myself for the inquiry, but Madge changed the subject.

"I'll tell ya what, I love animals, more than I love people, but I could not stand living with a bunch of monkeys. They're just like toddlers 'cept strong as bears. That is my idea of hell. I don't know how Jim stands it. Between you and me, I don't think he's right in the head. Take a look at his belt sometime. Them leathery things hanging there? They's two of his fingers a monkey bit right off. If you don't believe me, look at his left hand and see what's missing. That's sick, if you ask me. He lives right over there in the next trailer. Shares a tub with his chimps, Daisy and Spencer. They play in the toilet then eat right at the table, or on top of it. Used to have him a gorilla in there, too. None of 'em housetrained. I kid you not. Goddamn, that place stinks! I hold my nose when I open my windows. Jim's Jungle, we call it. It ain't decent. He don't care. Furballs! Monkey shit!" She sprayed some ammonia on a sponge and began to wipe her clean counter, shaking her head all the while. "Nasty, nasty, nasty! I hope ya didn't spend the night in there. Was he hairy?"

She set a plate of bacon and eggs in front of me. "Eat this while it's hot. I got to get back under that sink. I watched her kneel on the linoleum floor, clenching a pair of pliers, and tried to imagine the day when her broad backside fit into a bikini. She was saying, "I told Tic Toc not to use them goddamned plastic washers, but he don't listen, that fucking drunk." Her head disappeared under the sink, and for a moment, listening the soft drone of her muffled voice, I leaned back in my chair and closed my eyes.

When I opened them, I saw Percy. The nine-foot albino python slid purposefully down a stripe in the wallpaper, across the floor, and up the table leg. It's body went on and on and on. Tongue flickering, it began to slide toward me. At the edge of the plate, it raised its flat, ancient face to mine and looked into my eyes with wet black orbs.

I screamed.

Knocking my plate off the table, I scrambled to the hallway and was out the door before I could catch my breath. A small hot wind came up, blowing a paper cup across the dirt lot, and the smell of Myrtle Beach hit me hard. Through the aluminum wall, I could hear Madge crooning, "Hush, hush, toodle; let Mama look. Does Percy toodlums have a boo boo from that hot coffee? Come to Mama. Mama will make Percy all better. Mama give kissy-kiss?"

As best I could, I wiped my face with the hem of my sundress. Hell—I might have gone to bed with a gorilla, who cared about a dress? A woman, probably a hermaphrodite, had almost beaten me up with a broom. The biggest snake I had ever seen in my life had stolen my breakfast. The only sensible thing to do was go home, take a shower, return to the Maude Wilson College for Women, become an art museum curator, and make up with Jesus.

I had taken three steps across the lot when I heard my name. A tall young man in a pair of faded shorts, with wavy red hair falling around his bare shoulders, stood on the cinder block in front of a trailer, waving a sparkler.

"Louise!" he called out, and grinned.

Then I knew him—Zane Wilder, the Human Dragon, with freckles. For some reason, they didn't show up on the poster. In another trailer, the door opened, a midget stuck his head out, scowled, and slammed the door shut again.

"Louise Peppers, I love you!" called Zane Wilder. His white teeth flashed in another grin, the sparkler sailed through the air, and I went to him, all the while hearing Florida's voice in the letter I imagined would come.

> My Dearest Louise,
> You have an orthodontist appointment on Thursday. Do you want me to change it? Call us collect. They charge you if you don't show up, so we need to know. That's just being responsible. You can't run off and leave everything behind for your parents to take care of. Your father is worried sick. So am I. We are supposed to go to the Guys and Gals Ball at church on Saturday night, but I don't know if your father will go or not. The men dress up as women, and the prettiest one wins a prize. Last year it was Reverend Waller—he wore a miniskirt and go-go boots—it was real cute. I made Henry a tea-length gown of midnight-blue crepe. He's conservative. White gloves. Used a McCalls pattern size eighteen that I got for you when you were heavy. Don't know what shoes he'll wear. I had a time with

the tiara. Finally threw it away. Just wanted to cover his bald spot. Please call us so we'll know where you are and that you are not hurt. Or kidnapped. I am praying for you. I guess you'll come home when you are hungry.

Love,
Mom

I WAS BACK in the red truck. This time Zane was driving it; we were going into town for supplies to make the torches he used in his fire-eating act. As we rattled out of the back lot, he blew the bicycle horn someone had screwed on the outside of the driver's door, and people began to trot toward us with requests. Tic Toc wanted beer. Lollibells, who came out of his trailer in a smoking jacket, his face smeared with cold cream, needed a razor, some hostess cupcakes, and a pretty little boy. "Get me one that just matches your pretty little girl," he said, winking at me. "A lil ole schoolboy."

"I'm not getting anything for a man wearing red lingerie except a plaid bathrobe."

"It's garnet, honey. Garnet silk." He waved at me with the tips of his fingers and winked. He was gorgeous, even in cold cream.

Felix, the midget, wanted cigars, vermouth, and a kitten.

"If I see one on the street," said Zane. "I'm not going to a pet shop for a goddamned kitten. I'm not Santa Claus. I'm going into town."

"Up yours," said Felix. He stuck his tongue out at me, then walked away with his hands in his pockets, head down. He turned around and hollered at us, "A gray-striped one with white paws!"

Striped kitten, I scribbled on the back of an envelope. The requests were coming fast. Daisy loped over to my window and handed me Jungle Jim's list, scrawled on an envelope grubbier than my own: "bannannas beer trysicle w/horn make sur it work." She watched me read it, and for added insurance, gave me a kiss on the mouth. Then Madge came out, and with her face purposely averted from mine, kindly asked Zane for washers, rum, and burn ointment.

"What did you do to her?" asked Zane after she had walked away. Before I could answer, a woman with a shaved head took his face in her hands and kissed him soundly on the mouth.

"Lover boy!"

"Did you meet Eva? Eva, this is—"

Through the open window, she pressed her nose into his neck and sniffed. "So smoky sweet!"

"Louise," he said, pushing her face away. "She's my friend."

"Ah . . . you sleep with my dragon?" She flashed a smile. I caught a slanted glimpse of her olive face—the Roman nose, curvaceous lips, sharp cheekbones. Everything about her seemed long: long nose, long neck, long arms, and long skinny fingers tracing Zane's ears. "Lucky girl. The fire-eater fuck you like flame?"

"She also goes by Spidora—because she's wicked."

Pleased, Eva laughed. "You fear me?" she asked, poking her head into the cab. "I am a bad lady. Ha! Absofuckinglutely. But you, I like. I know already I like you very much. Zane likes you—I love you. Like that, see? Dragon and princess."

A girl came to my window. She looked about twelve. "Get over it. Zane got laid. Yippee. You going to town, hon? I need a ride."

I looked at the girl, then at Zane, and back to the girl again. She stared me down. Then she flipped her hair, stepped back, and put her hand on her hip: a skinny white-trash girl with lanky hair and sharp features, practically naked in a pair of cut-offs and a dirty yellow scrap of bra.

Eva was giving Zane her list: "Oven mittens, some creme for the eye—in the little blue pot, you know, not the pink one; the pink one makes me sneeze, Pop-Tarts, the big box with sprinkles, some cotton balls, and darling, last thing, I need a little perfume. I let you pick for me." She took a last sniff of his hair and added, "Something hot and smoky—like you."

The girl came back to my window with an unlit cigarette and reached her arm across me so Zane could light it. "Aren't you going to introduce me?" she asked.

"Louise, Sunny. Sunny, Louise," said Zane, blushing as he lit her cigarette. "What do you want?"

"She wants to fight," said Eva, then waved gaily at me and walked away. Only then did I notice that Spidora had a third leg under her skirt.

Sunny lowered her voice, making the hair itch on the back of my neck as she purred, "I need a bra." His eyes went to her chest. "And some panties." I didn't write it down. She didn't leave. It seemed like forever that the three of us hung in balance in the cab of the red truck with the sun beating down, her head in the window, her arm reaching across me to him. It seemed like my whole life.

ON MAIN STREET in Myrtle Beach, I sauntered along-side Zane, who looked wild and beautiful in flip-flops and faded shorts, with a spangled vest open over his bare chest. His red hair caught the sun in tiny flames, his sequins danced. Everywhere we went, people stared. He was like a fish on the shore, shimmering, sparkling, flip-flopping. Beside him, I was the freak, wearing a new blue-and-gold-striped gym suit with a MWCW stamp and a wet ponytail.

He bought me a hippie dress. It was made in India, of bright-orange embroidered cotton, and covered with bells and beads.

"I don't wear orange," I informed him.

"Try it on." He pushed me into the dressing room, and with his mouth on mine, stripped off my gym suit. The dress was perfect. He put a pair of sandals on my feet, and in the store, braided my hair. The saleswomen crowded around us, amazed to see a man braid. "Earrings!" he called out, and one of the women arrived with a tray. Deftly, he removed my gold hoops and offered to trade them for the dress, sandals, and a pair of dangling crystals. "Real gold," he said. When he lightly bit the hoop between his teeth, he looked just like a gypsy. On his way out, he pocketed a bottle of perfume.

In the hardware store, he purchased an ice-cube tray, five bottles of lighter fluid, and a box of votive candles. He had a long discussion with the clerk about a sixteenth-inch-diameter brass rod and some file handles. He tried on tubular bandages until he found one that fit his finger perfectly. After much deliberation, he added a package of red dye to his basket. Then he went into the store's bathroom and came out with the cardboard cylinder from inside a roll of paper towels. "We're going to make a torch!" he said, and his eyes shone. They weren't exactly the same shade of green as Roderick's eyes, but they were close.

On the way home, we found a gray cat with white feet stuck in a tree and put it in the truck for Felix.

"It's not a kitten," I pointed out. "It doesn't have a stripe."

"You're not with it, baby," said Zane, "but you will be. Then you'll understand that in a carnie's life, everything is a suggestion." The cat crouched on the back of the seat with his hair standing straight up. Apparently, he smelled chimpanzees and pythons. I sucked on my cigarette, desperate for something cool to say.

We rode in silence for a while, drinking Goebel beer, and then Zane began to piece last night together as if he were recounting our honeymoon.

"So, I'm on the back lot, smoking a J with Sunny and Lollibells, when I hear that damned Sinatra. We'd closed the gates an hour ago. Lollibells says, 'Oh hell, Tic Toc's drunk again,' so we go over there to get him before he decides to hit the town. Arthur bails him out three times a week. What the fuck? The chaise volonte is running at one o'clock in the morning—burning free gas. No sign of Arthur. Probably nodded off on Valium. We figure ole Tic has passed out on one of the chairs, and the thing is running on auto. But we get over there, and the old geezer is sitting in his cage working the gears like he has a mile of rubes waiting in line. Sunny sniffs out Female.

"'Rufus got him a girl,' she says. We all run up to see the fool who would kick boots with Tic Toc, and there you are, swirling through the stars like an angel. Sunny gets all jealous. She's been the only chick on the lot—under fifty and with the standard number of parts—all summer. But there you were . . . so beautiful up there in the lights with your hair flying.

When that car swept down, and I saw you up close, I said, 'Yikes!'"

Self-consciously, I touched my new braids. Then I asked the question that had been torturing me since we left the lot.

"Is Sunny your ex-girlfriend?"

He laughed. "No, Sunny has never been my girlfriend."

"Good." I leaned back happily sniffing the salt air.

"She's my ex-wife."

"You're divorced?" The ring! He was still wearing the wedding ring on his left hand! And the way she had looked at me in the cab of the truck. I was the Other Woman!

"Separated, divorced, whatever." He began to talk to the cat. "You ready to be a carnie cat? Wait till you meet Felix. A little rough on the outside, smells like a dead cigar, but he's really a sweetheart. Hey, kitty kitty?" The cat hissed.

In my brief experience with men, I had come to understand that they were not artful creatures. In addition to the sound advice Florida had given me that boys would find me interesting if I talked to them about themselves, she also warned me that males required patience. She had often demonstrated this with Henry by a sudden and complete dissociation, during which time she would reapply her lipstick or resume her knitting with the air of someone who is utterly alone in a room. Therefore, I did not mention the ring on Zane's left hand. Instead, I asked nonchalantly, "How long were you married?"

"Married is a strong word for it," said Zane. "Carnies usually hitch up on the merry-go-round. It's the closest we come to going to church. One ride on a pony with your sweetheart squeezed between your thighs, and it's for better or worse. Usually worse, in my case." He lit a cigarette. "To answer your

question, we were together about five years." Raindrops began
to hit the windshield. "Hell," he said. "Pull your wiper, will
you? This rain is killing Arthur. We need a blowout tonight,
just to get the gas to get to Rock Hill. Rock Hill, South Carolina, what a dump."

I stuck my arm out the window and pulled my wiper string,
but it wasn't as fun as it was last night with Jungle Jim. My legs
were crossed under my new dress, and my mouth had tightened into the straight line of a hard-nosed Baptist. I had for-
nicated with a married man.

"What's the ring for?" I asked.

"What? Oh, Christ! I don't need this, okay? Don't play cop
with me. If you wanted to deflower somebody last night, you
got the wrong guy. I ain't asking *you* every little detail. What
the hell do you want?"

"I want to get out of this truck. Pull over."

"Just like a woman! You wait until the downpour hits and
leave me with one wiper." He squealed the truck to a stop on
the shoulder of the road. It had begun to hail. "Louise, I can't
let you out in this. Not in your new dress and everything."

"Take your damned gypsy dress!" I screamed, tearing it off
and throwing it at his face. "Take your tacky fake earrings and
these piece-of-shit shoes! I don't want anymore of your low-
rent beer, either!" Naked, I jumped out of the car and began to
stomp away in the mud. The cat followed me.

Honking the bicycle horn on the truck, Zane puttered along
beside us. When we began to draw a crowd, I got back in.

"Where's the cat?" he asked.

"Gone."

"I love that cat."

"You just met that cat. How can you love it?"

"I just met you, and I love you."

We got out and chased the cat up another tree, so Zane could climb up and get it.

"I love this cat because it has faith," said Zane. "It has no idea how to get out of a tree, but it goes straight up every time."

"That would be stupidity."

"Yes," said Zane, dabbing some blood from a cat scratch on his face. "But this is an old cat. Stupid cats die young."

Hail the size of golf balls bounced against the truck. The wet cat shivered behind the seat. Zane took off his spangled vest and hung it around my shoulders. "May I offer you another low-rent beer? How about a Pop-Tart?"

"How old is she?"

"Who, Sunny?"

I gave him a long, patient stare.

"She was sixteen when we married down in New Orleans. I was playing the horn with her daddy, Earl Boudreaux, plays tenor sax. When he's not drinking, he's the best. Earl the Pearl. I was in high school, had one of those old silver Conns with a goofy bell."

"Do you play now?"

"Naw. I thought I was gonna be the best, ya know? Played eight, nine hours a day. Never even thought about women — well, almost never."

"What happened?"

"Life happened. Gotta bring home a paycheck when ya got a wife." He laughed bitterly, and the dream left his eyes.

"You're not exactly selling insurance."

"No, Zane Wilder, the Human Dragon don't sell insurance."

"Why did you marry her?"

"It wasn't my idea. Everywhere I went—she was there."

"She followed you around New Orleans," I offered.

"You could say that. Sunny has had a tough time. Her mama ran off when she was a baby, and Earl the Pearl isn't Daddy material. He has too much talent. Talent kills relationships."

"Is that what happened to you?"

"Oh, none of us around here have any talent, except Lollibells, and he's too fucked up to use it. The Arthur Reese Traveling Show is one big unhappy family. We drew a good crowd for a while, but lately we've had a run of bad luck: rain, inflation, flat tires. Snakes getting coffee burns." He grinned and took his hand off the steering wheel to ruffle my hair. "But when I saw you swinging on the chaise volonte, I had a feeling in my gut. I thought, She's going to change our luck! This girl is going to save the Arthur Reese Traveling Show!"

"You haven't seen my act yet," I said.

"Clown," he said firmly. "You told me last night when I hijacked your car on the chaise." A shadowy memory surfaced: tall man swinging by one arm on the side of my flying chair. "That fool Tic Toc wouldn't stop the rig. I don't know what you gave him, but he was off the planet. He kept screaming, 'She parachutes! Watch out!' I was afraid you might jump. We've had that happen more often than Arthur would like to admit. So I'm swinging there by one arm, trying to get in your seat, and you look over cool as you please, like you're in the supermarket, and we just met. 'Hi,' you say. 'I'm Louise Peppers. I'm a clown.' You didn't crack a smile."

"I'm not really a clown."

"I'm not really a dragon. Just swamp mix from South Louisiana."

We parked on the back lot and ran into Zane's trailer, which was soon crowded with carnies, shaking off the rain as they grabbed cans of beer. Zane stood on top of his bed, vest thrown open, tossing out the loot. I gaped at the things he pulled from the ample lining of his vest. I didn't think I'd taken my eyes off of him all morning. "Swischer Sweets for the Sweet," he called out, tossing a package of cigars to the room. He threw some condoms at Lollibells. "Whirlie whirls at the tip, plays a tune when you come. Sorry they were all out of little boys. Cats, however, were on sale . . . where is Felix? Step on up here, lit-tle fellow, and get your furry friend."

"Kiss off," said Felix. "I said kitten. This is a cat."

"This is Faith. She loves you." Faith, however, did not love Felix. When he picked her up, she scratched his face and then ran under the bed and wouldn't come out until Jungle Jim called her with a long strange meow. Soon, Faith was purring on Jim's lap, paying no mind to Felix, and this made the midget fall desperately in love with her. When Sunny breezed into the room, I watched closely to see if Zane would produce lingerie, but she helped herself to a pint of gin and left.

After the gifts were distributed—apparently no one paid the person who went to town—we all went to work. Although I had been perfectly useless around the house at Owl Aerie, I had learned a good work ethic at Southern Board: Move. Even Dopey made it a policy not to stand still, at least not where he could be seen. At the Arthur Reese Traveling Show, I moved. Squatting the way Henry had taught me, so I wouldn't damage my back, I moved crates, shovels full of chimp poop, and heavy tarps folded like flags. I moved in and out of lights, so Tic Toc could check for shadows. With a clenched jaw, I moved elec-tricity through unlikely conduits.

"Just don't lick the wire!" yelled Tic Toc, guffawing as he staggered away. I moved a paintbrush across a backdrop for four hours without stopping until Felix screamed that I was using the wrong color. Often, I just moved out of the way. When we had everything set up, word came from Arthur that we were to tear it down and set everything up in the tent, in case of rain.

"Who ever heard of a grab joint in a tent," complained Tic Toc as he dismantled a red-and-yellow hot dog stand and hauled it beneath the canvas. "Far be it for me to say!"

"Cats up!" exclaimed Eva in disgust. "Cats up on their mouths, cats up on their fingers, cats up on my web!" She wasn't wearing her wig, just a bandanna over her shaved head, and she had hiked her skirt up to use her third leg, somewhat shorter than the others, to roll up a rug.

I didn't see much of Zane, and when I did see him, he didn't seem to see me.

"Zane is zee real artist," said Eva with glowing eyes. "Zee how he disappears inside of himself? Zee how the world falls away from him? Like a coat." She nodded firmly. "This was my grandfather. He swallowed the sword of Caesar. Fire was nothing to him. He used to say, 'How can fire burn fire? I am fire.' When he was working, the world was as nothing to him. A great man. An asshole, but a great man."

Tentatively, I offered to help Zane set up his table. "Sure," he said with a curt nod, as if I were Felix, or Tic Toc, or just some rube who had walked into the tent. Lovingly, I taped up the broken leg, and with a sigh, spread the ugly cloth over it. Someone, probably Sunny, had painted a bad portrait of the Human Dragon on the dirty vinyl tablecloth. Clearly, his beauty was beyond her scope. Following his terse commands,

I dumped lighter fluid into the pan, lined the torches on the rack, and hung the bayonet on a nail. I tossed the blowtorch under the table. I couldn't figure out what to do with the light-bulb, so I stuck it in the pocket of his vest, which I kissed and hung over the chair. To warm up for his act, he stood in front of a full-length mirror, took five deep breaths, rolled forward on the balls of his feet, and stuck his finger down his throat. He did this until he stopped gagging. Then he used a banana, un-peeled, and after that, a cucumber.

"Hell of a way to make a dollar, ain't it," said Lollibells, strolling over. He stood beside me with his fingers hooked into the bib of his white overalls and watched Zane in the mirror. "The sword enters the glottal chamber, passes to the epiglottis, the pharynx, and enters the esophagus, where it must be pushed —a little—past the muscle that closes the stomach, and then as far as Zane will allow it. Zane knows how far he can go into the depth of the stomach because he's touched the bottom with the tip of his blade—just once, we hope. One never forgets that feeling, or so I hear." He looked down at me and smiled. "I ain't fool enough to try, is you?"

Warren—it was hard to think of him as Lollibells when he was talking like a doctor—continued his lecture. "The thing that separates the sword swallowers from sane people is the ability to control the gag reflex, put in place by whoever de-signed our wonderful bodies to prevent foolishness of this kind. It's not perfect; hospital emergency rooms overflow with babies trying to swallow buttons, vacuum cleaner parts, gerbil tails, you name it, but for ages three and up, it's automatic. Zane has not only learned to overcome that reflex, he's gained control over some of the muscles in his throat. No one can tell a human being how to control those muscles. It just one of those things, like wiggling your ears." Warren wiggled his ears for me. Just then, Zane turned toward us, pulling a long cucumber from his throat.

"Oh you fine-looking thang, you!" cried Lollibells, putting his hand on his crotch. "I got something right here for you to practice on. Be a lot sweeter than that nasty ole cucumber. Bigger, too."

"Go to hell," said Zane, grinning.

"Now dont be shy lil' white boy. Come on over and sit on Uncle Lovely Balls's lap."

Zane pulled out a tube of Instant Tan and began to apply it to his chest.

"Let me help with you that," said Lollibells. "Let me rub that on the hard-to-reach spots."

"Don't you have any work to do? Don't you need to practice being funny or something?"

"Oh no, honey, that all comes natural. Jus' like my bronze skin. White boy, you going orange now. Watch out with that shit."

"Really?" Zane lifted his arm to examine the effect of the Instant Tan.

"Ain't he pretty?" said Lollibells, glancing in the mirror. Then he lowered his voice. "Uh-oh. Here come trouble."

"Am I interrupting something?" asked Sunny. Zane busied himself with the bayonet while Lollibells studied a hangnail. She wore nothing but a tiny black-lace bra with matching panties. The effect was shocking, but not erotic. In her underwear, she was definitely skinny, with big knobby knees and a hard, flat ass. Fresh nail polish lacquered the toes of her dirty bare feet. Her nipples poked pertly through the black lace.

"Law, chile, get you some clothes on!" cried Lollibells, pretending to peek through his fingers.

"Zane gave me this," she replied. "He got it in town this morning. How does it fit, Zane?"

When she put her hands on her hips, one rough, chalky elbow pushed me aside. Sunny Boudreaux. Balls to the wall.

"It's nice," said Zane without looking up from the sword he was polishing. I felt my ears growing hot; instantly, Sunny turned to me. She had a rat's face: sharp chin, beady eyes, and wide, red mouth. I remembered a nightmare. I'd go into the kitchen and say, "What's for supper?"

"You," Florida would say, knife in hand.

"My husband tells me you're going to be with us for a while," said Sunny. "What is it that you do?"

Lollibells let his mouth drop open, either at the mention of a husband, or the bad acting. Silently, looking at no one, Zane racked his sword and slid his vest over his shoulders.

"I'm a clown," I said, choking on the word.

"Oh my God," said Lollibells. When he looked at me, his eyes narrowed. "Did I hear this? You're a clown?"

"Aren't we all," said Zane in a flat, cold voice that made tears stream down my face.

"You bastard!" screamed Sunny, swinging a punch that missed his jaw and landed squarely on the lightbulb in his pocket. A stream of blood ran down her bony wrist, and she began to wail. From all corners of the tent, carnies crowded in to see the action, raising a din that was finally hushed by the deep, smooth voice of Arthur Reese himself.

He was a tall, stout man with a head full of wavy white hair and a neat goatee. He appeared in a tuxedo, with Felix by his side pushing a cart of mint juleps. "My dears," the old gentleman said, looking calmly all around him. "I'm afraid it's nap time. Off to your beds. Felix will bring your drinks around, and he will return to wake you promptly at forty-five minutes from the hour. We're going to have an excellent show this evening. Night night."

Chapter Eleven

WHEN I WOKE up on Zane's narrow bed, it was dark, and the carnival was in full swing. Through the thin walls of the trailer, I heard "Le Sabre" playing on the calliope, the chatter of Jim's monkeys, the clatter of the roller coaster, and the roar of the motor drome. The talkers cried, "Step right up, Ladies and Gentlemen! Never seen before in the history of man! Only two dollars, that's right, see the Most Beautiful Teenager in America!"

"Pitch till you win!"

Grinders, most of them local, called out, "Doughnuts! Doughnuts! Get 'em while they're hot!" Somewhere, a child cried. As I lay still, I began to hear the softer sounds, the underlayer—a flap of canvas, the sizzle of meat, and faintly, the sweet refrain of Sinatra from chaise volonte.

Then I heard Zane's knock on the door. "Hello," he said, smiling shyly. He'd put on a clean vest and braided his hair with a scarlet ribbon. His eyes were on fire. "I was afraid Sunny might have scared you back to school." Kneeling beside the bed, he held me, pressing his face into my neck. He smelled of smoke, butane, and doughnuts. "Don't leave me," he whispered in my ear. "Please don't leave until you've seen my act." I wrapped my arms around him, feeling the taut muscles beneath the silky back of his vest. I touched the smooth hollows beneath his cheekbones.

"You're not faithful," I said.

"I'm a cat in a tree," he said. "Save me." He took his wedding ring off and swallowed it.

We walked arm in arm through the drizzling rain, into the packed tent.

"Madge Olinick," boomed Arthur Reese, "is a native of Chicago, the daughter of a policeman and a baker. She never saw so much as a garden snake until she eloped with her high school sweetheart to the swamps of Louisiana. There in the bayou, where the sun casts an eerie green glow through the black swamp grass, where the buzz of insects is the breath of the land, where the black panther stalks beneath a yellow moon, Madge Olinick first discovered love."

Arthur was a born orator. He had boom. "Who was the lover of this pale city girl, lovely, nubile, just seventeen? Alas, it was not the bridegroom, who fell into the jaws of an alligator, leaving the nymph alone and frightened in the thick jungle. Young Madge fell prey to serpentophilia. Serpentophilia—a long word for the love of snakes. Ladies and gentlemen, I invite you to see Madge with her lover, Percy, the nine-foot Burmese albino python who shares her bed today. Let your imaginations play freely as you see the lovers here on the stage, caressing each other, intermingling their fine bodies. Keep in mind that this reptile, the *Python molurus bivittatus,* weighs over sixty pounds; he can swallow a baby and squeeze a grown man to death."

The crowd was silent, staring at the red curtain behind him. "I ask you, Ladies and Gentlemen, not to content yourself with a quick glance. Take a second look, and a third. You may need to return and see the act once more in order to answer the question, Who controls this relationship? You will see Madge hypnotize Percy and bend him to her will. However, there are those who say that Madge is not free to leave. She is entangled with the snake, in body and heart. But you will have to decide. So keep your eyes open, my friends, and please, stay away from the fence." A drum rolled. "And now, may I present—the strangest couple in the world! Madge and Percy!"

I almost didn't recognize the lady who stepped out in a spangled harem suit and high heels, wearing her snake piled on top of her head. A shiver ran through me as he slid his yellow head over her bare shoulder. Although Madge hadn't seen seventeen in some time, the image Arthur had painted colored the entire act, and as the thick serpent entwined himself through her legs, coiling his strange yellow body around her waist, I found it impossible not to see a blonde Lolita in the bayou. She did a fair hypnotist act with him although she played the flute badly, and Percy was an awkward dancer—pythons are a little heavy for this routine—and Percy was getting on in years, but they were definitely a couple.

When the curtain went down, we shuffled along the fence to the Tunnel of Love, which I had helped patch together with tinfoil, red lightbulbs, and pinups. The marks loved it. They laughed at the recording of Jungle Jim's voice saying things like "Darling, I can't live without you, but I want to try" and "Honey, please don't leave me with the bills!" We'd rigged up a heart-shaped button that kids could push to hear "Violets are red, roses are blue, you're mine, and that's a lie, too!"

Stepping out of the tunnel, we ran smack into Eva's web. From the shadows, Arthur emerged smoking a pipe.

"Spidora," he said gravely. "Born Eva Pisano, in the small village of Positana, Italy. Mother Nature plays her tricks; no one knows why. Here a child is born with two heads, or an elephant ear, or perhaps a tail. Perhaps our creator has some lesson to teach us, a lesson in tenderness, compassion, and mercy. A lesson from the Almighty. Shall we throw it away?"

"His dad was a preacher," whispered Zane. "Baptized the entire state of Mississippi—two or three times."

"That's what the people of Positana did with Baby Eva. They threw the three-legged child into a Dumpster."

Arthur sighed. His pipe smoke filled the room, and we all squinted to get a better look into the nine-foot web. Spidora, lit by a black light, wore a short black dress, black-lace gloves, and three black stockings fastened to garter belts. She swayed above us. Onstage, she wore a black wig plaited into tiny braids, which somehow gave the impression that she had more than three legs. If anyone leaned against the fence, she smacked her lips dangerously.

"In the Dumpster," Arthur said sadly, "behind the KFC in Positana, Italy. She was eleven months old, surviving on chicken bones." He shook his head and drew on his pipe while we stared at Spidora and imagined her as a baby in a Dumpster. "Yes, friends, in Positana, a picturesque Italian village built on ancient cliffs spiraling up from the sea . . . can you hear

Homer's sirens singing from the Isle dei Galli? Listen . . ." Off
cue, Spidora spit a long rice noodle from her mouth. "Positana
could tolerate a KFC, but not a deformed child. And this is
what we call progress." Eva waved her third leg.

"No honey, that ain't real," a mother whispered to son as we
were leaving. "That's rubber." The child, however, did not believe his mother and continued to whimper.

Behind them, a stranger tried to help. "Third leg! That was
just too fake for me. Believe me, if a person was to have another leg, it wouldn't go there."

"Well, where would it go?" demanded his wife.

"Well, it wouldn't go there. On the other side, maybe. Or on
the back. That's where I'd put it, right in the back." The child
cried more loudly.

"That rubber snake killed me," someone said. "Did you see
the stamp, MADE IN KOREA? That just killed me." Several people agreed that they had seen the stamp on Percy's belly. "I can't
believe I paid ten dollars to see that piece of junk. They git ya,
don't they?"

In staging the ten-in-one, Arthur had anticipated the marks'
disillusionment at precisely this point. Pretending to open a
curtain by mistake, Arthur swiftly unveiled Lollibells. Decked
out in bows and polka dots, Warren sat in a dunking cage on
a springboard over a tub of water. For just fifty cents, anyone
could buy three balls and hurl them at him.

"Hey you!" he called out to a large man. "Fat guy. Porker.
No, not you. The other bubble butt. The one with the ugly
girlfriend. Yoo-hoo! Can't catch me."

Quarters clanked; the balls began to fly. Lollibells splashed
into the water and came up grinning. "Hell of a way to make

a living, ain't it," I said, rapping on his cage, but he didn't hear me.

In a few minutes, Arthur ushered us through a tent flap into some makeshift stands placed in front of a mattress ringed with chicken wire. Red, white, and blue crepe paper streamed from the ceiling, and a large sign announced DAISY AND SPENCER, THE BOXING CHIMPS.

"Ah," cried Zane. "The monkey smell! I love it! This is the best act in the ten-in-one!"

"Except for yours," I said.

Shrugging, he blushed beneath his Instant Tan. Backstage, Tic Toc slapped in a tape of jungle sounds. Arthur paced in front of the empty ring with his hands clasped behind his back, inexpertly followed by a green light.

"The esteemed physicist Stephen Hawking said, 'We are just an advanced breed of monkeys on a minor planet of a very average star. But we can understand the universe. That makes us something very special.'" He rubbed his goatee and faced the audience. Lecturer, the carnies called him. "I don't know if I understand the universe or not, but I do know that although it may be hard for the average man to believe he has descended from an ape, it's even harder for the ape to believe."

"Here comes the Bible lesson," whispered Zane. A couple of toucans squawked over the drum beats, which were increasing in tempo.

"Did we come from these hairy beasts? Did we once swing from branch to branch, picking each other's fleas as a sign of affection? Did we, too, sometimes brutally attack our mates?"

Behind me, a woman rose and answered him. "No sir, we did not! We come from Adam and Eve and they was made in the image of the Lord! The Bible says it. Genesis 1:26. And God said, 'Let us make man in our image, after our likeness: and let them have dominion over the fish of the sea, and over the fowl of the air, and over the cattle and over all the earth, and over every creeping thing that creepeth upon the earth.' That means monkeys!"

"Ma'am, you are absolutely correct," said Arthur Reese, nodding at her. "Thank you. Now let us pose another question—"

"Jesus weren't no monkey, I know that much," interrupted the woman.

No one volunteered to go in the ring.

"Let me ask you one question," the woman said, standing up. She wore pale-blue slacks and a pink-striped shirt that outlined her drooping bosom. A series of bad perms had turned her hair into hay; blue eye shadow swept glamorously toward her ears. Her face was red with excitement. "You tell me," she called out to all of us, "if God is a monkey, then how could He write the Bible? You answer me that."

Beside her, a lumpy teenage girl in thick glasses hunched her shoulders and dropped her head.

"Anybody here go to church?" challenged the woman.

"Mother!" hissed the teenager. "Sit down."

"You hush. I just asked a question."

"Second Pentecostal," said a skinny man with a pocked face.

"That don't count, honey. Anybody here go to the Baptist church?"

"Don't count for what?" cried the skinny man, but just then Arthur motioned backstage, and the music rose to a level that drowned out every voice but his own.

"Ladies and Gentlemen!" he called out. "Meet two very special members of the Arthur Reese Traveling Show." As he bowed, he made a wide sweep with his arm; bashfully, the two chimps stepped out from behind the curtain and climbed into the ring. Daisy wore her yellow sundress with matching ruffled underwear and curtsied for her admirers. Spencer, butt-naked except for a bow tie similar to Arthur's, bowed. The audience clapped, and several women cooed.

"These two pygmy chimpanzees, brother and sister, came from south of the Congo."

"Ain't he cute," said a huge man beside me. When Daisy and Spencer wrapped their arms around each other and began to dance to "Feels So Good," the audience buzzed with admiration. Every child in the crowd asked his mother for a chimpanzee.

After the dance, Jungle Jim hopped over the chickenwire and instigated a comedy routine. Hooting and squealing, Daisy and Spencer chased him around the mattress. They did flips and somersaults, and Daisy did a headstand on Spencer's shoulders, proudly showing us her ruffled panties. Spencer yawned, exposing his enormous yellow teeth, then scratched his ass. We were all laughing, even Zane, who had seen this show hundreds of times. When Arthur asked if anyone wanted to box with Spencer, he received a round of giggles and snorts.

"For a mere five dollars, Ladies and Gentlemen, you are welcome to challenge our chimp. If you can stay in the ring for five minutes, I will give you one hundred dollars." He pulled a wad of money from his vest pocket and flipped through the crisp green bills.

Spencer raised a hairy arm to show us his skinny muscle.

The Pentecostal stood up. "I'll go a round with the little fellow," he said with a kindly smile on his face, as if he were about to play with a toddler.

"I must warn you, sir," said Arthur, pocketing the five. "Our hairy little brother is a champion boxer. He may inflict pain; he will certainly leave bruises." With a mocking grin, the challenger signed a waiver. Then he removed his cap and did a boxing step, winking at Spencer. "Your glasses, sir," said Arthur, holding out his hand.

"I gotta see my target, don't I?" protested the man, but he was laughing. "For all I know, this fellow gets real quick in the ring."

Everything happened so fast that afterward I perceived it as a single instant—a scream and a whorl of blood. Zane, who had set his watch, told me the fight lasted one minute and three seconds. First, Jungle Jim hauled Daisy out of the ring, pretending to be jealous when she blew kisses over her shoulder. Then he straightened Spencer's bow tie, gave him a whack on the butt, and led him to his corner. The challenger, grinning sheepishly, went into another corner. When Jim was out of the ring, Arthur blew a whistle. In a flash, Spencer was on the man's chest, giving him rapid blows to the head. Blood spurted, a fountain of blood. When the man screamed "Oh, God, please make him stop!" Arthur blew a second whistle, and Spencer wandered away from his victim and began to pick his teeth. Jim switched tapes and slid the man away on a gurney to the tune "Dog and Butterfly."

"Do we have another challenger?" asked Arthur.

I elbowed Zane. "Not on your life, sweetheart. And you're not going up there, either. Do you know what that waiver says? In case of injury or death. The lawyer cut accidental."

Beside me, the big man was heaving himself out of the stands.

He walked toward the ring with his jeans sliding down his hips. Numerous cans of Skoal had worn a ring in his rear pocket. His belly was the size of a watermelon, and when he raised his arm in anticipated victory, his hairy white flesh gleamed under the lights. His face bore the expression of a bulldog. With fondness and embarrassment, I thought of T. C. Curtis.

"Ed Larkin," he said, shaking Arthur's hand.

"No need to crush my bones, Mr. Larkin," said Arthur, recovering his hand. I can see that you are a strong man. How tall are you, if I may ask?"

"Six three and a half, last time I measured. Weight, 296."

"Very impressive. Your opponent, Spencer of the Congo, is three feet two inches tall and weighs 55 pounds. Do you really think this is a fair match?"

Larkin shrugged. "You all set it up. I get a hundred bucks right here if I stay in the ring five minutes, right? I don't want no check in the mail."

Arthur patted his vest pocket. "It's right here, waiting for you. And if you stay in the ring for six minutes, I'll double it. Two hundred dollars."

"Let me at 'em."

Spencer took an immediate dislike to Ed Larkin. He circled him in the ring, baring his teeth and spitting. His hair stood straight up. When Larkin took a swing, Spencer lifted him up and threw him over the chickenwire.

"I ain't outa the ring!" screamed the man, jumping back on the mat, and that is when the real beating began. With my hands over my eyes, I heard bones breaking.

"Holy shit," said Zane. "Where's Jim? Holy shit."

When I looked again, Spencer had ripped off the man's shirt and was scratching his back, leaving long red stripes on the flesh. Blood bubbled out of Larkin's mouth as he cried out, "Mercy!"

Zane looked at his watch. "Two and a half minutes—counting the time he was thrown over the wire." Another gurney appeared. Daisy climbed into the ring, put a towel around Spencer's neck, and then handed him a banana.

Beside me, a woman in a pink seersucker pantsuit sighed and said, "And he paid five dollars for that."

Suddenly, the teenage girl who had been glowering beside her mother stood up and made her way to the ring. She wore a T-shirt that said I LOVE NEW YORK and a friendship bracelet on her thick wrist. When Arthur took her glasses off, he had to help her find her way into the ring.

"I'm not going to tell you how much I weigh," she told Arthur in a serious voice.

"I would never ask a lady such a question."

In the stands, her mother was going nuts. "Linda!" she called. "Linda you get back up here right now before I have to come get you. You hear me? I won't have this. I will not. Young lady, I am counting to ten!"

Linda sighed. When Arthur whispered something in her ear, she scowled and turned reluctantly to her audience. "I love you, Mother," she said sullenly.

"Don't you smart off to me," said her mother, making her

way through the bleachers with her pocketbook in hand. "Mister, if you put my girl in there with that animal I'm gonna call the police. You all hear that? I'm gonna call the police!" The crowd gave appreciative murmurs.

Before anyone could stop her, Linda had hauled herself over the chickenwire and stood in the middle of the mattress facing the killer chimp. In his corner, Spencer crossed his arms over his chest, watching her closely. She was a big girl, with thick dark hair pulled into a tight ponytail on top of her head. Her jeans looked painfully tight, and the I LOVE NEW YORK T-shirt stretched over her ballooning chest. Without her glasses, her face seemed sleepy and naked. She just stood there.

Cautiously, Spencer approached on all fours. He examined her tennis shoes and untied one lace. Then he tried to look up her pant leg. Jumping up, he circled her, pulled lightly on her ponytail, grinned, and did it again. She held out her hand.

I shut my eyes. Would he bite off her fingers? I didn't hear a sound. When I opened my eyes, he was on his knees, kissing Linda's hand. The rubes went wild. Linda's mother, who had been restrained by the side of the ring, wept.

"Five minutes," called Arthur, but Linda stayed one minute more and made two hundred dollars.

The Boxing Chimps were followed by the Most Beautiful Teenager in America, starring Sunny, who turned into a gorilla at the end of the act. Even with Tic Toc furiously working smoke and mirrors backstage, the appearance of Jim in a gorilla suit timed to coincide with the disappearance of Sunny in a bathing suit was not convincing. Then there was the snake. It was a rubber snake, the kind sold in bins at discount stores:

kelly green on top and white on the belly, with a long red forked tongue striking between two flimsy fangs. Sunny was terrified of it. She wore the toy around her neck, stroking it only when someone backstage hissed out an order. Then she shuddered.

As Tic Toc dimmed the lights to a rosy pink, Arthur announced, "Ladies and Gentlemen! I present Sunny Boudreaux! The Most Beautiful Teenager in America!" Scowling, Sunny slouched forward in a beige bikini that sagged over her flat bottom. The rubber snake hung around her neck like a towel. Tic Toc had snuck in his favorite Jimmy Buffet song, and now Sunny was obliged to dance to "Why Don't We Get Drunk." She stroked the snake once, twice, and then gave her hips a lethargic wiggle.

"Her act sucks," I told Zane, who was watching her closely. "It's fake."

"People need a break from reality, especially after watching the Boxing Chimps. That was real blood. Real pain. Arthur is a genius at manipulating the marks' emotions. They need this. You'll see." He added, "Don't take this the wrong way, but she's very sexy."

"She's tacky," I said hotly.

"People like tacky. You've probably spent your whole life trying to develop good taste. You think all the tackiness you see in the world is evidence of your progress in refinement. You refuse to believe that people hang air fresheners shaped like Christmas trees from their rearview mirrors because that makes them happy. Oh no, they do that because they have poor taste."

"You're calling me middle class."

"A wild guess. You went to prep school, but no one's ever

heard of it. Your family belongs to a country club that calls the toilet a powder room and can't afford a doorman. Middle class is in the damn middle. Middle of the road. Do you know what's in the middle of the road?"

He looked at me, eyes blazing. "Roadkill," he said.

"Your tan looks fake. It's orange."

"Is this a fight? Are you starting a fight, Louise?"

"You bought her a bra," I said, my eyes smarting with tears. "And panties."

"Oh, fuck! Fuck me! I knew you were going to do this. I just knew it."

As the music played on, Sunny's indolence became sultry and hypnotic. The corners of her wide mouth turned down, and as she stroked the snake, her lackluster eyes took on a faraway glaze. Zane watched as she stroked the snake.

"Do what? What does roadkill do? We sit and rot, right? We stink. That's what I'm doing, I'm—"

"I'm sorry, okay? I didn't put that the right way. I just meant that people are different. You need to be open to that."

"Shut up." I was crying, so I covered my face with one hand, but I kept the fingers slightly spread to see Sunny. She had the snake's head between her boobs now and had closed her eyes. As she swayed back and forth, her stringy hair fell into her face, and her bathing suit bottom sagged further down her hips. The snake slipped down to her belly, and then around one white thigh. Zane was all over it.

I kept telling myself, *It's okay. She's going to turn into a gorilla. She will go away.* I waited. Finally, Tic Toc crossed the lights, sent up some smoke, and after some noisy fumbling on the dark stage, showed us that yes indeed, the Most Beautiful Teenager in America had turned into a big ugly gorilla.

I turned to Zane, ready to make up, but he had disappeared.

"WHAT IS NORMAL?" Arthur asked when he gathered us before the sign ZANE WILDER, THE HUMAN DRAGON. I glanced at the table to make sure I'd set it up right. "Most of what you've seen in our show tonight requires that you change the way you ordinarily think about the world. What you are about to see will challenge your most basic assumptions about the human body. I will do my best to prepare you for the startling revelations to come."

"'Scuse me!" called Lollibells in falsetto. Then he pranced through the crowd on stilts, dressed as a nun. "Oooh, you bad boy!" he said, bending down at a terrifying angle to slap Arthur's head. "Don't look up my dress!" Warren danced on his stilts, raising a leg high to poke a man in the ribs, then to remove a child's hat. He hopped on one leg, then on his hands, revealing a pair of Satan-red underwear, and then on one hand. "Oooh, sword swallower," he called out. "Here, dragon! Here, kitty kitty!" Then he leapt into the air and did a back flip, landing on Zane's table, perfectly balanced on the stilts.

"What is normal?" continued Arthur after he had chased Lollibells off. "We all know that it's not normal to lay a hand on a hot object, such as an iron, but wetting a finger to check an iron is normal, isn't it? Sticking pins in one's body is not normal, but diabetics do it every day. Sword swallowing is done every day in hospitals when an anesthesiologist inserts an airway into a stomach tube. If you take a bead, say a pearl, and feed a piece of string through it, you'll find that you can easily snuff it up your nose, catch it at the back of your throat, and pull the whole string out of your mouth. Now, if you tie the ends of the string together, you can make a loop; you can run it around and around, into your nose and out of your mouth. In India, this is the way people clean their nasal passages. To them, it is normal. I see this young man eyeing his mother's necklace; please don't try this at home.

"What is abnormal is to find men and women with the courage to pursue these talents. I have found such a man. May I introduce to you, the fire-eating, sword-swallowing, ultimate wonder of the Arthur Reese Traveling Show—the Human Dragon, Zane Wilder!"

Zane stepped into the spotlight, hair braided, spangled vest open as usual over his washboard belly, pirate earrings glinting. Silently, he put on his white gloves, dipped his finger into the pan of lighter fluid, and lit it on the votive candle. He put the flame out in his mouth. By the time several rubes had concluded, in stage whispers, that the glove was the trick, Zane removed it and lit his finger. He used the flaming finger to light his first torch. Even though he had told me that only vapor burns, I cringed as he put the flaming torch in his mouth. Next, he lit a cigarette, pumping it until the head was red hot, touched it to his tongue, and then held it out with his finger on the glowing red cherry. Lollibells had said something about an insulator cap created by the wet tongue, but this only lasted a few seconds. I held my breath until he bit off the cherry.

"Eat a lightbulb!" yelled a mark, and I glared at him.

Zane moved with the rhythm of a sleepwalker as he lit one torch, and then another, and began to pass them back and forth from his mouth, lighting one with the other. I almost missed the sleight of hand when he squeezed some lighter fluid onto his tongue. Holding his chin high, with his legs spread for balance, and his mouth partly open, he exhaled softly, producing a fountain of fire.

He lit the next torch from the fountain of flame at his mouth. Again, he lit his tongue and lit a torch from that flame. The rubes were clapping madly, and Arthur Reese smiled. Zane threw the torches to the ground, stomped them with his feet, and bowed.

Then he turned his back to us, a smoking statue with a single braid down his back. People began to shuffle and whisper; to my horror, someone coughed. "One cough and I'm a dead man," Zane had told me.

When he finally turned around, he held his grandfather's Civil War bayonet. It was eighteen inches long. The nickel plating he'd added to it to make it glide more smoothly glimmered. He spread his legs, tilted his head back, opened his mouth. Slowly, with his eyes shut, he inserted the point of the blade into his throat. Down it went, behind the gently bobbing Adam's apple, down, down, down, until he held the hilt between his strong white teeth. It was all I could do not to cough.

After the show, while I was having a glass of red wine outside the tent, Lollibells stepped out from the shadows holding a white rat by the tail. I screamed.

"Oh you hush," he said. "I been watching you, girl; you ain't afraid of nothing! You waltz in here telling everybody you're a clown! Right in front of ole has-been Lollibells! Now that is funny." He dangled the rat in front of me. "You want to be with it. Don't fib to me. I seen it in your face. You have made the foolish decision to go on the road with the Arthur Reese Traveling Show. You already sleeping with Smokey the Bear, bless yo little pea-picking heart. Ain't that what they say back home, Georgia peach?"

"Georgia roadkill."

"Excuse me?"

"That's what Zane called me."

"Tsk, tsk . . . that little firecracker. Well, I cannot speak for the Human Dragon, but immodest mockery of those I love is one of my defects of character."

"Love is pretty cheap around here."

"Take it or leave it." He held out the rat.

Gingerly, I grasped the tail between two fingers, flinching as the thing jerked. "See what I tole ya? Courage. That lil ole hook-wormy thang from Louisiana ain't got nothing on you. Now you run this mouse over to Madge Olinick. You ask her real nice if you can feed it to Percy. Be sweet now. Girl, if Madge don't like you, you ain't going nowhere."

I turned away.

"One more thing . . . there's a gentleman here to see you. A fine-looking colored gentleman from Georgia. He's having a hot dog."

Chapter Twelve

"I HAVE TO feed this mouse to a snake," I explained when Jeremiah offered to buy me a hot dog.

"Well, I won't keep you. I was just in town and thought I'd drop by. You working here now?"

"Not exactly."

"I see." He wiped his mouth with a napkin, threw it in the garbage can, and then put his hands in his pockets and leaned back on his heels. Except for some distinguished streaks of gray in his temples, he looked the same as he did two summers ago at Southern Board. "Looks like you caught you a rat," he said, smiling.

"I think it's a mouse," I said, dangling it by its tail. Around us, barkers shouted, children shrieked on rides, and the faint strain of "Le Sabre" played from the merry-go-round.

"Your mama and daddy are looking for you. They been right worried. Got all the police in Wapanog County out looking.

Your daddy got him a police radio. Listens to it all the time. Figuring you might be kidnapped."

"Did they send you after me?"

"Naw." He took a toothpick out of his pocket and began to suck on it. "I just brought my family down here for a little vacation, and I saw that Ferris wheel and got to thinking." I looked around for his family, but he was alone. He was the only mark on the lot who looked like he couldn't be cheated. He looked like Henry.

"I have to go," I said. "I have to feed the snake."

"Caught you a rat after all, didn't ya?" He put his broad hand on my shoulder. "Now I want you to do something for me. I want you to get to a phone and call your mama and daddy. I imagine they'll take it collect."

"How did you know I was here?"

"You not the only chile that ever ran off to the circus. I tried it myself once."

I STOOD BESIDE Madge as Percy followed the mouse around the bottom of her bathtub. It took over an hour for him to open his jaws and swallow the shrieking rodent, and by that time I was ready to faint. Madge and I watched the snake swallow, slowly squeezing the mouse down its long yellow body. Finally, she said, "I forgive you."

"Thank you," I said. That night I dreamed of the fire and snakes and Jeremiah, who kept saying, "You ever seen a cat catch a rat?"

THE NEXT MORNING, on the way out of town, the caravan stopped at a gas station, and I called home.

"Living with whom?" asked Florida. I shifted the receiver to my other hand and took a drink.

"With a friend," I said in a small voice.

"With a black man? What did you say? I can't hear you? Where are you?"

"South Carolina. We're on our way to Rock Hill this morning."

"We'll see about that. You ask your father. He turned this town upside down looking for you. I told him you'd taken the bus. Or hitchhiked. Rebelling against your mother. You could have been killed or mauled. I've lain awake every single night. Had nightmares. I guess that doesn't concern you, does it? You just please yourself. Mark my words, one day you will be sorry. Here's your father."

I heard her murmur, "Living with a black man in North Carolina. She said something about somebody with three legs. I don't know what-all. Circus, it sounds like. Maybe she'll listen to you."

There was a silence on the phone. Then Henry said in a deep, steady voice, "Hello, Louise."

"Hi."

"How are you?"

"I'm fine. How are you?"

"I'm doing all right, honey. You're mother's been worried to death." In the background, over the clatter of dishes, I heard Florida's monologue: "Didn't hear a peep about college. Guess she gave up on that, too. Does she have any money? Oh, I could just wring her neck. I'm going to get my purse and go to the car."

"Sit tight, Florida," said Henry. "I'm talking to her." In a professional voice, he began to ascertain my situation. First, he took down the number of the pay phone, in case of disconnection. Then he asked for my address.

"Dad, it's the Arthur Reese Traveling Show," I said impatiently. "We don't have an address."

"He must have an address. Everybody in this country has some kind of address. How does he pay his bills? Spell his name for me."

"He has a patch man to pay his bills."

"A what?"

"A guy who pays people off."

"What's his address?"

Florida picked up on another extension to ask if I wanted her to reschedule my dentist appointment. "The Good Lord has answered my prayers," she said. "I thought you might be in pain." She began to cry.

"I'm trying to talk," said Henry.

"Is there a law that only one person can talk? I have something to say, too. I'm her mother. Boss, boss, boss, that's all you do Henry. I'm going to the grocery store. You all are driving me crazy. Bye."

"Yes, he went to college," I was saying when Zane walked out of the gas station and handed me a fresh beer. "He probably got a degree. I don't know."

"I went to all the colleges," said Zane, popping open is beer. "I can count to ten backwards, but I only do it for cops."

"Would you like to talk to him?" I asked Henry.

"Not right now," he said, but I handed the phone to Zane. Then, with a mixture of wonder and shame, I looked at the caravan lined up at the Texaco pumps. Arthur's limousine had been obtained, somehow, from a funeral home in Texas. Eva had replaced the black curtains with purple and gold ones, but you can't hide a hearse. Most people maintained a respectful distance, but while I was standing on the curb I saw a child edge toward the window. Then he fled, screaming "Snake! Mama, they's a snake in that car!" Madge claimed that Percy could not get comfortable anywhere except in the back seat of the limo, and Arthur, who had in fact traded in her mountain lion for a couple of hot dog stands, felt guilty enough to ride with an albino python for the rest of his life. Spencer and Daisy rode in Jungle Jim's trailer. Theoretically, they were in car seats, but they'd managed to unfasten each other and dash into the store. Daisy came out first, waving a fistful of lollipops, and was followed shortly by Spencer, who was chased out by the cashier. Someone screamed, "Call the police!" drawing a crowd around our sputtering rigs and the rusty, patched-up trailer homes we pulled behind them.

"You get them stinking gypsies outa here."

"Gypsies and niggers and monkeys, too."

"What's the damn difference?"

"Don't you leave that register, Brittany. Them folks are dangerous. I had my cousin Peewee out here one Sunday on the morning shift, and one of them circus ladies give him the evil eye. She snatched twenty dollars clean out of the drawer. Didn't touch nothing. Did it all with her eye."

"He tell you that?"

"He stood right there where you are."

On the pay phone, Zane was slowly repeating a phone number he had made up.

• • •

ON THE RIDE to Rock Hill, squeezed between Zane and Lollibells, who had snatched some Valium from Arthur and was snoring quietly, I asked Eva about her third leg. Until now I had been too bashful to ask, but since it was hanging over my shoulder, and everybody was in a good mood, I risked it.

"All of Eva is real," she said. "No rubber parts. Right, Zane?" She tickled him with her toes.

"You bet," he said, tossing her a handsome smile.

"Here, Louise. Give me a foot massage. My feet are clean. I am not like Tic Toc. It is how long since he has bathed, Zane?"

"He got caught in the rain a few years ago."

"A little harder, dear, yes, there, that's it." I rubbed her foot, which was small, smooth, and white, with blue polish on its little toenails, like Puff LeBlanc.

"She's nice! Nice hands, huh Zane? You have the hands of a lady—Eva's hands. We should have many of these fine hands; two is not enough. Do you know what a famous man with three legs, four feet, and sixteen toes said when he was asked how he coped in the world?"

"Lentini!" shouted Zane. "I love him!"

"He answers to this man, 'If you lived in a world where everyone had only one arm, how would you cope with two?'"

"So you weren't really found in a Dumpster?"

"No, I was in a convent, which is much, much worse. I did not eat chicken. I ate—how do you call it? Cruel."

"Gruel."

"Yes, that. And at night they locked me in a closet. The sisters said my parents have sinned—so I have three legs. Some of them thought I was a devil. They were afraid I would get out

of the closet at night and eat them up. That was correct." Clenching her jaw, she snapped her teeth and growled. Her eyes were dark corridors.

As we crossed the Catawba River, she brought up the subject of Sunny. "You can tell it's the end of the season when nobody will ride with nobody else," she said as we bounced along the rutted road. "Sunny wants to ride here, with Zane, but Zane cannot let her because here is his new wife, Louise Peppers."

"We're not married," I said pointedly.

"And you," continued Eva, "you hate that girl, no? You want to scratch out her eyes?"

"I could take her or leave her."

"Leave her to the wolves!" she cried, poking me with her foot. "All night you lie in his arms, thinking, Did she hold him like this? Did he like her smell? Is this her smell on the pillow?"

"Let's change the subject," said Zane.

I lit a cigarette for courage and asked, "Did you go to their wedding?"

"Oh, yes! It was a carnie wedding on the merry-go-round, in New Orleans. The horses were in better shape back then; they had shiny new paint and most of their teeth. Sunny's father bring his band to the lot, and they play beautiful music; everyone is dancing and drinking champagne. We make toast. Sunny, she is throwing up. We are joking with Zane—Is she pregnant? Because why else would he have married such a trumpet?"

"Strumpet," I corrected, watching Zane from the corner of my eye. He was mad. Eva didn't seem to notice.

"You see, Louise, he come to me the day before and say, 'Eva, Potrebbe mi aiutare? Can you help me? I think maybe I make a mistake.'

"I say to him, 'Ferma! Stop! The marriage is not . . .' andato e ritorno, how do you say in English?"

"Round-trip," mumbled Zane. "I don't want to talk about this."

"So don't talk," said Eva, opening a beer. "I am talking because I tell the truth, and this girl who leaves her family to join us needs to know the truth."

"That's very Italian, or something," said Zane.

"How do you know? I am a woman. This is what I know." Turning to me, she said, "I love Sunny. She is like a daughter to me. Her father—what music he plays! When I hear him, you understand, I am flying. But she is not the woman for Zane. She is too afraid. Afraid of everything. Always pushing people. Trying to be the one, as you say. Not like Zane. He dreams big dreams, like you. He loves. Sunny's father love only his music. Her mother love only her wine. Poof. Not like your mama, no? I see her now; she is hurting in her heart for you."

"Here comes the fortune," said Zane. "Give her a dollar, Louise."

Eva took my hand, running her fingers over my palm. "No money this time. Next time. This time, I am talking to you as a daughter. I see fire in you, a terrible hot fire you cannot put out with whiskey. It gets hotter and hotter. Big, big fire. Zane cannot swallow this fire. The dragons across the sea, they run from you. Inside, you are burning, burning, burning. Nothing can stop you. You are crazy. Do you understand what I am saying?" I looked into her eyes. She hissed, "Il cotella!"

"Give her a dollar," said Zane.

"You insult me," replied Eva.

"I try," he said. He rubbed his eyes and stared tiredly at the

road. The birds were flying south in unwavering black V against the blue sky. At dusk, we drove through a town where the houses sat close together behind neat picket fences, and I looked at each softly lit window, wondering what they were doing inside, if anyone was thinking of joining the carnival.

IN ROCK HILL, I received a real letter from Florida:

Dearest Louise,

I am sending this General Delivery and don't know if you will get it or not. Please let me know. Your father and I do not like it that we cannot reach you. We might have an emergency, and no one would know where to find you. We are trying to let you be "independent" but you will have to prove that you are capable. Mature. Please call us collect. Henry wants to know if you got your check.

It is raining here. It is something like a "rain forest." It was very hot in Atlanta and warm here but not hot. Last weekend we went to the lake with Mary MacDermott and her husband, Phil (I always call him Bill), who taught you math at Bridgewater. He said that it's not unusual for female students to have a math block. I don't know if that's prejudiced or not. He wore his socks the whole time we were on the boat. Maybe next time we'll invite her when he's out of town. They are new members of our church but don't come regularly.

"The fool hath said in his heart, There is no God." Psalms 53:1. Try to make some Christian friends in the circus who will be a good influence on our morals and not lead you down the wrong path (premarital sex). Do you work on Sundays? See if you can get to a church service. Stick your neck out there. Smile. Fix your hair and your makeup. You can do it! No one wants to be around someone who is down in the dumps. You were very unhappy at home. I know you don't like me to tell you this, but you have hardened your heart against JESUS CHRIST YOUR LORD. I'm sending you a hairbrush that Agnes recommends for fine hair. I'm back with her now.

Mary thinks it's wonderful that you are studying to be a "clown." People are driving from Atlanta and all over to buy MacMe clothes. Her prices have gone sky-high. I bought a pair of socks from her that you can have if you want them—I can't afford anything else. I know you don't like her style, but these are real cute. She asked me if you got your sense of humor from me, and I told her no, you aren't very funny at home, just around other people. You get that from Henry I guess. He mopes around the house now that you are "away."

I shooed our owl away last night. We think he's the one who ate Puff. Then I had a bad dream about a big bird carrying me away. Got up at three and went back to sleep on the couch. Don't know if we'll get another pet or not. They're more trouble than they're worth, but now that you aren't in your room, the house feels empty. Found one of your argyle socks behind the dryer. Do you have the mate?

I can send it to you. I'm taking a painting class, but I'm the dumbest one in class. I may quit. Henry doesn't like the mess I make.

Remember all the good qualities you have when you make an effort and all that you have to be grateful for. Have you spoken to anyone at Ringling Brothers about your ambitions, desires, and goals? You know who to talk to better than I do. Put your best foot forward! Have a positive attitude! Let me know if you would like me to send you Billy Graham's tape on that (the one I got for Mother). She never listened to it. Please don't take any drugs if someone offers them to you.

Love,
Mom

P.S. I saw Drew's mother yesterday at a shower for Barbara Groche's daughter (the fat one) who is getting married to a piano player from Cartersville. Barbara tried to discourage that but failed. She said Drew is working hard at Harvard and is running for vice president of her class. Drew has always been outgoing and bubbly. Have you talked to her lately?

P.P.S. Dr. Frommlecker married and divorced a nineteen-year-old Vietnamese girl. People say he was mean to her. I don't know what happened to the secretary, I guess she ran out on him. It just about killed Shirley (the marriage) but she went to a spa in Asheville, North Carolina, and is much bet-

ter now. Henry says she took an arm and a leg off
Leo in the divorce. She looks great! Skinny and tan
with a manila frost in her hair. I've gained ten
pounds right around my middle. I'm old and fat—
not young and cute like you!

I HAD BEEN with the Arthur Reese Traveling show for
three weeks and was no closer to being a clown than I was
when I stepped off the bus in Myrtle Beach. Each day, I lowered my standards. In Asheville, North Carolina, I accepted
the temporary position of donniker manager. *Donniker* is the
carnie word for toilet.

"I have ESP," I confided to Arthur Reese. "Let me tell fortunes."

"Fortunes, eh?" He rubbed his goatee. "I've been consider-
ing a mitt camp, but Eva's our man for that. People appreciate
a foreign accent when they're being lied to. Softens the blow.
It's like sitting in a big velvet chair at the bank."

"I could be her helper," I offered.

"What? Oh yes, the mitt camp. Dear, I would never allow
you to step foot in a mitt camp."

"I can read minds. Eva is teaching me. Let me show you."

"Don't you dare read my mind. That's rude. No, you
wouldn't do as a fortune-teller. The best thing for you to do is
run on back to college. Don't dillydally around with Shakespeare and such. Study genetics. Cloning, the future is in
cloning. Oh, the lawyers and shrinks will have their hands full!
Imagine: You could kill yourself and still be alive. No end to
the entertainment."

"How about Guess Your Weight and Age? I could do that."

"No, dear, you'd tell people the truth. We couldn't have that."

I didn't have the nerve to tell him I wanted to be a clown.

One night after the show, while I was scrubbing a donniker, I looked into the sudsy blue water and thought about Lolli-bells. What compelled such a smart man to let people dump him in water night after night. They didn't even know that he put ice in the water. It wasn't even funny.

Zane opened the door. "Why, it's the donniker fairy!" He stepped behind me and put his hands on my breasts, kissing the back of my neck. "The door's locked," he whispered, taking the toilet brush out of my hands. "We have an hour before the show. Look at these fine hands—much too pretty for scrub-bing. Oh, they're cold! Let me warm them." He unbuttoned his jeans and slid my hands into his crotch. I smelled the smoke in his hair, and the red wine he drank to clean the lighter fluid out of his body. His cock burned in my hands.

"Why doesn't Lollibells do a regular clown act?"

"You wench. How can you talk about another man while I'm disrobing you?"

"The dunking station is a cliché. It's not even funny."

"Not even funny, says the donniker fairy." He pushed me up against the cool concrete wall and looked into my eyes. His muscles were taut, and his breath was hot on my cheek. "Listen. Warren is a genius. He could do anything he wanted. Don't believe that crap he tells you about dropping out of med school because he couldn't pass chemistry. The man has a pho-tographic memory. He reads a book, and Zap! It's printed on his brain. You don't find many bookworms who can do triple flips, flat on their feet, but Warren can. I've seen him jump off the merry-go-round, do a triple flip, and land in a handstand."

"Why doesn't he do that at the ten-in-one?"

"People have their reasons. Some of them are ugly reasons, and some of them are wrong reasons, but they're reasons all the same. After a while, the reasons make a story. You know why Arthur Reese plays that Sinatra crap on the chaise volonte? Old Blue Eyes himself came to Arthur's wedding. Art the rich old fart. He was in *Who's Who*. Poured it all down the Arthur Reese Traveling Drain. Married some debutante who ran off with his brother—balled him right at the wedding, in the water fountain. She had her reasons." Lightly, he stroked my nipples. "Some people might ask what a smart beautiful woman like yourself is doing in the john screwing a carnie."

"Am I screwing you?"

"Oh, yes," he said. "Very hard. Screwing me to death."

As we walked out of the donniker, I heard faint strains of "Send in the Clowns" coming from Arthur's trailer. Tic Toc had convinced him that it was too depressing even for the chaise volonte. Ahead of us, Spencer, dragging his tie in one hand, kicked a beer can across the empty lot. One by one, lights clicked off; motors droned to a stop. The gates closed. Nothing was left of the screaming, surging, spending crowd except a few drunk girls, hanging around.

"So you want to be a clown," said Lollibells, when I finally knocked on his door to ask for career advice. The garnet silk smoking jacket was tied around his slim waist, and he was smoking a Havana. "Please, have a seat. Fait comme chez-vous." He'd done a lot with his trailer. He'd pulled up the crappy brown carpet, painted the plywood floor a soft yellow, and hung the walls with tapestries. Somewhere, he'd snagged an oriental rug, which had to be folded in half to fit into the room. Shyly, I examined his book collection: *Color Me Beautiful, Proustian Space,* and the copy of *King Lear* I had loaned him. I was about to pull *The Nine Lives of Marcel Marceau* from the shelf when Warren pressed a smooth hand on my shoulder. Waving his cigar at the black-and-white portrait of Barbra Streisand on the wall, he said, "That is my mother."

"She's beautiful. Your father?" I pointed to the picture next to Barbra—a photograph of Tony Curtis.

"Uncle. My father left us when I was quite young. I didn't know him. Now my sister—" he produced a framed photograph of Whoopie Goldberg—"she's something else! We both decided to be black. A streak of rebellion. Please, have a seat."

I sat stiffly on the edge of his fouton, afraid to wrinkle the damask cover, but he sprawled across it, ashing his cigar into a wing tip oxford.

"Marital problems?" he asked, plumping his pillow. "Is Smokey misbehaving? Or have you come to ask for a vial of my special Sunny poison? I brewed it up last month when she destroyed my curling iron. Never lend anything of value to these people. They have no respect. They live in abysmal squalor. Hair in sinks, skid marks on shorts, yesterday's lunch under the fingernails. Tic Toc is filthy. Just filthy." He ashed his cigar on the floor. "Now what is it you came to ask for, darling—money? Or have you decided that you're an alcoholic?"

I took a deep breath. "I don't want you to think I'm competing with you—" He grimaced. "I admire your talent, Warren. You're a clown, and a genius, and of course I'm not either one, not yet—the clown part anyway, I mean—do you have a drink?"

"Splendid idea." He poured cognac into two shot glasses. Exhaling a luxurious stream of blue smoke, he said, "Charlie Chaplin defined comedy as Knowing Who You Are and Where You Came From. He added that it has to be perfect. Perfect, that's the key. In comedy, there is no room for error. Now in tragedy, you can fuck up all over the place. No one notices. Once you get a good boo hoo going, it's hard to stop it. But to draw laughter from the fickle human heart—ah, that is a delicate operation. You strike me as the tragic type. Religious, almost moral."

"I'm an atheist."

"And I'm a straight white man. Don't look so disappointed. If I may quote Reinhold Niebuhr, 'Humor is a prelude to faith and laughter is the beginning of prayer.' Now tell me about your deepest religious experience."

"Brief stint as a missionary. Second grade at Pruitt Elementary. I set out to convert Robert Robertson, who was electrocuted last year—double murder. After I converted him, he thought I loved him, so I gave him a bloody nose."

"Was he a black boy?"

"No, he was white-trash white, like Sunny. Bluish skin, pinkish hair. One brown eye, one blue eye. Frazzled genes."

"Sunny Boudreaux! I thought we'd never get to her. Now, she should be a clown! Funny name, big funny feet, thinks she's married to your lover."

"She's deluded."

"You know what they say: There's always three in the bed."

"You should try your wit on the dunking stand. Maybe you wouldn't get so wet."

"Louise wants to hear something funny from the clown.

Let's see . . ." He rubbed his chin then snapped his fingers. "How about this one? Uncle Lollibells hears it from the grapevine that Madge washed Jungle Jim's gorilla suit."

"Washed it?"

"She and Jim used to be married. Joined the show together. Either her snake got tangled around his monkey, or his monkey got tangled around her snake, but they split. She wants nothing to do with the man, but when it's laundry time, she's after him with the clothes basket. You'd think she'd know by now that the man was born dirty. He'd fall down and die in a clean house. Eva swears his grandmother was an ape. I guess they do that in Italy. I wouldn't know." His cigar had gone out; he tapped it in the shoe and relit it. "But," he said, taking a long drag, "that's not the funny part. The funny part is . . ." He began to giggle. "The thing I wanted to tell you is . . . the gorilla suit shrank in the dryer. It's a teeny weeny little gorilla now. Just your size. Arthur thinks it's perfect. Of course it would also fit Sunny, but she's busy being the Most Beautiful Teenager in America."

"I am not going to be Sunny's goddamned gorilla!"

"Disappointing! I thought you would be excited. But that's right, you came here to be a clown, didn't you?"

"You fucking faggot! You did this. You shrank the suit. I hate you!"

"Tsk, tsk, tsk. Why you wanna talk so ugly to Uncle Lollibells?" He put on a giant pout. "You wanting to call me a nigger, too, I bet. That be coming next. Ugly, ugly, ugly. And I thought you was a sweet girl. You sounding just like a big mean ugly old gorilla!" He burst into a cackle as I threw my glass against the wall and ran out of the room.

In the morning, I wrote Florida and Henry a letter, inform-
ing them that I had been promoted.

The gorilla suit was unbearably hot. It was as heavy as a shag
carpet and so rough on the inside that I had to wear long underwear and a knit cap. Sweat poured down my face, back,
arms, and legs. It was hard to move around, and when I fell
down, as I did often at first, someone had to help me to my
feet. The mask was too big and would shift around on my face
until I was blind and choking for air. Inside the big hairy mitts
my hands were useless.

At dress rehearsal, Tic Toc tried to pep me up. "You're a hell of
a lot better in there than Jim was, even if you do trip now and then.
Jim wasn't quick. I'm not trying to criticize, but that's the truth.
Plus, he'd get to coughing. You ever heard a gorilla cough?"

Behind the curtain, Sunny screamed, "Eat my shit! I did not
take your razor. I bought this one with my own goddamned
money, motherfucker."

Lollibells replied, "White trash, White trash, born and bred!
Beat up yo mama, take yo daddy to bed! Welfare, welfare, give
me some bread!"

Sunny flung back the curtain and stomped on stage mum-
bling, "Mother-fucking coon."

Tic Toc smiled at the sight of her in her bikini and said, "If
Sunny weren't so goddamned beautiful, with every guy in the
stands goggling at her, Jim would have tripped us up every
time. Course nobody really looks at the gorilla."

Sunny took the compliment in stride. Straddling a stool beside Tic Toc, who sat cross-legged on the stage, she removed
Lollibells's razor from her pocketbook and began to shave her
legs. Inches from Tic Toc's nose, she began to work her bikini
line. He was tortured.

"I was just telling Louise that it ain't so bad in the gorilla suit, once you get used to it," he said, dipping his head to hide his red cheeks. "It might be good luck that Madge shrunk it in the dryer. Louise is a damn sight better at it than Jim, and I don't mean to criticize."

"That's not what I heard," said Sunny, smoothly drawing the razor around her thigh.

"What did you hear?"

"Oh nothing." She rubbed some lotion on the edge of her crotch. "I didn't hear a word, did you, Rufus?"

Tic Toc looked confused. After searching unsuccessfully for the right answer, he glanced at Sunny and said, "Don't that sting?" Then, realizing that he'd been staring, he motioned toward the gorilla suit piled at my feet.

"This here is a good one," he said. "Some of 'em stink pretty bad, but Arthur got this one brand new for ya."

"Whoops," said Sunny. "Cat's out of the bag."

Tic Toc pulled the gorilla mask over his head.

"THE GORILLA IS a clown, Louise," said Eva as she walked across the stage with me. "A very big hairy wonderful clown. "The gorilla is funny, no?"

"I guess," I said through the mask.

"Your voice is muffled; speak out. Now, tell me what do a clown do to be funny?"

Wrenching off the hot mask, I faced her and said, "He knows who he is and where he comes from."

"Same as Spidora! Spiders, gorillas, people, all the same. So, tell me. We practice."

She sat on a stool with her legs sprawled around her, while I stood before her, unable to sit down in my suit.

"Who are you?"

"I am a gorilla."

"No, no, no. Who are you . . . never the mind. Who is your mother? What does she teach you?"

"Don't wear white before Easter or after Labor Day, say your prayers before you go to bed in case you die in your sleep, and always ask to see the manager."

"Good. Good mother. Your papa?"

"He taught me how to whistle."

From behind the tattered curtain, I heard Sunny snort.

"Ignore her. Whistle."

I wet my lips. I tried Henry's whistle for Puff, two long blasts followed by a short one, and then his whistle for Roderick—a referee's staccato call for foul play. He did not whistle at ladies, at least not to my knowledge, but when he was really angry, he whistled hymns. I had a good start on "A Closer Walk with Thee" when Sunny stuck her head out the curtain and broke into raucous laughter.

"Talent," she said, snickering behind her hand. "Real talent. You've come a long way for a rube. Most of the little sluts Zane picks up never get past donniker cleaning. And look at you!"

I saw myself in one of Tic Toc's distorted mirrors: sweaty red face, hair on end, huge, bulky, hairy body.

Then I looked back at Sunny's pale rat face and screamed. It was a shrill rattle that hurt my own ears, burned my gut, razed my throat. And still, I hollered. Other carnies stepped up, poked their heads through the curtain, moved their mouths, gestured with their arms, and finally left. Only Eva remained on her stool, watching me with the dispassion of a music teacher. When I was finished, she nodded her head and said, "Now we are ready."

That night, the Most Beautiful Teenager in America was so beautiful and the Gorilla was so beastly that the rubes gave us a standing ovation. We drew such a crowd that Arthur decided to spend an extra night in Asheville before moving on to Johnson City, Tennessee.

Chapter Thirteen

ZANE ASKED FOR my hand in marriage in Johnson City. We were on the chaise volonte, just the two of us, after the show. Earlier, Zane had scored a bag of cocaine, and we'd been doing lines for hours. On the flying chairs, we ditched the razor blade and snorted it through a straw straight from the bag. The painted lady above my head smiled as Tic Toc washed her in green and purple lights. Tic Toc, bribed with his own small bag of toot, played "Fly Me to the Moon," spinning us around and around the sky. The stars were so bright that my eyes ached. Zane could not stop talking.

"I told you about my friend Herman, right? Herman Lamont. Everybody called him Skip except his dad. Paul Lamont, chief of police, president of Little League. Mr. Lamont came around when my parents died; I was seven. All the sudden, he takes an interest in me. Shows me how to choke a pat. Cuts the meat on my plate. Takes me frog gigging with Skip. Crab boils in his backyard. Every Saturday afternoon, in his basement, he gives me a glass of bourbon and fucks me. Tells me if I tell anybody, he'll tell Aunt Mary Esther that I've been drinking. On Sunday morning, he picks me up and takes me to mass. He lights one candle for my mom, and one for my dad." Zane began to cry.

"You were seven?"

"Seven, eight, and nine. Then he stopped coming to the house. Maybe I got too old, or maybe he found somebody else."

"He doesn't deserve a dick!"

"I don't think they're issued out for good behavior."

The chaise volonte turned around the starry sky. Suddenly, it all seemed sinister: the purple and green lights, the painted ladies, Sinatra. I wanted to get in a car and find Paul Lamont and kill him.

"Have a cocktail," said Zane, handing me the bag and straw. "I've upset you."

"How did your parents die?"

"Car wreck. Drunk probably. Good Catholics at Mardi Gras. Aunt Mary Esther moved in to take care of all five of us. She'd never had any children, and she had no idea what to do, so she just played the piano all day. Played "On the Sunny Side of the Street" and "Ain't Misbehaving."

"Inspirational stuff."

"Yeah. Whenever she went to the bar, she brought home an accompanist. 'Children,' she would announce, 'this is my accompanist.' He might actually sit down beside her on the piano bench for a few minutes; then they'd go to the bedroom to fuck or fight. She beat up several guys."

"Didn't the neighbors help?"

"I told you about the neighbors. Here, you take the straw. My nose is going to bleed. I can always feel it." I took the straw and snorted a long cold line. The sky was gorgeous. "The Catholics in Villa Platte let us slide for a while because Aunt Mary Esther was a good Catholic. Whenever they forgot this, she dropped a load in the collection plate. But the Baptists got her."

"You have to watch out for them."

"They snuck right up on the old girl. Sent her to a rest home. All the way there, she yelled, 'I am not tired!' So they put her in a straitjacket. Can't play the piano in a straitjacket. When they took her bourbon away, she died. Want to hear the sad part?"

"No. I want to laugh some more. Let's laugh."

"The piano went to the Baptist church."

"Where did you go?"

He shrugged. "Here and there. A roundabout way to you. And who might you be?"

"Same as you."

"But with breasts." He pushed his hands under my shirt. "Warm, round, wonderful breasts. What happened to your Aunt Mary Esther?"

"Didn't have one."

"Mom, Pop, a closet full of ex-husbands?"

"I had a brother, but I killed him."

"Shit."

"It was an accident."

"Fuck."

"You would have liked him." I kissed him slow and deep,

past the cool frost of cocaine to the hot flames he licked, the broken glass, the red wine, the warm wet flesh. I stroked his thigh, hard beneath his worn jeans. Tic Toc turned off the music, and I could hear Zane's breath as I touched the zipper, in and out, between the rapid beating of his heart. The chair lifted; I pushed my hand into his pocket and through the lining felt the stiff rise of his cock.

"Go down," he said, unbuckling his belt.

"Not here."

"Here." When he pressed my mouth against the metal zipper, I felt my nipples tighten into points. As I took his penis into my mouth, I imagined that it was a sword, and I was him, that I could die any minute.

When we came, the car jerked on the rail, and Tic Toc shouted, "I'm turning this thing off! You want me to leave you up there?"

"Marry me," said Zane. He was crying. "Please be married to me."

It seemed like a good idea.

ALL EVENTS FALL short of their anticipation; my wedding was no exception. The preparations went on longer than expected because on Sunday night, at the scheduled hour for the carousel ride, we were all too drunk to stay on a horse. Arthur bitched and moaned about renting the lot for an extra day, but he'd been the one to open the case of champagne on Sunday morning, and he was secretly pleased to extend the celebration. Beside the fact that Arthur loved a carnie wedding, he considered his odd assortment of employees a family, himself the father. "How many more of these girls do I have to marry off?" he'd groan as he proudly counted us on his fingers: Eva, Madge, Sunny. He spared no expense.

It was Arthur who designed my wedding gown. "That is a marvelous ensemble for a kootch show," he told Eva when he saw her design. "File it." He drew up something elegant and chaste, and then barked directions over Eva's shoulder as she stitched it up on her treadle sewing machine.

"Put it in reverse!" he cried like a backseat driver. "Go left! Not there! There's a ruffle over there! Stop!"

Eva ignored him. With her dark head bent close to the cream silk, she treadled with one foot, held the train on the floor with the other, and kicked Faith away with her third foot. "Felix!" she cried. "Take this cat away before I make a guitar!"

Felix was photographing the scene. He insisted on being the photographer even though he cut off heads in all of his pictures. We all tried to help him tilt the camera, but he was an impossible student; he cursed our mothers, then stomped off in tears. Finally, Arthur declared that headless was the artist's style, and we let him be.

Lollibells and Madge created a cake in the shape of a man and a woman copulating. You couldn't really tell that was what they were doing after the frosting went on, but the thought was there.

Tic Toc repainted all the horses on the merry-go-round. Jungle Jim, who felt guilty about saddling me with the Gorilla Girl suit, tried to throw a bridal shower, but no one would go into his trailer because of the smell. We ate cashews and pillow mints outside, and he brought me my presents, one by one, whenever he felt inclined. There was a big bag of leftover pillow mints, and a smaller one of cocaine. Wrapped in newspaper, tied with a piece of dirty string, was a gold-plated Tiffany alarm clock with someone else's initials engraved on the back.

"I tole 'em your name, but they must of got it wrong," he said bashfully.

"I love it," I said. "I'll change my name."

"I got more stuff for ya," he said, "but I got to go work with the kids." Daisy and Spencer were in training to become flower children. They were to ride on the roof of the car—a souped-up Oldsmobile with huge speakers and a new paint job—which Zane had gone to purchase. Arthur had decided to buy the car from one of his nephews and give it to us for a wedding present.

Sunny had disappeared. Rumor had it that she planned to quit the show and go to culinary school.

"Now you tell me who's gonna pay good money to eat that girl's food," said Madge as she added the final touches to our cake. "She don't know how to boil an egg."

"Someone can teach her," I said, feeling magnanimous. Madge pushed a raisin into the spot where Zane's belly button was supposed be and said nothing.

Zane had gone to get my wedding present and didn't get back in time for the wedding supper, but we all crowded into Madge's trailer and ate anyway: filet mignon wrapped in bacon, twice-baked potatoes topped with melted cheddar cheese and sprinkled with dried parsley, and two spears apiece of canned asparagus. On the side of each plate was a wedge of lemon, which most of us squeezed into our tequila. I ate in Lollibells's smoking jacket so I wouldn't get my dress dirty.

"Now," he said, when we had finished eating, "come into my trailer and let me do you."

"No, me," said Tic Toc, who was drunker than usual and had lost his shyness with women. "Let me do you."

"Hush y'all dirty minds." Lollibells brushed a crumb from the collar of my dressing gown. "I am going to dress her hair, apply her cosmetics, and help her into her gown."

"Then you come right over here and do me," said Madge, snorting helplessly.

"Do me right . . ." someone began to sing, but we were out the door.

When he wanted to be, Lollibells was an excellent girlfriend. He was frank: "I am not even going to try to curl that stringy hair. We're going up." He was lavishly supportive: "To die. Look at you. Turn around one more time. Gorgeous. You are *it*." And he was practical: "Hush. I am putting this bib on you. Don't sass me. I've worked too hard on you to see you wearing that margarita."

When I was dressed, with a towel clipped to my dress and a fresh drink in my hand, he put on Diana Ross and the Supremes and asked me to dance. I declined. He demonstrated. In the small trailer, he rocked on his heels, twisted his hips, waved his hands. Rhythm coiled through his body. It was as if he couldn't stop moving. "Come on," he said, pulling me to my feet, swinging his lean hip against mine. "Dance, little sister, dance!" My face burned to the tips of my ears. How could he know what it was to be a Peppers on the dance floor? We were like frogs in danger: dead still. There was no dignity in it, and no escape. You had to try not to try. I began to rock on my heels, like a child who has to go to the bathroom, and to clap my hands shortly after determining a beat in the music. I didn't know what to do with my face, so I closed my eyes. Lollibells turned off the music.

"Stop laughing."

"No, it's cute."

"I can't help if I can't dance. It's not genetically coded. I'm sure there's something you can't do."

"Don't pout. If you can screw, you can dance, and y'alls trailer be rattling every night. Come here."

He pulled me close to him and held me tight against his chest and hips as he swayed back and forth.

"One, two," he was saying as he turned us around the room. "One two, relax goddamnit, one two . . ." I stepped on his foot. I backed us into the bookshelf. I missed the beat, every time.

When Eva walked in, I was standing alone on the floor, trying to clap when he clapped.

"Stop!" she cried, "Stop! In the name of love . . ." and began to swing me around as she danced. When I could get free, I sat on the edge of the bed and watched her shimmy and twirl. She lacked the athletic grace of Lollibells but had her own three-legged rhythm, and her face was ecstatic. That was the worst part of not being able to dance, you saw how much fun people had doing it, how they forgot themselves. I fixed myself another drink and left to find more philosophical company. It would be nice to find the groom.

"Louise!" called Eva, running after me. She was breathing hard and still breaking into shakes and twists from the dance, humming "Love Child" under her breath. Fucking cheerleaders.

"What's the matter, darling? You feel sad?" She adjusted my dress. "Don't be sad when you are so pretty on your wedding night."

"You can't have a wedding without a groom."

"Oh him!" She waved her hand as if Zane were a fly.

"That boy always late. He think of this, then he think of that, then he go here, then there, and *vroom!* The time. You know? I bet right now he is buying something very nice for you."

"I bet he is at a bar."

"That, too."

"Funny that Sunny isn't around either."

"We are not interested in Miss Sunny. She bores us, no? Tonight, we find interest in Louise and Zane, bride and groom." She smiled brightly and did a half-step turn. "You want to dance with Eva?" I watched her.

I had reached the point of intoxication where I knew the truth. Each time I got drunk, I reached this point, and each time it was the same, but each time I thought it was different. The truth! It hit me like a rock. I had to share it.

"Eva," I said quietly as I staggered toward her. "Zane is an alcoholic. Everyone in the Arthur Reese Traveling Show is an alcoholic."

"As we say in Italy, you have discovered water."

AT TEN O'CLOCK that night, I opened a fifth of bourbon, and by midnight, I was drinking straight from the bottle, alone in Zane's trailer. Outside, fireworks lit up the sky. Someone was playing "Here Comes the Bride" on a harmonica, and someone else was singing a Zappa tune. Every once in a while,

Felix would climb up on a stool and try to take my picture through the window.

To carnies, a wedding was a wedding, groom or not. They brought the cake to my door, shouting for me to cut it, but I told them to go away. Once I heard Eva at the door, calling out to me in drunken sympathy, "He's the son of a pig!" I wondered if anyone else would take this opportunity to get married, since the carousel had been painted and all. I passed out on the bed with my nose buried in Zane's smoky shirt.

When I came to, the party had quieted down; I heard only a faint strain of "Le Sabre" through the thin walls. Somewhere Sunny was arguing in a high-pitched, drunken voice.

I heard Lollibells laughing and then Zane. I was out the door like a nail flying to a magnet.

I ran barefoot across the gravel, to the sound of Zane's laugher. The bastard! But Madge caught me in her thick arms. "Listen," she said, shaking me. "Listen to me. Percy is gone." I tried to focus on her face, a white blur of tears.

"Who?"

"I have looked everywhere. He ain't in the drain. Or on the fence. Or under the bed. He ain't at yous guys place?" I told her that I hadn't seen a python in our trailer, but she had to come over and look for herself. We checked the box where Zane kept his torches, and our suitcase, already packed for Gibson. The posters on the walls mocked me: THE ARTHUR REESE TRAVELING SHOW! THE MAN WITH ELASTIC EYEBALLS, FIFI THE HEADLESS WOMAN, THE MOST BEAUTIFUL TEENAGER IN AMERICA, ZANE WILDER, THE HUMAN DRAGON! I was Louise Peppers, the groomless bride. Percy wasn't in the shower or beneath the refrigerator, where he sometimes went to get warm. He wasn't on the windowsill. We called the police, but they hung up on us.

"You and me kid," said Madge, throwing her arm over my shoulder. "We lost 'em. Losing Larry was just like this. Awful." She picked up one of Zane's socks and mopped her eyes with it. "I called and called. Dreamed about him every night. Still do, but it was easier with Percy wrapped around me. Took my mind off things. But I ain't never forgot ole Larry. You don't forget a cat like that. Him with his tail on fire, going on with the show." When she moaned, I stepped back, thinking she might puke on me, but she only cried, "Oh God! Oh Jesus fucking Christ I loved that little snake!"

To get rid of her, I suggested that Percy might be on one of the rides.

"He gets carsick," she said hesitantly, but her eyes grew bright, and she began walking rapidly toward the carousel calling out in a thin, raspy voice, "Percy! Percy, come to Mama!" Staggering behind her, I kept a lookout for Zane. What do you say to the man who has just stood you up at your wedding? It needed to be memorable. Maybe he'd ask me again. Then I could say no. With painful clarity I saw that the engagement ring was a down payment. Sunny didn't have one either. In my mind, I heard Henry saying, "Why, he's no good. Shiftless, lazy, irresponsible—you're better off without him." Behind him, Florida said succinctly, "Trash." But then I heard his voice, ringing out clear over "Le Sabre"—a smoky tenor touched with a fading drawl, and I was ready to negotiate. Maybe Sunny had kidnapped him. Maybe his car had broken down. Possibly he had the dates mixed up. I strode forward.

In the faint light of a broken Japanese lantern, the carousel spun brief, grotesque shadows in the dirt. Around and around, grinding out that mad gypsy tune, horses with flashing white teeth shot into the light and dipped away. Zane was on a gray mare with a broken tail and a red mouth stretched into a silent scream. He was with Lollibells. They were spooned in the saddle.

"Go Blixen, go Vixen!" cried Lollibells, kicking the wooden horse. "Giddy up, reindeer!"

Rocking in his arms, Zane tossed his head and sang, "Rudolph with your nose so bright, won't you—" then he saw me standing there in my dirty wedding dress. "Aagh!" he cried, holding his hands over his eyes as the horse pumped out of sight. "The gorilla is here! Watch out!" When the horse circled back around, the men covered their eyes with their hands, screaming, "Go away, gorilla! Go away!"

Madge jogged beside them yelling, "Stop it! Get off that merry-go-round. Get off right now!"

"Oh lady, we are getting off!" said Lollibells.

"Can't stop," slurred Zane. "Lost the stopper."

When she came back to me, her face was red. "Don't cry over those fools," she said with one hand on her hip, looking back at the carousel with an evil eye. "Goddamned children. Where's Tic Toc? Somebody needs to turn that thing off. Stop that crying now. Come on back to my place. I'll make us some coffee. Goddamned idiots. I ought to spank both of them. They sure do know how to spoil a party."

When she put her arm around me, I sobbed into her chest, "I thought it was Sunny."

"Aw baby, that was over a long time ago, him and Sunny. That damn Warren has been chasing his tail for—well, it don't matter. I'm sorry you had to see it this way, dressed up and all. But we're carnies, see? Around here, the saying goes, I love you baby, but the season's over."

Chapter Fourteen

SOMETIMES I IMAGINED Roderick watching us. He'd be stretched out on a cloud or something, looking at Pepperses the way he used to lie in the grass and study lizards. He'd scrunch up his nose, slit his eyes, and freeze—just like the lizard. When a chameleon turned green, to hide from him, I half expected Roderick to change color, too. If the dead can see the living, Roderick was watching.

IT IRKED FLORIDA that Louise was worshiping a lightbulb. She'd been carrying her to church since the day she was born. Glued a ribbon to her head when she was a baby, and after that she curled her hair every Saturday night even if it was straight as a stick in the morning. Henry polished the children's shoes and set them on a piece of newspaper by the door to dry overnight. She had her own Bible, white gloves, and a dime for the tithe. Every single Sunday. She could have stayed home if all Louise needed was a lightbulb.

"I have found a power greater than myself," Louise told her after she'd been gotten out of the drunk tank in a wedding dress.

"His name is Jesus Christ, Son of God," said Florida.

"Not necessarily," said Louise. "But yes. It's big, bigger than we can imagine, so big it can be anything. God can be Jesus or Buddha or a lightbulb, or a chair—"

"Shoot," said Florida. "Is that what they taught you at the circus?" and they went at it.

None of those lightbulbs kept her out of jail. Arrested for drunken driving. Where had they gone wrong? Henry spoiled her. Couldn't say no to her. She told him, but he didn't listen. And now she was going to have to go back and serve a ninety-day sentence. Her little girl in a cage.

"I wash my hands of her," Florida said aloud, wiping her tears. She switched on the light in her studio and strode over to the easel. For a week, the canvas had remained blank. Mary MacDermott said to look at a white canvas like a cloud. Try to see something in it. Florida looked hard. She saw a lightbulb. Who wanted to paint a lightbulb? She didn't want to paint Jesus—that had been done so much. Everybody else was so original. She was saying *Dumb, dumb, dumb* to herself when the phone rang.

It was Agnes, trying to change her appointment on her. Said she had to take her granddaughter to tap dancing. Last week it was something else. That was how Agnes did—tried to see what she could get away with.

"No," she said crisply in the receiver. "I believe I'll find someone else to do my hair. I need to have it done by Saturday because Southern Board is giving Henry a retirement party. He's worked for them for thirty years."

Agnes gushed over that awhile, and then she said, "I hope Louise will be able to go. Will she still be in . . . town?" Florida knew that was coming. Blabbermouth.

"We expect so," she said.

There was a silence. Finally, Agnes said sweetly, "Well, I didn't know what your situation would be. Can you swing by tomorrow morning? I think I can work you in."

"I think I'll just have someone else do my hair. I don't want it to go flat before Henry's party. He's worked for them for thirty years. It's very important."

"Shoot, then. Let's keep the appointment the way we had it."

"That would suit me better. I'm right in the middle of something, Agnes. I have to go."

Louise would have been proud of her. You need to define your boundaries, she said. Good Lord. She'd get her fill of boundaries in jail.

She couldn't stand to look at that empty canvas another minute, so she squeezed a tube of sienna paint onto her pallet, mixed it with soleil, and picked up a brush. Nothing happened. In her Special Art class, Helen Olfinger picked up a paintbrush like it was a fork and went to town. Those paintings were selling for a thousand dollars apiece now. Florida looked at the white space in front of her: nothing to spring off of, no boundaries. Glaring at the canvas, she remembered her daddy's words: "You're Brack Deleuth's daughter; you won't amount to nothing."

Then Florida did something unthinkable. She hurled the pallet of paints against the wall. For a moment it stuck to the new wallpaper. Then, slowly, it slid down to the floor leaving a trail of rusty blood.

That's when she saw the bird. Stepping closer, she looked at the giant claw: thick and ropey, covered with bumps and scales, the way it would be if you were a rabbit in its grip searing with pain as you soared over the pines. With a few dabs of her brush, she pulled out the wing.

All day, Florida painted. When Henry got home from work, he stood in the studio doorway watching her until he determined that she had lost her mind.

"How's the artist?" he asked in a cheerful voice.

She mumbled a reply and kept working.

He watched her paint on the new wallpaper for a few more minutes; then he went into the kitchen to open a can of soup. If that was oil paint, it would not come off, but she probably knew that. It took all of his strength not to go in there right now with a damp sponge, but he had a feeling that this was it. One word and she would crack. He didn't need a wife in the nuthouse and a daughter in jail. Not with a son in the grave. When he finished his soup, he washed the pan, his bowl, and the spoon. He put the paper napkin in the drawer because he hadn't needed it. He glanced into the studio one more time, but she was still going at it, so he went downstairs to watch the news. After he had listened to the same report on several stations, he switched to the Weather Channel. When he was current on the wind patterns moving across all fifty states, he watched the late night news. At three o'clock in the morning, he said good night to Louise, who was doubled up like a pretzel on her bedroom floor in meditation, and checked the locks on all the doors and windows. Finally, he knocked on the studio door. When she opened it, light flooded over them.

For the life of him, Henry couldn't remember his retirement speech. He looked around the civic center, which was filled to capacity with Southern Board employees and their families. Along the back wall, on a long table covered with a white cloth, sat a roasted pig with an apple in its mouth. The apple was Florida's idea. She sat up straight in the folding chair beside him; her hair was perfect.

"You're as nervous as a cat," she said. "Did you forget your speech?"

"No," he said, frowning at her.

"Most people in here are deaf anyway. Maybe it won't matter."

He nodded as if he hadn't heard her and looked over at Louise. He had asked her not to close her eyes in public, but she said she couldn't meditate with them open.

"What are you meditating on?" he'd asked when she first started.

"God."

"Well. That's important, but do you have to do it all the time?"

"Without ceasing," she said.

He wouldn't let her walk on the street for fear she'd be hit by a car. She had trouble paying attention even when she was

trying. She was wearing a sleeveless linen dress, and her hair
was cut in a pixie. He couldn't imagine her in jail.

At the podium, Raymond Patch said a few words of introduction through his voice box. He'd had a laryngectomy last
year, paid for in full by Southern Board insurance, but the doctors couldn't get him to quit smoking. Briefly closing his eyes,
Henry prayed that Louise wouldn't pick up cigarettes again in
jail. She'd quit smoking and drinking. Jail was no place for a lady.

Florida poked him in the arm. "Get up there. He wants to
give you a present."

Smiling, Henry walked up to the podium where he and Raymond shook hands and patted each other on the back. He was
presented with a stiff new pair of overalls—"the working man's
tuxedo," Raymond called them—an electronic mosquito zap-
per, an ice chest filled with venison steaks from the deer Polecat had shot that morning, and a gold watch. Then they shook
hands and patted backs again, and Henry was left alone to face
the crowd. He hadn't been this nervous since his wedding.
Although he strictly avoided looking at his family, he felt
Florida's presence as always, tugging at him. His awareness of
Louise was different; he was pulling her. He felt the pull move
back and forth, Florida to him, him to Louise, all around the
gap of Roderick.

Henry's speech was entitled "Service and Dedication." He
remembered that part clearly. "Service and Dedication," by
Henry Peppers. The rest was a blank. To calm his nerves, he
tried to imagine the audience in their underwear, but this made
him more uncomfortable. He drank some water from the glass
on the podium. Finally, he took a deep breath and began to
make something up.

"The first word I spoke was light. My first memory is watching a man hang on the square in Perrytown, Kentucky, where I was born. His head was covered with a black cloth sack. I guess I was four years old. Later on, when I was eight or nine, there was a big flood. I remember the water sloshing in my shoes as I ran down the street calling after a family stranded on the roof of their house—the house was floating down the Okawhalla River. The river rose over the banks and kept rising on the street. People were trying to run, but they kept falling in the water. It was up to my knees by then. A block of ice fell off a car and came at us like an iceberg, knocking people over. A dead chicken floated by, legs straight up in the air. I kept watching the people up on the roof of that house. The whole family was there, the mother and father and son and even the dog, waving their arms and yelling, 'Help! Help! Help!' The house went around the bend. By then the water was up to my chest, so I swam over to the Baptist church. My father was the preacher, and I knew how to climb up into the bell tower. You wouldn't believe what all I saw from that bell tower. I saw horses and cows—the cows were all upside down—and fences and wheels and a lady's parasol streaming with ribbons. I saw an uprooted tree, a bag of basketballs from the high school gym, and a baby carriage. The water just kept rising. A piano bobbed around the bend in the river. Maybe it belonged to the house. I never saw that house again."

On the long white table, melting iced tea had reached the rim of the pitchers. Somewhere, a door slammed shut, and the apple fell out of the pig's mouth.

"Let us pray," said Henry. He bowed his head. Lord, we thank you for the bountiful gifts you have bestowed upon us and the nourishment we are about to receive."

Chapter Fifteen

ON THE DAY I was to be driven back to the Wapanog County
Jail, Florida brought me a basket of Oscar de la Renta soap,
powder, lotion, and perfume. "I don't know if they'll let you
keep the basket or not," she said. "They don't want you to have
anything you could use as a weapon. That perfume has alcohol
in it, so don't drink it. They give you soap if you need it, but I
expect it's harsh. When this runs out, I'll get you some more."

Henry handed me a catalog: The Wapanog County Contin-
uing Education Program. "They've got all kinds of courses," he
said. "Not just the basics, which of course you've already taken
at Bridgewater. A Bridgewater graduate has the education
equivalent to a sophomore in college. They've got some real interesting classes." He thumbed through the pages. "Psychol-
ogy, typing, computer science, and art and all that. It will all
transfer to college when you enroll." He smiled broadly. "Why,
I'd like to go out there and take a course or two myself."

"Your father wants to go to jail with you," said Florida.

"You can even get a Ph.D. out there," he added, "but of course you'll just be there for three months. You'll be done before you know it. Just do everything they tell you, and don't associate with anyone. You're not out there to make friends. You want a fresh start when you come out." He patted me on the back, pressing his Masonic ring into my spine. "You can do it. I know you can. Remember who you are. You're a Peppers."

"The lady I got on the phone out there said she could have a sketch pad and acrylics," said Florida. "They're afraid you might swallow the oils."

"You don't want that kind of paint anyway," said Henry, who was still working on the stains Florida had made in her studio last week. The painting was hanging in a show in Atlanta and had been written up in several papers, but they'd had to tear the wallpaper off the wall. "Even turpentine won't get those stains off the floor."

"They are not going to let her have turpentine, Henry!"

"That's what I said!"

"No, you didn't. You can start a fire with turpentine, honey."

"I know that." He tightened his jaw.

"Don't fuss at me, Henry."

"I'm not fussing."

"Yes, you are. You're all tensed. I can feel it."

Sighing, Henry turned back to me. "They must have fire drills out there. Florida, make a note for me to check on the fire escape plan."

ON THE DRIVE to jail, I sat in the back seat of the Ford Taurus letting thoughts float through my brain like balloons. If

I wanted to, I could hold on to the string of a balloon and watch it for a while, or I could let it float up into the sky and disappear. I let Zane float away. The whole Arthur Reese Traveling Show floated on by except for Lollibells. For some reason, I caught the string of that balloon and held it. I wanted to tell him what had happened to me after I drove off the lot in the red truck—Lollibells always liked a really bad love story.

So I'M DRIVING down I-85 seeing double, and I have to go to the bathroom, but I can't get off an exit ramp because I don't know which ramp is real. One of everything is a joke— one of the blue cars in my lane, one of the yellow lines beside me. If I get on the joke exit ramp, I'll fall through the air. Unless I go up the joke ramp in the joke car. But there is only one of me. By the time I get this all figured out, I'm seeing triple, so I just pee in my seat.

Why didn't you stop?

I forgot where the brake was. I tried to pass the blue cars riding three abreast in front of me, but it was too scary, so I had another beer and decided to drive through them. I studied the cars, trying to remember which one was the original, but I couldn't tell. I could drive through the joke cars because they were made of air, but the original—then I realized that everything is made of air. What appears to be solid mass is a spin of molecules.

Atoms.

Right. Whatever. So, if I aimed right, I could drive through a car like a swarm of gnats, without hitting a single one.

You wanted to die.

Yes, it was good to die. We all had to die that day. It was time
to get off the planet. I was careful not to pray, not even to say,
Oh God. I had worked hard to become an atheist.

I told you about that.

I know. I'm getting to God. I ran that car off the road. That
car shunned me.

Girlfriend, I hope you be under lock and key.

I sped up to the next car, and then I blacked out. When I
came to, I was parked on the side of the road, surrounded by
patrol cars. One of the cops rapped on my window. We looked
at each other through the glass, and I knew that he loved me.
I was going to marry a cop.

Might as well since you're already dressed for it.

We'd live in a trailer. When he came home from work, I'd un-
buckle his holster.

Don't forget the handcuffs. What's your friend's name? Harvard girl?

Drew.

Drew St. John is appalled but secretly fascinated. Watch out!

Someone said, "Christ, it's a bride." Someone leaned into the
front seat of the truck and said, "Phew! Get a whiff of this."
They went on all around us talking about expired tags, open
containers, stolen vehicles.

And y'all didn't pay no mind.

He touched me. He pulled my wrists behind my back. "Now
I'm going to put these on real loose, so they won't hurt," he
said. "If you act up, I'll have to tighten them." In the front seat
of the patrol car, I slipped my wrists out of the cuffs and waved
to him. He said, "Louise, what did I tell you about that?"

Father figure. Here we go.

I asked how he knew my name; he got it off my license.

Clever. Y'all stop off for a cocktail on the way to jail?

He said no. He wanted to ask me a personal question. He wanted to know if I was an alcoholic.

Did you smack his hand?

Then he wanted to know if I thought I was different from other people.

In what way?

I don't know. I told him I was both. Different and alcoholic.

IN THE FRONT seat, Florida asked Henry if he was low on gas. "We can't run out today. We can't make her late. They'll come after us. Pull over here and fill up your tank. I mean it now. Louise, are you asleep back there?"

"Yes." Behind my closed eyelids, I watched balloons fill the sky. Everything was an illusion. A balloon, a thought, a breath. Pull it it in, let it go. In and out, in and out. I was telling Lollibells: Locked in the bathroom of the Wapanog County Jail, I banged on the steel door and screamed until a woman hollered, "Quit making that noise, you're messing up the radio waves!" It was a small room and it kept getting smaller. No windows. No lid on the john. Nothing to kill yourself with. Nothing but walls squeezing tighter and tighter around me; the floor came up and the ceiling came down, pressing the air out of my lungs. I tried to breathe, but I couldn't remember how. I curled into a tight ball and tried not to look at the walls. Then I knew something. God breathed for me. I didn't have to worry about it.

"Henry, up here on your right," said Florida. "Ninety-two cents a gallon, honey."

You got religion? asked Lollibells, and I let his balloon go. More balloons floated past: the dark eyes of Eva, Zane's bare throat as he leaned back to swallow the sword, Daisy's wicked grin, Sunny. More came. Drew throwing a left in her grandmother's pearls. Mr. Rutherford crouched in a tackle position in front of a room of seventh-graders as he introduced Shakespeare. Regina Bloodworth reading a magazine behind dark glasses. T. C. Curtis in a tired light. And more: Mrs. Gubbel on the organ, Sunday after Sunday. Mary MacDermott breaking plates. Raymond Patch wheezing into his box, another voice moving out of his throat. Daddy-Go in a tobacco field with the tall green plants high over his hat, and Grandmother Deleuth in the chicken coop pushing hens off their eggs.

Finally, Roderick came. There was no picture, just the sense of him, raw and familiar at the same time.

I'm an alcoholic, I told him.

I know, he said.

I told him about the black man singing on the corner, the last day I ever drank. Like a knife slicing through the canvas of the universe. A light. A sound like no sound I ever heard. Black man singing "Amazing Grace" on the corner of Front Street and Magnolia. Suit and hat, frost on the ground and no gloves. Blasting it out straight to God. Everybody on the sidewalk stopped. Maybe there was a red light, I don't know. Someone said, "He should make a record. He could make a lot of money." He sang it over and over; maybe that was the only song he knew. I never heard the human voice sound like that. It was inhuman. A God. A Love. A Big Love. So big I could just see the tail end of it, and that shook me up. He didn't even take his hat off for money.

That's love, said Roderick. You'll get used to it.

"Henry," said Florida. "What was wrong with that gas station?"

HENRY STOOD OUTSIDE the processing room wearing Florida's pocketbook over one shoulder and mine over the other. They wouldn't let Florida carry her bag into the ladies room, and I was handcuffed. I was wearing the bright orange pajamas I had been issued.

"I like this uniform better than the old zebra suits they used to use," said Henry, making conversation. "Orange is a good color on you." Gently, he touched my wrists. "Are they tight? I think that fellow was new. The older officer just wanted to show him how to handcuff a prisoner, in case he ever had to. They were using you as an example for procedure." Again, he pressed the cold metal against my skin. "Aw, you've got all kinds of room in there. You could get out of those in a minute if you had to. Now don't you try that. You'll get in big trouble. But in case of emergency, if there were a tornado or a fire . . . I asked them if they had fire escapes and they said they did, but I don't see any."

"What are y'all talking about?" asked Florida, returning from the rest room with sharp clicks of her heels on the tile. She took her purse from Henry's shoulder. "I always tried to get you to wear orange. That's your color."

"We were talking about fire escapes."

"Henry, they can't have fire escapes in a jail. They don't want people to escape. That black girl was so ugly to me in the rest room. I ought to tell somebody. I guess she's just doing her job, guarding everybody, but I don't think it would kill her to be a little more courteous."

"Black woman," I corrected.

"Her name is Yolanda. I asked because I was going to report her. Louise, you stay out of her way. Meaner than a snake. All I said to her was, 'This commode is stopped up. You might want to take a look at it.' She jumped all over me! Told me she was not the cleaning lady; she was the guard. Big fat old thing, too, about to pop every button on her uniform. You stay away from her, Louise."

"They can't keep her locked in here if there's a fire," said Henry. "Of course they don't want inmates escaping, but they have to have an evacuation plan. That's the law. Why, there aren't any windows in here. She'd smother to death in the smoke." When I touched his hand, my cuffs clinked.

"I can't look at those chains on you," said Florida. She turned her head away. "Do they hurt?"

"They don't hurt," said Henry. "I checked them. That fellow put them on real loose. He was just demonstrating the procedure to a rookie."

Sniffling, Florida went through her pocketbook looking for a Kleenex. "I brought some crackers. I don't know if anybody is hungry or not. Henry, go up to that window and see if she can bring crackers inside with her. I'm not talking to these people again if I don't have to. That black lady was so rude to me. Just awful."

A guard approached us with a clipboard. She wore mahogany lipstick and had ironed her hair into sausage curls. On her holster, she carried a baton and a pistol. "Frances Louise Peppers?"

"She's right here," said Henry, standing up tall.

"Excuse me just a minute," said Florida as she stepped between the guard and me.

"Ma'am," said the guard.

Florida put her arms around me. My handcuffs clinked
against the zipper of her purse.

"Ma'am, I'm going to have to ask you to step out of the
way."

"I love you," said Florida. "You don't know."

Henry wrapped his arms around both of us.

The guard tapped her pen against the clipboard. "I need the
prisoner to identify herself. You're obstructing her."

"Tell her who you are," said Henry, brushing some lint from
my back.

"Can't you take those things off her wrists?" asked Florida.
"They bother me."

"We will ma'am. Once she's been processed."

"They will," said Henry, handing his handkerchief to Florida.
"This is just how they organize everybody. This place would be
a madhouse if they didn't." Two tears ran down his cheeks.

"You telling me," said the guard in a softer voice. "Are you
Frances Louise Peppers of 711 Mount Zion Road, Counterpoint, Georgia?"

"I am."

"Y'all can hug once more, then you need to come with me."
Henry pressed me so hard against his chest I couldn't breathe.
He kissed me on top of my head. When Florida kissed my
cheek, I tasted her tears on my lips.

Finally, the guard took my arm. She led me through a grated
iron door into a cell block. Pulling out a ring of keys, she un-

locked my handcuffs and then the door to Cell 11. Inside the cell, the concrete-block walls were painted the color of scrambled eggs. On top of a steel bunk bed, a female prisoner, with a shaved head and GOOD tattooed on one arm and EVIL on the other, sat reading a magazine.

"That's Gabriella," said the guard. "She's a little strange, but she don't bite. Gab, this is"—she looked at her clipboard—"this is Louise."

"Thrilled," said Gabriella without looking up from *Southern Living*. I took a tentative step forward and stopped. *Breathe*, I told God. *Breathe, damn it.*

"Proceed on in there, Louise. I ain't got all day." The guard jangled her keys, and I passed through the pearly gates.